CRIMEUCOPIA

The Cosy Nostra

A Murderous Ink Press Anthology

****

Murderous-Ink Press

CRIMEUCOPIA

The Cosy Nostra
First published by
Murderous-Ink Press
Crowland
LINCOLNSHIRE
England
www.murderousinkpress.co.uk

Acknowledgements

To those writers and artists who helped make this anthology what it is, I can only say a heartfelt Thank You!

And to Den, as always.

Contents

*Live Free or Die appears as part of the *Live Free or Die: A collection of three short mystery stories* (Superior Shores Press 2016)

They Don't Write 'em Like That Anymore...
(An Editorial of Sorts)

Actually they do, Aunty Jean. Cosy Crime has spanned the literary centuries and now due to its popularity, over a physical century as well.

But what constitutes a Cosy? Is it bounded by the Golden Age as presided over by Queen Agatha, Dame Sayers or Countess Marsh? Georgette Heyer stepped out of the Regency period to complete six very passible crime novels...

But is the Cosy now something that has actually transcended the Golden Age time period and matured into an acceptably modern crime sub-genre. Does it always need the Downton Abbey touches of country mansion, old upper crust family, downstairs unrest, and the usual collection of nefarious butlers who always seem to have 'done it', whatever 'it' might be?

Or is that 'predictability' what makes a cosy comfortably cosy? Or annoyingly so? And let's be honest, who hasn't at some time wished that Lord Peter would take a .32 between the eyes when the plot becomes more twisted than a corkscrew hazel?

Certainly writers such as Simon Brett, Ann Cleeves, and Caroline Graham – to name 3 off the top of a variety of heads – have given us what are now considered to be 'classics' in their own rights. Alexander McCall Smith has been presenting the genteel African cosy for some time now, along with his outings into Scottish cosy, while Minna Lindgren even gives us Scandi-cosy – and OAP cosy – way back in 2013 – before *The Thursday Murder Club* pulled the sub-genre back into the bestselling spotlight.

Or is Cosy what we – the readers – decide it is, and to Hell with genre stereotyping?

In support of that, in this anthology, Gina L. Grandi gives us something that could be described as Cosy-NOIR – though the jury's out regarding Wendy – while Eve Fisher puts us firmly back in time to something with a more traditional historical setting.

Alexander Frew takes some time out from writing novels to give us something that is as Scottish as whisky, bagpipes and the Loch Ness monster, and Andrew Humphrey presents a more modern view of semi-rural life, though possibly the expression NFN* may well apply.

Tom Johnstone manages to lead us down a very dark garden path, yet later Matias Travieso-Diaz also shows that Lady Luck can have a more than a passing influence on anyone's life.

Eamonn Murphy puts us back into the Modern Day, just after Gary Thomsom takes us to ancient Greece, and Ella Moon guides us firmly back to traditional Cosy Country once more.

Madeline McEwen has a modern spin on an Ogden Nash

line, before Lyn Fraser gives us criminal intent at the Sun Glo Care Home, and Louise Taylor presents us a story of village life, USA style.

Judy Penz Sheluk recounts a tale of misadventure – or is it more like revenge? – and Joan Hall Hovey returns with a story that may be more Suspense than Murder Mystery, but has all the trappings of a modern day Cosy.

Bringing this anthology to a tail wagging finish is Judy Upton, who deftly proves that sometimes it can be a dog's life being a Private Investigator.

As with all of these anthologies, we hope you'll find something that you immediately like, as well as something that takes you out of your comfort zone – and puts you into a new one.

In other words, in the spirit of the *Murderous Ink Press* motto:

"You never know what you like until you read it."

*Oh, and NFN? Medical annotation – *Normal for Norfolk.*

Truth & Turpitude
Murder at Abbey Mill Farm
Eve Fisher

1

I was out riding with my dear sister, Selina Suckling of Maple Grove, in her barouche-landau just the other day, and she suggested that I write a narrative of my involvement in the events of last July. That was when Robert Martin was murdered, shot to death while standing in the north paddock of Abbey-Mill Farm. A very vulgar crime, to be sure, and certainly not a subject for a lady to write of. But, the more I thought of it, the more I felt that dear Selina was right. After all, it was I who solved the mystery, practically single-handedly.

It all began that fatal Thursday. I heard the dreadful news that evening. A murder in Highbury! I was completely overset. I shrieked, I positively shrieked! And then I fell fainting on the chaise-lounge and my husband (Mr. Elton, Vicar of Highbury) had to run for the doctor while my stupid maid nearly set the curtains on fire, burning feathers to bring me around. My sensibility has always been acute.

Mrs. Knightley did not shriek or faint when <u>she</u> heard the news. (My housekeeper and hers are second cousins.) Instead, she put on her shawl and went for a walk, which argued to me of a strange indifference. Yet there had been a time when Harriet Smith was her boon companion, and Mrs. K practically shoved her protégée down everyone's throats. Of course, that was back when Mrs. K was Miss Emma Woodhouse and queened it over Highbury as if she were of the blood royal, before she entrapped Knightley into making her an offer. I happen to know that Miss Woodhouse and Miss Smith fell out over a most unsuitable attachment for either of them: Frank Churchill! Who married that lovely, sweet, pitiable Jane Fairfax. ("Not a connexion to gratify," said her mother-in-law, Mrs. Weston – quondam governess to Miss Woodhouse – as if she had been such an unexceptionable match herself!) I have always felt that Miss Woodhouse married Knightley in a fit of wounded vanity.

Nor did Mrs. K show any better behavior the next night at the Coles' dinner party. The Knightleys were practically the guests of honor, which was disgusting, considering how very recently Mrs. K had put off her black gloves – I cannot tell you how sincerely I mourned her father, <u>such</u> a gentleman – and how very obvious it was that she would soon have to return to seclusion. (I refuse to use the old, vulgar term "great-bellied," no matter how apt.) I was civil to her, of course, which was more than she was with me. She positively ran – such a mistake, in her condition – to her former governess, Mrs. Weston, and clung to her like a limpet, as if they did not see each other almost daily. I really have no patience with such behavior.

But poor Knightley. He looked like a ghost. I asked Mr. E, "Why, pray tell, does Knightley look so worn?" For he did look worn, white and drawn and thin. I am sure she does not feed him as she ought. Mr. E was singularly obtuse, saying that Knightley seemed just as usual, but then men never do notice those small, important details of life. He added that Knightley was very much upset by the murder.

"Pshaw," I said. "Robert Martin was a very good sort of tenant, I have no doubt, but there are in Surry 'many better than he.' No, depend upon it, it is something else."

But Mr. E absolutely contradicted me. "No, Augusta, I think not. I believe him to be genuinely distressed. He had to attend the inquest, and then there must be an investigation."

There are times when it does take a man to set things right. In a trice I saw what my *caro sposo* was saying: A murder had been committed; the murderer had not been found; the murderer was still on the loose. It quite took my breath away, and if I had not been in such a public place, forced to self-command, I believe I should have fainted again. I looked around the Coles' drawing room. Where was the man capable of the delicacy, the discrimination, the instinct necessary to discover the felon? Knightley was absolutely shattered; my husband was entirely devoted to his duties as Vicar; Weston has always been in my mind a nonentity (after all, he married a governess). No, none of them were suitable, and as for the women! It was obvious that only I could discover the secret of Robert Martin's murder.

2

It is a truth universally acknowledged that no one has a better entrée into all levels of society than a clergyman's wife. For example, even though ranked among the highest both by marriage and (I must confess it) birth, I have always found it easy to converse with the lower classes. A compliment upon the shining brasses, an inquiry into their parents' well-being, and their heart is yours. My servants all know that I am ready to hear their little trials and troubles, although of course they know their place and do not presume. And for a matter such as this, the servants were of utmost importance. Naturally the movements of such a person as Harriet Martin would be beneath the notice of the elite of Highbury, but servants are another matter. Always idling, always curious, always on the look-out for scandal among their betters, the servants would know everything.

The next morning, therefore, while I was closeted with my housekeeper, I spoke to some purpose.

"Wright, we must have something extremely tempting for Mr. Elton's dinner today. His appetite has been sorely disturbed by all this unpleasantness with the Martins."

"Indeed, ma'am, but I hadn't noticed," the obtuse creature replied. "He took second helpings of ham this morning."

"Because I told him he must keep up his strength," I said sternly. "He is greatly upset."

"Well, ma'am, I dare say that's natural. Him being a clergyman and all."

"I am sure everyone in Highbury is upset by it." Wright sniffed. "By the bye, Wright, isn't the upper-maid at the Martins a cousin of yours?"

"Betty? A <u>third</u> cousin, ma'am."

"A third cousin is a blood relation, Wright."

"I dare say." Wright sniffed again. A very irritating habit, and sufficient to explain why I spend as little time with her as

I can. "To say truth, ma'am, my family and hers have had little to do with each other. Betty's father came from Loamshire."

"No!"

"Yes, ma'am. What would you think of shepherd's pie, ma'am?"

"I should think we might as well be in Loamshire ourselves. Shepherd's pie? On choir night?"

"No, ma'am."

"I should think not. A turkey poult, perhaps."

"I dare say, ma'am. But the weather being so hot and all –"

The wrangling that went on before we had decided on a turkey poult, nicely dressed, with devilled bones to start and apple tart to finish, completely exhausted me. And I never did get a word out of her about the Martins. But then, as Wright said, they were only third cousins. I'm sure Wright knew nothing of the matter at all.

3

But servants never know anything. Luckily, there are many ladies in our friendly little community who are always willing to share their keen observations of daily life. I am sure that I can say in all honesty that no one despises gossip more than I. But after all, I must stay *au courant* with the events of our little village. How else could Mr. Elton, with his heavy responsibilities, be kept properly informed? Especially on such a subject as Harriet Martin. You may not believe it, but in her single days she set her designing eyes on my *caro sposo* himself! A woman of such breathtaking ambition could hardly be expected to keep herself happy on a mere farm. One hardly knows what such a woman would be about. It has obviously been my duty to keep an eye on her, while at the same time carefully shielding Mr. Elton from her unwelcome company. That is why I am so thankful for my many friends in Highbury.

Thus, from Mrs. Coles I had learned that Harriet "often yearned, poor girl, for the delights of Hartfield. Such society, such gentility, such cultivation, and what had come of it? Mr. Martin and Abbey-Mill Farm. True, it was a better marriage than one of her birth and breeding could ever have hoped for, but still… I dare say Miss Woodhouse, I mean, Mrs. Knightley, meant well, but it spoilt her, I fear, for a quiet home."

Mrs. Ford thought that things had been going hard for the Martins of late: "I know he had some plan for breeding horses, ma'am, but then something happened with the stud horse, and they never did get the piano, which she'd had her heart set on, poor girl."

Miss Bates – whose garrulity must be heard to be believed – had been "pleased to give Miss Smith, I mean, Mrs. Martin, details about turning and buttering the cheeses – something that should never be left to servants – my mother always insisted on my doing it – would not even trust Patty – and then of course the hams must be wiped daily – and the cheeses – and I warned Mrs. Martin to always make sure her feet were well wrapped and dry when she went into the dairy – I would not have her catch cold for the world – colds always come when the feet are damp – thankfully, I have never been troubled much by colds, but poor Jane – dear Jane, she wrote me the prettiest letter, just the other day…"

And then there was Anne Cox, spinster. (I fear her only hope of marriage now is a better dowry than her father has provided her.) She had once had hopes of the bachelor Robert

Martin and there is nothing like an old love for clear-eyed observation.

"What strikes me as most curious is Mrs. Martin's walks," Anne told me. "Every Thursday, rain or shine, wet or dry, out she must go, leaving the baby to be looked after by a ten-year old brat from Oakham."

"No!" I said, suitably shocked. "Do you think it was for her health?"

"She is strong as a horse," Anne said. "And if it was for her health, why not every day? No, Mrs. Elton, although it pains me to say it, I fear there must be another reason for Mrs. Martin's constitutionals." We looked at each other across the teacups. "She must have been meeting someone." My eyes widened. "Considering the tastes she learned at Hartfield, it must have been a gentleman." I gasped. "And we must not forget that it was on a Thursday that Robert Martin was murdered."

I set down my tea cup with my hand positively shaking. "I hope, my dear Anne, that you have shared this information with the suitable authorities?"

Anne gave me a wintry smile. "Alas, Mrs. Elton, who would listen to someone of my humble position? Now if _you_ were to mention the idea, or perhaps the Vicar…"

"My dear, I understand perfectly. It would come much more properly from the Vicarage than from you. Well, I shall do what is necessary. It is all most painful and distressing, but I have never shirked my duty."

"I knew that you would do all that is right," Anne said, and I passed her the seedcake.

4

If a young married woman – I cannot believe that I am even contemplating such immorality – meets a gentleman secretly, it can only be for one thing. The identity of such a monstrous commandment-breaker must be known, for the good of the community. But how to find it out? It is not a thing that any man, no matter how shameless, would boast of over the port, lest he be publicly hissed. And I felt certain that this man (for I really could not call him a gentleman any longer, knowing what I did), was both shameless and shameful. Skulking around the woods with Harriet Martin! What a come down! And then, of course, the confrontation with Robert Martin, with its hideous conclusion…

"What do most of the gentlemen in Highbury do with their afternoons?" I asked Mr. E.

"Stay indoors out of the heat, if they have any sense," he positively snapped at me.

I pointed out to him that I was not accustomed to that tone of voice, and he apologized, as well he ought. I have always made it plain to Mr. E that one must maintain a standard, even in the privacy of one's own home. Dignity, decorum, duty, courtesy are never relinquishable, no matter what the situation, or the weather, or –

"But my dear!" my husband cried, "I don't believe I told you what happened at the Crown today."

"Something further about Robert Martin?"

"No. Nobody seems to know anything about that at all. No, I happened by and saw Weston's carriage there, so I stopped to speak to him, simply out of courtesy. Anyway, he was outside, having a word with Abdy ostler. You know, young Abdy, whose father we put on parish relief?"

"I am certainly aware of Abdy ostler," I said, "considering that we have had to hire the Crown chaise three times in the last month because our carriage horse continues lame. We have had some talk, as you may remember, about the expense of feeding such a wretched screw instead of replacing him, and I foresee that we may soon have to have another."

"My dear," Mr. E hastened to say, "I have thought more carefully of the matter, and I have decided that you are absolutely right."

"I am gratified that you have at last come to your senses, Mr. E."

"Yes, well… Anyway, Weston was out in the yard arguing with young Abdy."

"What on earth could a gentleman like Weston have to argue about with an ostler?"

"I do not know."

"Could you not hear?"

"No," he said. Just like a man. "The only thing I heard was, as Weston was coming back towards the inn, Abdy called after him, 'Oh, aye, I'll send the bill, you may be sure of that!' The bill!" Mr. E cried. "As if Weston needed to hire a horse!"

"How curious. Did you ask him about it?"

"No, I had not the chance. Instead of coming inside, he met Knightley, and the two walked off together."

"Hmm," I murmured, my mind racing. I certainly could see that hiring a horse might be the ideal thing to do if one were a well-known local gentleman and yet wished to go somewhere incognito. And I have never trusted Mr. Weston.

I might not have mentioned it before, but Mrs. Weston was Emma Woodhouse's governess. I have been told that Mrs. Weston, when they first married, looked very well for her age, but that has changed. Since her hymeneals were celebrated, she has gained two daughters and three stone, as well as losing some of her teeth and all of her looks. Weston himself is still a fine figure of a man, still youthful, indeed, somewhat boyish for his years in both personality and behavior. To look upon Weston, buoyant and hearty, and his wife, aged and gray, is to see living proof that a man should never marry a woman near to or greater than his own age, unless considerable wealth favors the match.

I think anyone can see where my thoughts were tending. But I needed more information. It was then that I remembered that Wright's niece was in service with the Westons, and it seemed as good a time as any to see if she were being well-treated. Randalls is a considerable distance from the Vicarage, and, with our carriage horse lame, I would have to hire the Crown chaise again. (I deplore wasteful spending, but sometimes one must make sacrifices in the line of duty.) And of course I would insist on young Abdy driving me, for one cannot trust the young men at the Crown. As the proverb says, I could kill two birds with one stone.

But Mr. E was yawning. "Well, Augusta, I believe I shall go begin work on my sermon."

"Certainly, my dear."

I watched him go, knowing that his handkerchief would be over his face in no time, and loud, rhythmic breathing would fill the house. Some trials of marriage no one ever prepares one for.

5

As soon as Mr. Elton was properly settled, I sent young Thomas down to the Crown, and told Wright that I was going to visit the Westons.

"So, if there is anything you would like to send to Sarah…"

"Well, ma'am, there is that scorched tablecloth you said was only fit for the scrap-pile. I thought as she might could make some pillowcases from it for her hope chest, if you wouldn't mind."

"Not at all!" I cried. "Bundle it up, and I will take it over with me."

Wright brought me the bundle, carefully done up, which I naturally undid once she had left the room. One must always keep an eye on servants, or they presume. But it was only the tablecloth, which was not nearly as scorched as I had thought it, but it would make Sarah happy. I had just finished retying it when the carriage came up to the door.

"And where is Abdy?" I asked, looking at the young puppy twirling his whip.

"He's mortal busy, ma'am," said he, "and said as I should be driving, seeing as it's only a short distance." I believe the insolent creature muttered 'and small pay' under his breath.

I set my jaw and my skirts, and said, "To the Crown."

"I thought as you wanted to go to Randall's," the creature said."

"To the Crown!" I snapped. "I wish to speak with your

superior."

I fumed all the way there, and surged out of the chaise, seething with righteous indignation at being fobbed off with a mere hobbledehoy. By the time I had done, young Abdy was in his coat and hat and, as we drove away, I saw the young puppy back at his proper job of grooming horses.

A couple of miles down the road, I said, "What is this I hear about Mr. Weston renting horses from you?"

"Mr. Weston, ma'am?"

"Yes," I said. "I understand that there has been a problem about a bill."

"I don't know how you come to hear of <u>that</u>, ma'am," Abdy said, glancing over his shoulder.

"Eyes on the road, if you please," I said. "As the Vicar's wife, I hear a great deal of what goes on in Highbury."

"Well, ma'am, I may have obliged him once or twice."

"Really? I heard it was far more often than that." True, it was conjecture, but with that class, it is always best to operate from a position of certainty.

"I don't talk about other people's business, ma'am. It's not my place to."

"Certainly in the normal course of events that is perfectly true. But considering the terrible tragedy that has lately happened among us, such... behavior raises questions."

"Questions, ma'am?"

"Questions. Such as, why a gentleman, who certainly has a carriage and horses of his own, would need to hire horses to ride to an unknown destination. Where was he going? Who might he be meeting? Is there any correspondence between a gentleman on a hired horse and a – well, I will not say a lady, but a woman, a married woman, taking long walks every Thursday afternoon. What do you think, Abdy?"

"I think nought about any of it. I hire out horses, that is all."

The set of his back seemed determinedly stubborn. "And what about Robert Martin?" I asked.

Once again, he looked over his shoulder, and his face was certainly apprehensive this time. "What would you be wanting to know about him, ma'am?"

"I heard that Robert Martin was thinking of setting up for horse breeding."

Young Abdy made the most peculiar noise. There are none of that class that can keep their nasal passages both clear and silent. "Aye, he was. But his stud horse failed him, strange to say. No business of a lady like yourself, ma'am. But here we are, at Randalls, ma'am."

Neither of the Westons were at home. Mrs. Weston had gone to visit Mrs. Knightley: really, their attachment is positively unhealthy. Weston himself was off. Gadding about, I presumed, but did not mention it. Instead, I asked after Sarah, and gave her the bundle.

"Oh, ma'am," she said. "Thank you ever so much."

"It is my pleasure, Sarah," I replied. "Mine and your aunt's. So, how is your situation suiting you?"

"Oh, ever so well, ma'am. Mrs. Weston is a kind mistress, and the little ones are ever so sweet."

"I am glad to hear it. And all is going well?"

"Oh, yes, ma'am."

"Excellent. I had heard that there has been some trouble with your master's stables lately."

"Trouble, ma'am?"

"Well, I have been told that he has had to hire horses from the Crown."

Sarah looked at me, then across the courtyard to the Crown chaise. "I wouldn't know about that, ma'am. But I do know that the master has said that John Abdy was never to set foot on this place any more. Of course, he was never referring to a lady like yourself, needing a carriage ride."

"Of course not," I said, smiling to myself. Obviously Abdy knew about more than just horses. "Well, my dear, I will tell Wright that you are doing quite well. Please tell your master and mistress that I called, and I will try to come back another time when at least one of them is at home."

"Yes, ma'am. And thank you again, ma'am."

I believe that I forgot to mention that this was a Thursday. I had already decided that, if Harriet Martin had been lost to depravity before her husband's death, it was unlikely that she would regain her morals after it. Weston's absence added weight to my conjecture. So, as we left the Westons, I told John Abdy that I felt in the need of some air, and to take me home the long way, through Donbury Wood, which lies, bye-the-bye, at the north end of Abbey-Mill Farm. I happen to know that there is a walking path from the Farm through the Wood, and out to the Turnpike Road.

My eyes were keen to catch the view that day, I can assure you. And industry and virtue were rewarded for, as we neared the Wood, I could see two figures standing in amongst the trees, one, a woman in black, the other a man in riding boots.

"Stop a moment, Abdy!" I said, in a voice that I hoped would not carry too far. "I see some fine flowers by the roadside that I simply must pick." I leapt out of the carriage at once, and went scrambling up the bank. So intent were they on their criminal conversation that they never noticed me. I picked flowers at random, as slowly as I dared, waiting for the man's face to become visible. All things come to he who waits, and at last, the man turned just enough for me to see who it was. I nearly fainted from the surprise, for there, before my eyes, drawn, thin, ashen white, was Knightley.

I was, of course, deeply shocked. I had always believed Knightley to be the soul of honor. But of course, there are circumstances that can drive a man to the utter depths. I cast my mind back and remembered how, when he first wed, he had moved into Hartfield! I had proclaimed it a shocking plan then, and knew it would never do. Mr. Woodhouse, with his extreme sensibility, would try the patience of a saint and that was the one virtue, obviously, that Knightley lacked. The last two years of Mr. Woodhouse's life saw a great deal of absence on the part of Knightley. He went to London, he went to Kingston, in fact, he was always gone on business. Emma Woodhouse saw more of Knightley than did Emma Knightley. Granted, that seemed to have changed after Mr. Woodhouse's death (such a gentleman, I miss him so), but I had the proof before my eyes that habits – and vices – once undertaken are hard to break.

These thoughts and many more raced through my mind. Weston had horses, but Knightley did not, except for those his wife had brought him. Who else but Knightley would be the one hiring from Abdy? Sending Weston for the bill was simply to throw sand in the eyes of anyone seeking to trace his steps. The guilt must be overwhelming, I thought, as Knightley looked out across the fields. I stirred not a hair, and he turned back to Harriet. They walked away. I scrambled back to my feet – grass stains everywhere, I noticed with dismay, on my delicate lawn – and ran back to the carriage.

"To Abbey-Mill Farm!" I cried.

"To where, ma'am?" Young Abdy turned and looked back at me, a picture of dismay.

"Abbey-Mill Farm," I repeated. "I wish to take these beautiful flowers as a comfort to Mrs. Martin."

"I don't think that's wise, ma'am," Abdy said. Indeed, he looked very peculiar. And then it dawned upon me: Abdy was afraid! He knew that the man who was visiting Harriet Martin was the man who murdered Robert Martin, and that man was at the farm right at this moment. He had no intention of putting himself at risk by meeting up with the felon. A coward, that was what he was.

"Nonsense!" I said, with a surge of righteous triumph. "Pull yourself together, Abdy. Knightley is there, at this moment. We have the perfect opportunity to wield 'the strong lance of justice'!"

To my dismay, my shock, my horror, Abdy jumped down from the carriage and said, "No, ma'am. I'm not going over to that farm, no, not for no amount of money. It's all been a trick, it has. I don't know how you found out, but I'm not going near there, and neither are you!" And he actually had me by the arm; he was dragging me out of the carriage!

"Help!" I cried. "Help! What are you doing? Help! He's gone mad! Help!"

"Shut up!" Abdy hissed, and placed a coarse hand across my mouth. He was dragging me across the road, muttering into my ear, "I don't know how you find out, you old besom, but by God, you'll not tell anyone else. First to Westons, then out here. All those questions. You think I didn't see Knightley over there in the trees? I know what you're up to, sure enough. You think you'll be having Mr. Knightley arrest me, but I'm not going to be hanged. But how did you find out? I swear I didn't go there to kill him. It was all just a stupid quarrel over a harlot, and now I've got to do something about you…"

I was struggling furiously – obviously the man was completely mad – and I managed to tear my mouth free for one moment. "Help!" I screamed. "Help!"

The brute actually struck me, tumbling me to the ground. I looked up, to see his hand raised again. I shrank back, and another man grabbed Abdy from behind, spinning him around. It was Knightley. I saw him strike Abdy, and then I fainted.

6

I came to my senses in the parlor of Abbey-Mill Farm. Harriet Martin, blowsy as a dairy maid, with grass and mud all over the hem of her black skirts, was sitting beside me while her maid waved a vial of hartshorn under my nose. I coughed.

"Water," I begged. I could still feel the ruffian's hand across my face.

"Here you are, ma'am," said the maid.

"How are you feeling?" Mrs. Martin asked.

"Shattered. Absolutely shattered."

"Mr. Elton has been sent for, ma'am," Betty said. "As has Mr. Perry. And that murdering ostler has been taken down to the jail and may they throw away the key! Whoever heard of the like?"

"And Mr. Knightley?" I asked, one eye upon Harriet Martin.

She did not even blush as she said, "He accompanied Harry, William and John into town, so that he could give evidence. He said to tell you that he hoped that you would forgive his attendance upon you, but he needed to ensure that Abdy would be in no position to threaten anyone again."

"I should hope not!" I exclaimed. "Might I beg for some tea?"

"Of course," Harriet said. "Betty, would you?"

"I'll run and put the kettle on this minute, ma'am," Betty said.

I lay there, after Betty had gone, trying to put all the pieces together. John Abdy, then, had killed Robert Martin. But then, what was Knightley doing out walking the woods with Harriet? And where did Weston fit into all of this? And how was I going to find out?

A carriage came clattering up the drive – undoubtedly Perry and Mr. E – and all was chaos. Harriet ran for the door, her handkerchief, scarf, gloves, and something white fluttering to the floor behind her. I managed to struggle to my feet and gather her belongings for her. The note I put into my pocket for safe-keeping, and sank back onto the sofa as everyone surged into the room.

My dear *caro sposo*, how shocked he was, how concerned, how devoted! He was all for Abdy being hanged that day, and everyone agreed. A little tea, and Mr. Perry decreed that I was quite fit to return home, so long as Mr. E drove carefully. I thanked Harriet and her Betty with a pretty little speech, and was helped into Perry's carriage. We all waved goodbye, and I wondered how long it would be before Harriet would miss her note.

7

Of course, all anyone talked about in Highbury for weeks was John Abdy. How John Abdy sold a stud horse to Robert Martin, but somehow the horse was not... Well, I think discretion demands we not go into that. There was a quarrel. Robert Martin made threats. John Abdy came out to see Robert Martin, and made certain... accusations. Robert Martin became violently angry. And Abdy, having a gun with him, shot Robert Martin in the north paddock. It was all irredeemably vulgar, and the conviction and hanging of John Abdy took no time at all.

Of course, the whole truth of it never did come out. I knew, but only because I had been privy to the note.

"My dearest," it read, "It pains me to the utmost to say farewell to you, sweetest of all creatures, but K has made me see that this has been a madness. Such a sweet madness! But all must be over, forever. Some day you will find someone worthier than I to whom you can give your heart..." And much more arrant nonsense, but at the end, the signature: "W."

So it had been Weston, after all, meeting Harriet in the woods every Thursday afternoon. Knightley must have gone to tell her that all was over. How like Weston, to palm off a reprehensible task on a man of such integrity. I have often wondered if Abdy had been blackmailing Weston. He certainly seems more cheerful these days, as does Knightley. It might also help that Harriet Martin has removed to Yarmouth, where her sister-in-law lives. I am sure she has made herself an adornment to that sea-side resort.

The only vexation has been that I cannot see any utility to our knowledge, other than my own private amusement. However, I have heard that Emma Knightley has hired a nursery-maid who is far too young and pretty for her station. Considering that "W" has entangled himself with Emma's governess and Emma's friend, I feel certain of the sequel. It may become my duty to warn someone. And, despite my acute sensibilities, I have never shirked my duty.

Darkness at Noon

Alexander Frew

There is a degree of consensus in many quarters that driving is a scourge and a modern menace. From the early 1900's, when the passage of the motor vehicle was said to be so fast that it would induce startled, pregnant women to go into labour, and make horses gallop off in sudden fury, killing their riders, the rise of the motor vehicle has seemed to coincide with a speedier, more frenetic society.

In the present bucolic surroundings of deep countryside and equally deep, rutted roads, any motor vehicle seemed like a startlingly modern intruder, as out of place amid green fields as a cosmonaut in the Mackintosh Tea Rooms, Glasgow, once owned and managed by the Edwardian lady, Miss Cranston.

The brand new Ford Zephyr 6, the four door version, in classic grey and maroon, or maybe it was it maroon and grey since it was after all two-toned, was driven by a man who was sweating under his soft black felt hat. And since this was Scotland, heading into the second half of the twentieth century, and a typical overcast day in the Borders country, there was little reason as to why this should be the case.

Beside him on the passenger side of the bench seat, lurked another man, and it was as if Lennie from 'Mice and Men' had come to large, equally sweating life.

The Ford was straining enough to take in the rough road into the fair countryside of the Lowlands, but the driver seemed to be of the mind that there was a challenge that was not being taken. Finally and he saw a signpost that indicated the road to the next town - or rather village - since their trip today had taken them to the only gathering of buildings around here that could be graced with that name. He noted that the road along which they were bowling with such bouncy élan was wide open and they would be seen by the few other motorists who tried this route, while to one side was a cart track that led between the trees of the forest that had appeared on their left hand side. With an adroit twist of the wheel, and with an approving grunt from his companion, the driver twisted his wheel to follow this path, entering the woodlands, slowing down as he did so, shifting and grinding gears in his haste.

'Hurry,' said his companion, holding on to the bag in his lap with a vice-like grip that indicated either he was holding a depository of some value or he had a deep attachment to a old leather satchel, the like of which might have been taken from a blind schoolboy.

'All right,' said the driver, who noted even as they went onwards that the daylight was diminishing rapidly around them to the point where if he could find the switch he would have to operate the headlights. He steered with might, he steered with main, but what he did not do was steer with any particular skill, and as he made the once-cherished Zephyr follow a path that had been made for sheep, cattle and horses, who tended to wander in a zig-zag conga line rather than one which could be described as straight. At a crucial juncture a recalcitrant fir tree decided to take issue with this strange intruder into the woodlands and appeared to jump out in front of them. In reality of course the driver had simply failed to take a particularly curvy bend with any kind of finesse.

The two men, who knew each other as Tam and Jock, mainly because these were their names, climbed out of their vehicle. They had little choice given the fact it had crashed into their nemesis, a tree. The name of the area, coincidentally rhymed with tree because they had crashed into a tree in Kirkinlee, in the Galloway Forest, situated in the county of Dumfries and Galloway in Scotland.

Not that either of them would have needed telling what region they were in. They knew they were not far from Dumfries because they had made a very specific appointment with that town, if appointments can exist in such a manner. They had planned for this day and even this very hour, but the devil, as always, is in the detail and the entry to the crime scene had been planned in much greater detail than the departure.

As they stumbled from the junkyard ready wreckage of what had once been a perfectly good Ford Zephyr 6, they staggered around for a short while like two drunks emerging from a Glasgow bar. Neither, it seemed was actually injured from their impromptu encounter with solid woodland, but they were badly shaken.

One of the victims glanced at the Ford, a vehicle that Jock had selected because it was lamentably easy to break into and drive away with a simple twist of the ignition wires, a fact the owner would point out to the insurance company when he was making a claim for his half inched property. Tam examined the front of the vehicle and saw that there was steam rising from the bonnet and the two front wheels were twisted in different directions. Also there was a smell of petrol that argued they should perhaps make haste from what was now their ex-getaway vehicle before it decided to act like the ones in a film and burst into flame.

'That didnae go well,' said Jock, a statement that earned him a good long stare from his companion.

'Ye should not have been driving as fast,' commented Tam, 'We're not trying tae be Bonnie and Clyde ye ken.'

'Mair like Adam and Eve,' added Jock. 'As in I can't Adam and Eve it. How could ye have been so stupid? Gettin' on ma case to go faster. Discretion, that's whit it needed, not beltin' through like we were oan one of them motorways.'

Tam looked as if he was going to make some sharp rejoinder to this, but it was obvious he was still shaken by the events that had just occurred.

The two men contrasted sharply in looks. Jock was standing at his full height, trembling with fury, but his fury was not impressive due to his height being that of an average fourteen year old boy. He had the gleam in his narrowed eyes of a man who was already assessing the situation, and he looked as nervous as a bad-natured greyhound straining to get out of the trap. His mouth too was a thin line as if he was holding back a rising tide of ire that threatened to burst through this makeshift dam.

Tam, in contrast seem to have been built on the lines of the vessels that were still being constructed in the shipyards of his native Clydeside. He was impressively broad across the shoulders with a back that seemed built for carrying coals and his arm muscles bulged through the thin cloth of his poorly made post-war demob belted overcoat. The whole assembly was let down by his belly. That bulged over the waistband of his worsted wool trousers, because Tam liked nothing more than spending his afternoons in the *Saracens Head* public house, quaffing pints, while displaying a marked disinclination to make his brow sweat, and forever looking for easy money. Hence the reason why he was now in this predicament.

While Tam's brow was unfurrowed, there was a shadow of anger that reddened his cheeks. He took a deep breath, made a step backwards, reached through a car window that had been shattered by the impact, and took out the black bag that was the ultimate cause of their trouble,

'See this? I could chuck it far enough me auld boy.' He gave an experimental heave and, given his prowess in this area, would have precipitated the bag an untold distance within the confines of the forest. It was equally clear that once the deed was done, given the unforgiving nature of the undergrowth, it would be hard, not to say impossible, to locate the object of their attentions.

'I widnae do that,' said Jock with a trace of alarm in his voice at the look on the other man's face. He knew that his companion was quite capable of carrying out such an impulsive action only to regret what he had done a few seconds later. His tone immediately became friendly, and he even managed to relax and smile properly. 'All right Tam, you're upset, but think about it, ye worked hard for whit you've got there. Dae ye really want to literally throw it all away?'

Now that something resembling a thought was echoing

around his skull, Tam saw the sense in what his companion was saying and lowered his arm while still clutching the handle of the precious bag. Jock breathed an inward sigh of relief, but maintained his tough guy air. It wouldn't do to let Tam know how worried he was making his companion. Jock gave him a nod and smiled at the result, while all the time wanting to strike him down.

'But we don't have time to hang around, do ye ken whit time it is?' He took out a pocket watch and looked at the large numbers on the dial. Luckily it too had been unharmed in the crash. He was amazed that they had both survived with only a few minor scratches and one or two sore joints, because the front of the car had gone inwards, nearly compressing the passengers in the same way as the bonnet. They might have both have been killed if the impact had been that much greater. And here was his watch, not even broken. 'One in the afternoon,' he said, 'and ye ken whit that means?'

'Not sure aboot that,' said Tam.

'It means that the polis will have reached the building society, found out what's happened, and they'll be well after us.'

'Aye, we have to get out of here,' said Tam. He staggered, then began looking around in a slightly dazed manner that indicated he might well be suffering from some degree of concussion. For a moment he seemed to forget the precious satchel in his hand and it looked as if he was going to drop it to ground. Jock stepped forward at this but Tam came to his senses and gathered the bag to his side again. Jock might try to wrest it off him and run, but he suspected that he would not get very far.

'I wasnae in the scouts,' said Jock, as he looked along the unobtrusive path that did not exactly loom before them. 'But I'm guessing that we head north and keep going an' that'll take us weel away from Dumfries. If we keep to the woodlands we should be fine I would think.'

'In whit way do you mean?' Tam scratched his head.

'How far did we get in here off the side of what they laughably call the main road?'

'Can't think,' said Tam, 'but we wis goin' a bit fast.'

'We're at least quarter a mile deep in the woodlands, and the ground wasn't wet, which means we wouldn't leave any tyre tracks. That means the polis might miss our little diversion altogether. We'll stay in the woodlands.'

'Why?'

'So that we can keep away frae the polis,' said Jock bluntly. 'They'll be all over the main road like you on auld Morrison's widow before the end o' this day. We got to keep going is all.'

'All right, I'll get the gun,' Tam reached in through the broken window again and pulled out the weapon that had done the deed. Now Jock had another regret, that he had been so busy planning ahead that he had forgotten to look for the gun, and now it was in the hands of someone who was dazed, confused, belligerent, and who was not a great thinker in the best of circumstances.

'Great,' said Jock, who was beginning to regret his choice of companion, 'dae me a favour and pick the nearest, deepest undergrowth ye come across and chuck that straight intae the middle.'

'But whit if the polis catch up with us?' Jock was not built in a manner that encouraged athletic activities, he was more a caber tosser than a runner, but he still managed a little jig of frustration.

'If we get rid of the weapon we get rid of one more piece of evidence, Tam. If they catch us with a gun they'll throw seven books at us. For a start we stole it just like the car, it doesn't have a licence and it was used in a robbery. That counts as a form of aggravated assault. We don't need it. Dae whit I say as soon as.'

'Nae,' said Tam. 'This is for if the dugs catch up with us an' we have tae mak' break for it.' He was clearly set on keeping the weapon, and he was telling the truth when he surmised the police might have tracker dogs to hunt down their quarry. This area was not known for crime sprees but it *was* in the country and dogs abounded, often used in the amateur hunt.

'Whit dae ye think this is? We *are* making a break for it dunderheid. Chuck the thing ur they'll throw the book at us.' Jock let forth a sudden blaze of fury, annoyed and in possession of knowledge he did not feel like divulging to his companion.

'Nae,' said Tam, 'this is ma insurance policy,' he heaved the bag, 'and this tae.' He looked thoughtfully at Jock and at the gun in his other hand. Jock was not slow at catching his train of thought and immediately jumped into the silence. If he was one thing, he was a fast talker and he knew the more the silence grew between them, the more time it would give Tam to explore the inside of his own head.

'So, my wee pal, you know exactly how tae get tae the next village?' Jock asked. 'We were oan a woodland trail an' crashed into a tree, do you ken where you are?' He had to wait for a moment while the wheels turned, albeit slowly in the head of his companion. At last the cogitation was complete, and Tam lowered the gun which he might have used to shoot his companion in the head. Or would have, he thought, so that only one person would benefit from their incursion into the Dumfries and Galloway building society. Five thousand pounds had made its way from their coffers into the very bag he was clutching at his side.

However, Tam knew his limitations, and that he was far from being the brains of the outfit. Indeed, when he had been in the *Saracen's Head*, it had been Jock who'd approached him, bought him a couple of pints of McEwan's, and outlined what they were going to do. Jock had heard about the warehouse job where Tam had used his great strength to load some of the new-fangled TV sets on to the back of a waiting lorry. The big man had been paid the princely sum of thirty pounds. Jock knew that if he had a large, somewhat terrifying companion, who would present a front, that would achieve Jock's ambitions.

Tam had been the key to success, to the extent that he was the one who'd marched up to the sub-branch counter, where he had thrust the weapon into the face of the terrified cashier. The gentleman behind the counter had been forced to carry out the satchel containing the money to Jock waiting in the stolen car. Jock was the instigator with his encouraging words and phrases and the painting of mind pictures, where the two of them were lying on a beach in the Bahamas with a sexy girl each in their arms. Like many of his type, Tam did not see the many pitfalls that lay between gaining the funds and actually leaving the country to pursue the dream, especially given that in this year of 1953 air flight was notoriously expensive and he didn't even know the location of the Bahamas or indeed the addresses of the sexy girls in question.

But now they were stuck in the middle of a forest surrounded by sitka spruce and fir trees and thick undergrowth given the time of year. Ever so gently – given that he was with a volatile companion who had insisted that he pressed on taking the wheel to drive *real fast and escape the polis* as he had phrased the details of the escape plans – Jock was hoping that they could at least put some distance between the two of them and the inevitable police presence. On the plus side, no one in their right mind would have tried to drive along a woodland trail in the middle of summer, when the undergrowth was at its thickest.

Jock was in possession of one major fact that might have altered the relationship between them quite radically, but Tam thought he held all the cards, namely the bag and the gun, as they started walking in the direction that would take them to the village of Dundrennan.

The pair of them hoped that once there they would find a source of transport that would help them get to the comparative safety of Glasgow. It was doubtful if they would find a car they could hire, which would be the better option, but Jock was a skilled break-in artist and always carried a length of wire coat-hanger that could open a car door. He was also adept at rewiring and starting them up, and was quite sure that, once they did so, they could simply start their escape once more.

Once back in the arms of civilisation – well, Glasgow at any rate – he was sure they could disappear into the underworld and become faceless, invisible and hopefully unarrestable.

They had walked along for what seemed like an hour but was probably less than half that time. Tam, who was a man built like a brick outhouse, started to slow down. He was not used to rural surroundings and although the forest mould seemed reasonably soft under their feet, branches and pine cones lay everywhere, traps for the unwary to stumble over, while the odd low-hanging branch would whip them across the face as they progressed. Because of his size, this happened far more often to Tam than his smaller, more agile companion.

'My back hurts,' he moaned. 'My feet hurt,' he added. 'How far is the next village noo?'

'Not too far,' said Jock, who, in reality, did not have any clue where it was, but had an inkling that if they stuck to the track all would be well. 'We jist have to keep going or we're in real trouble.'

'Ach, tae hell wi' it,' said Tam. 'I'm gonnae sit doon an' rest for an while.'

One of the features of most woodlands is that the wind blows heavily during the winter and knocks down the occasional tree – so there was no lack of seating for the large-framed man. He lumbered over to a moss-covered log at the side of trail and sat down with a belligerent look on his oversized features that made him rather resemble Rondo Hatton, he of the acromegalic features, who had starred in the horror films of the thirties. The play of shadow across said twisted face now put an equally heavy shadow on the heart of his companion.

Jock wanted to shout and yell at his companion. Jock was

also weary because he, too, rarely walked further than he needed, mostly for his morning Daily Record and then to the pub for a pint of heavy. He gave a weary sigh and sat down beside the man he had pretended was his friend. Maybe it was all right to stay here for a while, rest and get ready to hurry to hurry on again. But Jock knew that the truth was simple. The police would not rest until they'd hunted down their quarry, and they were bound to have tracker dogs.

He had to find a way to put a rocket under the backside of his companion. They had to keep going. Then he managed to dredge something up from the back of his febrile mind. This was by no means the first time that Jock had been in trouble and had been forced to use his twisted wits.

Tam was from a lovely scheme outside Glasgow, called Pollock, where a four legged dog was a stranger and everyone, including the grannies, carried a cut throat razor. However part of the reason he had taken on the job was because he'd known the lay of the land since he was a child. Indeed he had lived here with his grandparents during the war. Their accommodation had not been fancy since it was one of those rural cottages with coal fires, and no lighting except candles. The old man, who worked as a farm labourer around and about these parts, had told the wide-eyed boy many dark tales about the region. Jock, on their journey through this benighted place, had remembered listening to the folktales of his grandfather, and was now able to bless the fact that he had recalled with good memory, the same one that told him they were heading in the right direction.

'We have tae keep going, I forgot to tell you about the Black Dog.'

'The black dug? Whit's that?' Like many of his ilk, Tam was quite a superstitious man and believed in the likes of ghosts, UFOs and not walking under ladders. In addition, he would throw salt over his shoulder if he spilled a salt container – much to the irritation of those behind him – always refused to work on the thirteenth of the month, particularly a Friday, and was careful not to break a mirror in case it brought seven years bad luck.

'The Black Dog is the size of the biggest mutt ye ever saw,' said Jock, 'plus anither fifty per cent. It has jaws that kin crush maist animals an' it hates intruders intae its domain.'

'Who ur the intruders and whit's a domain?'

'Us. We're the intruders and this forest, it's a domain.'

'Naw, naw, that's all rubbish!' Tam was beginning to show fear, even though he fought against his feelings.

'These woodlands is thoosands o' years old,' said Jock. 'Kin ye imagine the things that exist here, the ghaists an' bogles, the deid that rise in the dark - here it's nearly dark the noo.' He had hit on the right tack, because Tam forgot all about his aching back and lumbered to his feet.

It was obvious that he had taken on the gist of the conversation, and began to stride along so briskly that his companion had some difficulty in keeping up with him. Jock did not really believe the story, if there really was something lurking in the forest then surely it would have been discovered by now? But then again the world was a big place and all manner of strange things were being discovered all the time. He had read somewhere that Dumfries and Galloway, as a district, was one of the most underpopulated. It was a hard thing to believe, but most of the population of Scotland - a country that at the present time numbered some 5.1 million people - lived within easy commuting distance from Glasgow or Edinburgh. Basically, the rest of the country, like Canada's expanses, was empty.

Jock had been right in pointing out how dark it had become where they were now. Definitely a lot darker than just twilight, even though it was barely gone 3 in the afternoon. Clouds had obscured the sun, and heavy foliage obscured most of their surroundings, which meant it was almost like being out at night. They appeared as a pair of shadows moving along as fast as they could, which was not quickly, because they were town and beer-bred idlers who were quickly running out of stamina.

'The Black Dog just appears out of nowhere,' said Jock. 'It can attack from the side or from behind, an' it kills by ripping your throat and tearing off your head.'

Despite his bulk, Tam gave a whimper that could have come from a small child and moved on, making a valiant attempt for a man who'd spent most of his days either in bed, signing on the dole or making useless forecasts in the local bookies.

Jock knew that at this pace they would be out of the woods - literally - in under half an hour. True, all was not entirely well, but at least when they reached the village he would be able to steal another car and get them out of here, his hot-wire fingers were already twitching at the thought.

That was when they both heard a sound behind them that made them suddenly halt in their flight.

It was a growl.

One of those low growls that would probably emanate from a creature the size of a small bull, or a particularly large dog.

A really large dog.

That was when Jock discovered that the hairs on the back of the head really do rise when someone is frightened, and that a chill can literally sweep through the body.

At that moment the sun broke free of the clouds and the rays of light came down through the trees, partially illuminating the undergrowth behind them.

There, briefly glimpsed and seen only as a movement, was a non-descript black shape, followed by that deep, rumbling growl.

This was enough for Tam, who raised the gun and pulled the trigger four times in quick succession, panic making the bullets fly anywhere other than at the intended target.

'What the hell? He asked no-one in particular as another loud growl followed the last one in quick succession.

'I thought a loaded gun would be too much,' spat out Jock from a mouth that seemed unnaturally dry with fear. 'I thought you were dangerous enough in that bank withoot a loaded weapon'. Tam gave a shout and threw the useless weapon at the heaving undergrowth - whatever was in there seemed to be getting closer and could jump on them at any time - and they both spun around, got their feet into motion and started running. It was strange how their energy, which had started flagging, was suddenly restored by the proximity of menace. The Black Dog was on their heels, they thought, and the image of heads rolling about untethered to a troublesome body was uppermost in their minds, even the mind of the man who had dreamt up the image in the first place.

While they were running the thought became too much for Jock, and he began screaming with fear. Tam, who was easily influenced in such matters, began screaming too and they were still hysterical with fear when they emerged from the other side of the woodland, straight into the arms of the grateful officers who had circled around via the main road, and who had just been about to conduct a search for the criminals.

The constables relieved them of the bag, which Jock was still holding, inside which was more than enough evidence to put them away for a good fifteen years for armed robbery, to be spent at Her Majesty's Pleasure, Barlinnie.

Back in the forest Fergus Flynn, gamekeeper to the local Laird and adept trout tickler, strode along the cart track, crooked stick in hand.

There was a growl from the undergrowth and a heaving black hide showed as he parted the mass of shrubs and briar stems with his stick. The growl rumbled out again.

'Ye daft bugger Sam,' said Fergus as he freed the animal from the tree roots in the ditch that had tangled on his paw, holding him tight in place like a woody rope – the rabbit he'd been chasing was now long gone, merely a distant memory to the canine.

'Ye got aw caught up again? I tell ye, ye must have rocks in your head, so you have.' He took out a large black-handled clasp knife and used the sharp blade to saw through a couple of the roots that held the animal. 'Noo let's get ye hame and get ye sorted.'

The big old black Labrador limped beside his master, wagging his tail, and gave a deep growl of appreciation.

Gardener's World

Tom Johnstone

Hoeing the patio is very therapeutic, she finds. After a few moments, she realises she is screaming in rage. The poor weeds haven't done anything to deserve her spite! They are a proxy for something else. Embarrassed, she glances around to check the neighbours aren't outdoors. If not, these days the chances are someone is in next door and heard the commotion. She waits for someone to come out and ask, "Are you all right, Sue?" But no one does. Instead, a shadow descends upon the concrete where the felled weeds lie.

"Having fun?" James asks.

She doesn't answer. She just carries on with what she was doing, as if he wasn't there. Let him suffer as she has. He shifts his weight uneasily from one foot to the other as she continues her rage-hoeing.

"Looking good," he says.

"Thank you!" she says with more than a trace of sarcasm.

"The garden," he adds.

"Only the garden?"

"You too of course."

He frowns uncertainly, then moves tentatively towards her, as if to embrace her. When she smells his scent, she flinches from him, despising herself for breaking her vow of silence. Not that she intended to stick to it that long: Just long enough to make him feel uncomfortable. His discomfort is nothing compared to what she is suffering.

"Everything all right?" he asks.

With a bitter half-smile, she begins clearing up the weeds she'd gouged out of the patio earlier. They look as limp and wrung-out as she feels. She wonders if he can see how red her eyes are, or if he even notices the streaks of dried tears that have left salty paths down her cheeks, leaving the skin tight and dry.

"Well, you've done a good job, Sue," he carries on, with the hopelessness of a man digging his own grave. "Lock-down's done wonders for the garden..."

He trails off. He hasn't worked it out. The penny hasn't dropped.

"You left your phone at home, James."

He blinks.

"Oh. So I did." He smiles guilelessly. "Good thing I didn't need it today!"

He looks towards one of the flower-beds she has renovated.

"These are new," he says. "What's growing there?"

"You're the gardener," she says. "You tell me."

She smiles to herself. She knows he doesn't have any real horticultural knowledge. He just works for the Council parks department, cutting hedges and mowing verges. It's not really gardening at all. More grounds maintenance. Over the last couple of weeks, she's learned more about different plants and their properties than he'll ever know. But then he's not really interested, is he? Understandable really. When you spend all day gardening, you don't necessarily want to come home and spend your spare time doing it.

Besides, he has other hobbies.

"Okay…" He looks at the flower-bed uncertainly. "The orange, red and yellow ones are… Nasturtiums?"

"Very good!" she sing-songs in her teaching voice. Not had to use *that* lately – except on Zoom. "They're edible too – so we can have some for dinner in the salad."

"Sounds nice," he says, sounding less then convinced. "Didn't know you could eat them."

"You can! As a matter of fact, I'm going for an edible landscape here. Come on – name me another! What about those purple ones?"

"Sue," he laughs, "I'm not one of your students!" He stares at the flowers, as if willing the name to come to him, but it won't. "No! Never seen it before."

"Oh well, you'll be seeing a lot of it," she smiles. "And tasting it too! Come on. I'm hungry."

She isn't really, but they go inside. He showers while she begins preparing the salad, after carefully washing her hands.

"How was your day?" she asks.

"Not bad," he says.

"Is that all you can say? Come on, James – tell me about the big, wide world out there! *This* is my world now." She gestures around the kitchen and out into the garden drenched by the late afternoon sun.

"Well, it was a bit depressing actually. Had to go around all the play parks chaining them up."

"Not as depressing as dying alone in an isolation ward I suppose."

He blinks.

"Sorry. Being morbid. Hard not to be at the moment. So that's what you essential workers do all day, is it? Lock up play parks?"

He nods.

"Well, not just that."

"It's just… What's so essential about a gardener? It's not as if you're a doctor or nurse or delivery driver or anything."

He smiles, almost embarrassed. It's amazing how awkward things are between them, almost as if they haven't been living together for the past ten years. Sue wonders if he's got any idea what she's been going through.

"I've been thinking that myself," he agrees. "But the parks are open. People need them for their daily exercise. And I suppose… Well, *someone's* got to look after the grounds. Are you going to put those purple flowers in?"

He points to where they lie on the sideboard.

"I haven't decided yet," she says, staring hard into his eyes. "I don't know," she adds, looking away again, unable in that moment to bear the sight of him with his anxious hang-dog expression. "The Nasturtiums are peppery enough. These might just be a little too bitter…"

"You okay, Sue?" he asks. "Not getting cabin fever here, are you?"

"Oh no, not at all," she replies, unable to keep an edge of sarcasm from her voice. "I've got Zoom classes to run, there's plenty to do in the garden…" She takes a deep breath before continuing, despising herself as she hears the tremor in her voice. "…And today, when I got bored, I had the pleasure of reading your Facebook messages to… Mary, is it? Or Milly? I can't remember off the top of my head."

"How did you…?"

"Unlock the phone? The pass-code's my birthday. Well, that's sweet anyway. And easy to work out. So you're not even going to try and deny it then…?"

"Sue…"

"Don't 'Sue' me, James. The sooner you explain these messages the better."

"We're just friends, that's all," he says, his eyes darting around as if searching for the phone. He's rocking his best little boy lost look. She falls for it every time. But usually, she's too busy at the school to dwell on what he gets up to when she's not around. Things are different now she's working from home

Usually he doesn't leave his phone lying about with the messenger app there for all to see.

"I'm allowed friends, aren't I?" he asks plaintively, but those messages were a little more than friendly.

"*I'm allowed friends, aren't I?*" she repeats in a parody of his whine. He flinches. *Poor baby!* "I'm not your mother, James. It's wonderful you've made a new friend, and that she's a woman. Well done!" Her anger spent for now, her voice softens to an almost pleading tone. "But just for once, couldn't you make friends with someone you *don't* want to sleep with?"

He sighs, covers his face with his hands, the drama queen. She's tempted to ask if he's washed them first.

"Sue, you've got it all wrong!" he cries out.

She smiles, feeling the dryness of her salt-tracked cheeks as the corners of her mouth push them upward, disturbing the residue left by her earlier tears.

"Good," she says briskly, not really trusting him, but prepared to give him the benefit of the doubt, this time.

He looks up, his eyes widening, as if relieved her fury has subsided. Perhaps he thinks he's been granted a reprieve. If so, he doesn't know the full extent of his good fortune. She looks at the purple flowers lying innocently on the sideboard. James wanders through to the dining room and slumps on a chair, as if exhausted by the row. Suddenly, she reaches out to grab the flowers and throw them away, before she's tempted to go through with what she contemplated.

Then she remembers, and puts on the rubber gloves with the long gauntlets. Can't be too careful. Not like James. Leaving his phone lying around like that. Sloppy with her feelings. Almost like he didn't care if she read those suggestive messages. Careless of him too not to know what the purple flowers are. He was like that when he was at horticultural college. Too lazy to learn his plant identification, a mistake that could have cost him dearly. It's an error she's not going to make.

She read about a gardener who died of multiple organ failure after just brushing against them. She wonders if he would have eaten them, or spat them out because of their bitterness, and if she would have gone ahead and swallowed hers despite knowing what she does. She wonders if it would have hurt more than the terrible emptiness that is now her constant companion. But still, on balance, living is better than not living.

Tomorrow, when he's at work, she will dig out and burn the Aconite.

The Judge's Wife
John M. Floyd

"Ms. Sanderford?"

"That's right."

The man on the porch took off his cap. "There's been an accident, ma'am." He turned and nodded in the direction of a second man, waiting at the foot of the steps. "The police sent us to fetch you."

Janice Sanderford put a hand to her throat. "Oh, no. My husband…?"

"Yes ma'am. They're working on getting him out of the car. They don't think he's bad hurt, but he's asking for you."

"Oh my God." She looked around a moment, dazed, then came out and pulled the door shut behind her. "I'm ready," she said.

A moment later they were headed east on Highway 12, in an old blue Ford. The first man was at the wheel, Janice in the passenger seat, the other man in the back. She sat straight and stiff in her Polo shirt and jeans, hugging her elbows. Her face was chalk-white.

"What happened?" she asked. "Was it that bad intersection on the edge of town?"

The two men exchanged glances. "What happened," the driver said, "was a kidnapping. And pretty well done, too." He looked thoughtful. "Imagine that: the wife of J.P. Sanderford, snatched in broad daylight."

Janice blinked. She studied his face, then turned to look at his partner. The man in the back seat held up a pistol so she could see it.

"I don't believe this," she said.

The driver was smiling now, his eyes glittering under the brim of the John Deere cap. "We been watching you. The plan was to wait till tomorrow morning, but when we saw your husband leave awhile ago, we decided—"

"Why not?" the partner said, from the back seat.

The driver gave Janice another grin. "We're the Mauronds, by the way."

"The morons?"

"Mauronds. I'm Eddie, that's my brother Nate in the back. We'll be spending some time together, the three of us, the next day or so."

Janice's face, so pale a moment ago, had turned the color of new brick. "You *are* morons," she said, "if you think this'll work."

Eddie narrowed his eyes. "What do you mean?"

"I mean you're idiots." She turned as if to make sure Nate knew he was included in her assessment. "You're going to hold me for ransom, is that the idea?"

"That's the idea." Eddie Maurond's grin had disappeared. "What's idiotic about that?"

"I'll tell you," she said. "Jason won't pay it."

"Your husband, you mean?"

"Yes, my husband. He won't pay it."

"How do you know? You don't know how much we'll ask for."

"Doesn't matter. Do you know anything about him? Anything about *us*?"

Eddie was quiet a moment. "We know he's rich. We ain't from here, but we heard of him. 'J.P. Sanderford, one of the most successful trial lawyers in the Southeast...' Anyhow, we got directions to your house, and—"

"We're getting a divorce. Did you know that? Jason won't pay to get me back because he doesn't *want* me back." She glared at him. "You beginning to get the picture?"

Eddie shot an uneasy glance at Nate, who looked even more worried. "I don't believe you," Eddie said to her.

"Fine. Wait till you call him, to ask for the money." She settled back in her seat, her color fading. Now she just looked tired.

Eddie braked, swerved onto a dirt road, and stopped the car fifty yards from the highway, in a thick stand of pines.

They sat there in dead silence. After a minute or so Eddie cranked down his window; birds sang and played in the trees beside the road. It was a warm, cloudless afternoon. The breeze through the open window smelled like freshly mown hay.

"This is crazy," he murmured.

"It's crazy all right," she said. "You made a mistake, Eddie or whatever your name really is. Why don't you just turn around and take me back to my house, and we'll forget this ever—"

"No. Not a chance." He removed his cap and ran a hand through his hair. "We've done this, we've come this far, we ain't turning back. He'll pay if we ask him."

"He won't. What he'll do is call the cops, and they'll find you. Or, more likely, he'll just do nothing at all."

Eddie's face darkened. "Then we'll kill you."

"Kill me?" She did a palms-up. "What good would that do? Then you'd be murderers as well as kidnappers, and you still won't have your money."

"Well, we're not letting you go. Not now."

"Why not?"

Eddie squirmed in his seat. "Because we left him a message already."

"You what?"

"We left your husband a message on his office answering machine. I called there from a pay phone after we saw him leave your house, and said we have you and we want a quarter million in cash, or we'll kill you."

"You called his *office*?"

"That's right. A woman's voice on his machine said leave a message, and I did."

"I guess you probably spoke through a handkerchief, like in the movies," she said.

"Don't make fun of me. Yeah, I disguised my voice."

Suddenly her eyes widened. "You called the house last night, too. Didn't you."

Eddie made no reply.

"You did. I remember now. You called and talked to me, and said you were doing a survey, and asked if we had any children or other dependents living in the house. And I said no." She pinned him with her gaze. "You asked me so you'd know no one else was there."

"Well, it worked, didn't it?"

She closed her eyes, shook her head. "Did you happen to notice, when Jason left—did either of you even *notice*—that he had a suitcase with him?"

Eddie frowned. "What?"

"He's not gone to the office. He's gone to our condo, on the Coast, for two days. He won't even check that message you left until Thursday morning."

A silence fell.

"Can we get in touch with him?"

"Why? I told you, he won't pay your ransom. He'll be thrilled to be rid of me."

"I said, can we get in touch with him?"

She sighed. "Not until tonight. He'll get to Pensacola around nine. But I'm serious, he won't even consider—" She stopped and stared off into space. "My God."

"What is it?"

Janice Sanderford looked stunned. After a moment her eyes came back into focus, and she turned to face him.

"I know how you can get your money," she said.

Eddie studied her carefully. "What do you mean?"

"I know how you can get Jason to pay your ransom. You're

just using the wrong approach." She paused, as if deep in thought. "I could help you."

"Help us? Why would you help us?"

"So I could get half," she said.

"What?!"

"Why not? Without my help you'll get nothing, and God knows I could use the cash. I'm a software installer, in case you didn't know, and my debts—"

"But you're the wife of J.P. Sanderford."

"Grow up, Eddie. He's a lawyer. You really think I'll be getting much out of this divorce? If I help you, I guarantee you can pull this off, and for a lot more than a quarter million."

"How much?" he asked.

"How much more?"

"Total."

"A million at least. Maybe two."

Nate leaned over the seat, watching them like a little kid. "I don't follow this," he said. "If he wouldn't pay to get you back… what *would* he be paying for?"

"His reputation." A slow smile had spread across her face.

"What?" Eddie asked.

"His good name," she said. "I know his secret."

"What kind of secret?"

Both men stared at her, waiting.

"The judge's wife," she said.

*****

It was early evening, and their meeting place had changed

from a rusted 1992 Ford to a first-floor room at the Comfort Inn. Janice had put on Nate's windbreaker and wrapped her hair in a bandanna from Eddie's glove compartment to walk the ten paces from the car to the room. If anybody noticed her at all, they didn't seem to care.

"So this affair he's having," Eddie said, "is with the wife of a judge."

"A justice, actually. State Supreme Court." Janice took a bite of the Double Whopper Nate had brought back from his trip through the BK drive-thru. The Maurond brothers had finished theirs and were sitting together on one of the beds, watching her. She was seated at a table the size of a bicycle wheel. "He's one of the most powerful men around."

"And he—this judge—don't know what his wife and J.P. are up to?"

"Nobody knows but me," she said, chewing. "They've been careful. If word did get out, the judge would destroy him. Jason's career would be over."

Eddie gave that some thought. "Wait a minute. If your husband's playing around, why ain't *you* divorcing *him*?"

"Because I have no proof. I told you, they're careful."

"But you're sure? About the affair, I mean."

"Yes, I'm sure." She took a swallow of Sprite. "This'll work, I tell you. We'll go to her house tonight, around midnight—"

"Whose house?"

"The judge's wife."

"Why would we go to her house?"

"Because that's where you'll call my husband from. The

judge and his wife are out of town, so we'll have the place to ourselves."

Nate still looked worried. "You mean we'll break in?"

"We could, but we won't. I have a key."

"On you?" Eddie said.

"No, not on me. It's at home, we'll just stop by there and pick it up."

"How is it you have a key to their house?"

She stared at him. "How do you think?"

"Oh. I guess she gave your husband one."

"And he doesn't know that I know he has it."

"But… you said you had no proof. Wouldn't the house key be proof?"

"Not in a courtroom. My husband and the judge used to be fishing buddies. Jason could say he had the key from back then."

Eddie shook his head. "I still don't get it. Why go to her *house*?"

"I told you, that's where you'll place the call to Jason. You'll tell him you broke into their house and you've found her diary—it tells the whole story."

"Does she have a diary?"

"Who knows? It doesn't matter, long as Jason believes she does."

"And why should he believe it?"

"Because you'll call him from her house," Janice said again. "Jason has caller ID on his phone at the condo. When he sees where you're calling from—believe me, he knows her number—he'll realize you're really there. He has to be paranoid anyway after walking a tightrope for so long, so this'll make perfect sense to him. He'll know the house is supposed to be empty while the judge and his wife are away."

Eddie nodded, thinking. "So I call your husband, tell him I'm onto him, ask for the money, then lay low until he delivers."

"Right. And believe me, he'll deliver."

"And you'll get a third—"

"I'll get half."

Eddie studied her a moment, but made no objection. "What about after?" he said. "Won't it look funny, you coming into a lot of money all of a sudden?"

"Why should it? I told you, we're in the process of a divorce. People will think I got a big settlement. Besides, I'm well thought of around here."

"How well?"

"Very well. I'm the police chief's sister."

"My, my. Your sneaky mind might be a surprise to your family."

"It's a surprise to me, sometimes. Now, is this a go, or not?"

The two men swapped a look and, almost at the same time, shrugged.

"I guess so," Eddie said.

"Good." She drained her Sprite and plunked the cup down on the table. "Now that that's settled, and we're partners, we need to get something else straight."

"What do you mean?"

"Is Maurond your real name?"

"Sure it is. Why?"

"Edddie and Nate?"

"That's us."

"And when you first kidnapped me—did you intend to let me go, eventually?"

"Yes. Why?"

She leaned forward in her chair. "Kidnapping Rule #1: Don't tell the kidnappee your real names."

Both men frowned, thinking that over.

"That was a mistake," she said. "Among others."

They looked embarrassed.

"And from now on, there'll be no mistakes. I don't plan to go to jail over this. Understood?"

Two nods. "Understood."

A silence passed. Finally she said, "Any questions?"

Nate slowly raised a hand.

"What?" she asked.

"You gonna eat the rest of them fries?"

*****

They hung around the motel room for the next five hours, catnapping and gulping coffee and flipping channels on the remote. At a quarter past twelve they piled into the Ford, swung by the Sandersons' for the key, and drove the six miles to the house Janice identified as the judge's. A two-story colonial, on a wooded lot. No lights showed in the windows.

Janice directed them to a deserted side street, where they left the car and doubled back through a patch of pineforest to the judge's back yard. Once, when she got a little too far ahead, Eddie caught up with her and gave her arm a hard squeeze.

"Partners or not, you're still kidnapped," he said. "I'd be disappointed, after all this, to have to kill you anyway."

"I would too," she assured him.

Her key worked fine. The three of them stood together a minute in the moonlit kitchen, waiting and listening. Finally she led them along a shadowy back hallway. They'd agreed to be quiet and cautious, even though Janice seemed convinced the house was empty.

They paused outside what looked like a bedroom door. She had visited this house in happier times, she'd told them, and this was the room where Eddie should place his call: its only window faced the woods, so a light here wouldn't be seen from the road while he was on the phone.

"Wait here," she whispered. "I'll find a lamp and switch it on."

Eddie was still standing there in the hallway with Nate thirty seconds later, when the light came on. What it illuminated, however, was nothing a burglar would ever want to see.

"Hands up, boys," a voice said. "You're under arrest."

The voice's owner was a really large man with a really large gun, and the gun was pointing at Eddie's chest. Closer inspection revealed puffy eyes, mussed hair, and green pajamas, but the voice and the pistol were both rock-steady.

Eddie and Nate raised their hands.

"Don't tell me," Eddie said to Janice, who was standing beside the sleepy-looking gunman. "The police chief?"

"Afraid so," she said. Then, to her brother: "Glad you haven't had your locks changed lately. Or had an alarm installed."

"I'm just glad my heart didn't stop when you woke me up. Any guns in this group?"

"Just one," she said. "Nate?" He handed it over, then he and Eddie turned and held their wrists behind their backs while the chief handcuffed them. Over his shoulder, the chief called to his wife to phone the station to have a car sent over.

"You ready to explain all this, J.P.?" the chief asked his sister.

Eddie blinked, and twisted around to look at Janice. "J.P.?" he said. "*You're* J.P. Sanderford?"

"That's me."

"Good God." He gaped at her. "You're quite an actress, ain't you?"

"Just a lawyer."

"And your husband—"

"He's the software installer. That's where he is tonight, putting in a system."

Eddie couldn't stop staring at her. "So there ain't no judge, or judge's wife?"

"Sure there is," she said. "But this isn't their house. And they're happily married."

"Like you and your husband?"

She nodded. "Hell of a thing, all this marital bliss."

"And I suppose that was *your* recorded voice on the office answering machine?"

"Why not? It's my office." She regarded him a moment. "Let me ask you something, Eddie." She tipped her head toward the open bedroom door. "If this had been on the level, and you'd gotten the money… would you really have given me a share?"

Though he didn't quite smile, his eyes twinkled a little. "No," he said. "But I wouldn't have killed you, either."

She just nodded. "I believe you."

"I hate to break this up," the chief said, "but I'm sleepy, and it's late. I'm placing you boys under arrest for—" He glanced at Janice.

"Kidnapping," she said.

"Kidnapping. If you'll step outside with me, one of my associates will escort your sorry asses to jail."

As they started away, she grabbed his sleeve and whispered, "Go easy on 'em, Bobby. They're more dumb than mean."

"Yeah, well, that makes three of us."

The chief's wife, a plain woman in a pink housecoat, came to stand beside her while the prisoners were marched outside.

"Who *are* they, J.P.?"

Janice thought a moment, watching them out the front window. "They're the Mauronds."

Her sister-in-law blinked. "Morons?"

"Yes," Janice said. "That too."

Vinegar Lake
Andrew Humphrey

The wind came in hard that night, hunting through the dark streets. It swept in low, close to the ground, slapping saplings flat, snapping fence posts, seeking the soft wood and cuffing it aside.

Jenny slept through it. I didn't try. I stood on the lawn to the rear of our house, in t-shirt and boxer shorts, waiting for it. The first blow drove me back a couple of steps, flattening cotton against chest and thighs, punching the breath from my lungs. I threw my head back. It was moments before I could breathe. I tasted warm air as small pieces of debris pin-wheeled past my face. Falling to my knees I tried to laugh but the wind wouldn't allow it.

The rain came later, as the wind dropped, soaking me instantly.

Around dawn the weather lost interest in our particular part of Norfolk. The sky emptied and the morning, when it came, was bland and innocent.

It was a Sunday and Jenny had already eaten breakfast by the time I rose. She was in the conservatory watering her pot plants.

"Here he is," she said, without looking up. "The storm chaser."

"You slept well."

"You could at least have wiped your feet before you came in. I don't enjoy cleaning your filthy paw prints off the kitchen floor."

"I'd have done it."

"You know I can't leave it like that." Her voice was mild. Her voice was always mild. I can hardly recall her speaking above a gentle, lulling monotone in over thirty years.

"The plants look well."

She almost looked at me then but instead she gave a soft snort and continued watering. "Name one."

"What? I dunno. Brian?"

"That's very funny, Stephen."

"They're your thing, my darling; as has long since been established."

"My thing," Jenny said, standing up straight, stretching a little, the small green watering can hanging limply from her right hand. "I suppose it is."

I ate breakfast and drank a pot of strong tea while Jenny showered and dressed. My feet were coated with dirt. I smelled of old rain and wet earth. I remembered how the wind felt during the night, the heat of it as it pushed into my open mouth. I remembered wishing that every one of my atoms could be torn apart and reassembled.

I was still in a reverie, arms braced against the kitchen worktop, head bowed, when Jenny entered. Her scent preceded her, something fresh and floral.

"You haven't forgotten, have you? We're hosting tonight. Richard and Sarah. Drinks and nibbles."

"Drinks and nibbles. How could I forget?" She cleared away my breakfast things, working around me, wiping down the worktop. "I think I'll go as I am."

She paused and turned to face me, arms at her side, hands linked in front of her. "And what would Sarah think of that?"

"She might fancy a bit of rough."

Jenny made a noise in the back of her throat and looked towards the kitchen window. Her clothes were soft-edged and elegant. The colours she chose were gentle, muted. Jenny met no resistance as she moved through the world. There were no edges to catch, nothing abrasive or difficult. Except me, perhaps.

"Anyway, church." Her head swept round and she glanced past me at the clock on the wall, at the print next to it; a bottle of red wine, some grapes. "You can come, if you like. There's still time, if you hurry."

"Every week the same," I said.

"I have to ask."

Yes, I thought, *apparently you do.*

After Jenny left I tidied the garden. Our fence posts were sturdily constructed so most of the debris I gathered into a rough pile was from neighbouring properties. Not that there was anyone too close by: we were at the edge of the village and wild meadows buffered our boundaries on either side.

We had too much land. Jenny may have been mildly obsessed with indoor plants but her interest didn't extend to our garden. We had a couple of acres, mostly rough, undulating lawn, with a few half-hearted flower beds here and there; some fuchsias, some roses, azaleas for later in the summer. I'd started a vegetable patch a couple of years back but it was forlorn and weed-infested now. George, an old guy from the village, dropped in a twice a month to prevent things getting too out of hand.

"This house," Sarah said as she swept past Jenny into our hallway, her eyes cast upwards at the high ceiling and the wide, immaculate, cream-coloured walls. She'd said the same thing on the previous occasions she'd visited in the half year or so since she and Jenny had become friends. They'd met through the church, of course. She cooed her way through the kitchen, fingers trailing across the marble-topped island, then past the Aga and towards the living room.

"Make yourself at home," I said.

"Stephen, darling." She came towards me and kissed my cheek. Her scent was much heavier than Jenny's. "I always do. You know that. You look terrific, by the way."

Did I? I'd made a bit of an effort, I suppose; a fresh new shirt, jeans, a light linen jacket. Sarah was vibrant in a flowered summery dress. She wore her auburn hair short, cut neatly around her ears. She was tallish and slender with pale skin and grey eyes that brimmed with a curious light.

When Jenny came into the room she seemed muted by comparison. Beautiful, but of less substance; not entirely of this dimension. The dress that she wore was a cornflower-blue that matched the walls of the living room. It was as though she was camouflaged. It was sometimes difficult to tell where the house ended and she began.

Richard trailed in behind Jenny. He was a big man, tall and broad. His hair was very dark and obscenely lustrous for someone in their mid-fifties. My hand went involuntarily to the soft, thinning burr of my own scalp.

"Stephen." He loomed towards me, his fist engulfing mine. "How the hell are you?"

His presence overwhelmed me, as did his scent, which was musky and expensive. I felt something tick in my blood as I tried to smile. "Fine. Thanks."

"Good man." He squeezed my hand. His face was too close to mine.

"Put the poor boy down," Sarah said from across the room.

He released his grip, laughing. The early evening sun dipped and refracted light filtered through the large picture window that made up one wall. Primary colours fell across Sarah's face and neck.

We ate outside. Jenny served Negroni's with ham and pear crostini's and bacon-wrapped dates. Then we had soft roasted peppers and artichoke with warm olive bread and a bone-dry Manzanilla sherry.

I listened mostly. It was mid-June and it was some time before the light softened and the shadows grew bolder, encroaching the decking and the bespoke sofa upon which Jenny and Sarah sat. They spoke about church matters; committees that they were on, fund-raising issues, the new vicar.

Sarah liked him, Richard didn't.

"He's black," Sarah said.

"Nothing to do with that," Richard said, folding his legs awkwardly. "I just don't like his energy, that's all."

Jenny leaned forwards. "His energy?"

"He's perfectly charming," Sarah said. "You like him, don't you, Jen?"

"He's fine."

"High praise," I said.

They all looked at me for a moment. I sipped my sherry. To the east, beyond Sarah and Jenny, the sun was setting in peach and cherry-coloured layers, like some indulgent dessert.

As the light died we came inside and drank brandy in the living room. We sat in couples, opposite each other, nobody touching.

Richard talked about work, as he often did. I admired his confidence, his unvoiced assumption that anyone would actually give a shit.

"Thing is, small businesses, we're literally drowning in red tape."

"Literally," I said.

"Don't be tiresome, Stephen." He said it indulgently, with a smile. I didn't mind. "We're a different breed, I suppose;

entrepreneurs." He stumbled over the word. The drink was showing in his face as well; his jowls were ruddy and his ample, handsome, nose had become veined and prominent.

I nodded. "I suppose you are."

He ignored that, although I wondered for a moment if he would. Richard, as he never tired of telling anybody who would listen, was a self-made man. This had mostly entailed, from what I could gather, taking an extremely healthy nest egg, left by his father, and eroding it steadily through a succession of increasingly desperate property deals. I ached to ask him exactly what he would be worth if he had simply invested his father's inheritance in the first place. Perhaps after a couple more brandies I would.

"You wouldn't know," he said, draining his glass. "Not your fault."

"Well, you can't be doing too badly," I said. "Sarah's still around, after all."

I felt Jenny glare at me. "Stephen."

Sarah's smile was angled and obtuse, while Richard's laugh was loud and sudden.

"Nice one, Stephen. It's a poor excuse of a man who can't laugh at himself. Isn't that right?"

"As I'm sure the good Lord himself would attest," I said, raising my glass and tipping it towards Richard.

He looked understandably puzzled but lifted his glass in response anyway. His puzzlement deepened when he realised that the glass was empty.

As Jenny got up to offer a refill, I saw Richard glance down the front of her dress as she leant towards him. Sarah noticed too, then our eyes met briefly and she suppressed a smirk as she looked away.

Jenny settled again. "I don't know what's wrong with you this evening, Stephen."

"This evening?" Richard said.

It was my turn to laugh. It was short and bitter but it was still a laugh. "Touché," I said.

"Richard," Sarah elbowed him in the ribs, "don't be like that." Then, turning to me, "You look tired, Stephen."

"Well, if he is, it's his own fault," Jenny said.

"Been communing with nature again, Stevie-boy?" Somehow Richard's glass was empty again. His eyes had become hooded and sallow.

"Last night's storm," Jenny said.

"I wasn't out for long. It wasn't much of a storm."

"The willow in our front garden would dispute that," Richard said. "I don't understand what you get out of it."

"You wouldn't know," I said. "Not your fault."

"Touché yourself," he said. His smile was small and dark.

*****

It had started soon after Ben died. Our son was in his first year at Nottingham. He was thriving, by all accounts. He called us often, but not too often. He made friends easily but assured us he was finding time for his studies too and we believed him. We never had a reason not to believe Ben.

The course he chose was Liberal Arts. Jenny was far from happy. She thought it was too woolly, too detached from the real world to be of any practical use. She argued quietly, but persistently, for a more technical choice. Or perhaps he could commit to the Church, become a vicar, as her father had? I remember Ben explaining, typically kindly and gently, that he didn't actually believe in God, so perhaps that route was not appropriate. I remember also our argument later, after Ben had gone; it was understated, of course, but it was intense too, and bitter. The fault lines that formed then would soon become cavernous and unbridgeable.

It's odd the things that seem important; that can cause loss of sleep and relationships to crumble. But then fate presses its hard, cold hand into your face and you know that these worries carry no weight, and are of no importance at all.

A week before he was due to come home for Christmas, Ben attended a party at the house of a friend of a friend. Someone spiked his drink with ecstasy. Just before midnight he said he was feeling ill; he was over-heating and finding it difficult to breathe. Someone called an ambulance and they got him to the Queen's Medical Centre on Derby Road within half an hour. It was two in the morning before the police were involved and someone got hold of our number and gave us a call. By then Ben was dead.

*****

After they'd gone Jenny started gathering glasses and plates.

"We can do them in the morning," I said.

She put a brandy glass back on the coffee table. "What exactly is wrong with you?"

"What?"

She sat heavily in the chair that Richard had been occupying a few minutes earlier. She stared at the wall opposite. "The sarcasm. The point scoring. Can't we just have a pleasant evening?"

I stood in the doorway that led to the kitchen. Sarah's scent lingered. "I don't like them."

"You seem to like her well enough."

"It's just another phase, though, isn't it, sweetheart? It's been six months, that's longer than usual. I'll give you that."

"I don't know what you mean." She still wouldn't face me. Her back was rigid.

"Kerry and Brian. Terry and Steve. Fiona and David."

"I'm entitled to friends of my own."

"They're not your friends, Jenny."

"What would you know about friends?"

"They're a fad. We were going to go on holiday with Kerry and Brian. Remember? They were round here every week for meals, drinks. Then you dropped them. Just like that. Not very Christian, if you ask me."

"No one's asking you, Stephen." Her voice was small and tight.

I hesitated. When I spoke I tried to load some warmth into my voice. "It doesn't matter, darling. You're getting by, that's what counts. Somehow, we both are."

Her posture stiffened further. However obliquely, I'd touched on the subject of Ben. This had become forbidden territory. I waited. Jenny didn't speak but the atmosphere became hostile, airless. When I could bear it no more I went upstairs to bed.

*****

There was a blizzard on the New Year's Day after Ben died. It hit mid-afternoon, a vast, relentless wall of snow and sleet. We were in the study, Jenny and I, arranging Ben's funeral. The light through the study window became thin and brittle as the cloud gathered. The radio played low in the corner; weather warnings repeated over and over. When the snow came we moved to the living room and watched it together wordlessly through the picture window. Jenny eventually spoke in a voice so low that I couldn't hear what she said. She drifted past me and back towards the study. The air did not stir. She carried no scent.

A little later she emitted a single sobbing scream that seemed to come from a part of her that neither of us knew existed. It carried from the study and filled the house with its echo. I didn't go to her; instead I went out of the front door, onto the long, gravelled drive, obscured as it was by fresh, startlingly white snow and towards the wrought iron gates and the road and fields beyond.

I'm not sure how long I stood there, in the shadow of our house. I was dressed in jeans and a light sweater, arms spread wide as if to welcome the snow and sleet that drove onto me and caked my face and hair. Perhaps, if I had been able to wait a little longer, it would have stopped my heart.

It was George who found me. He was coming to check if we needed anything. He doted on Jenny. He shook me to my senses and pulled me back into the house. Jenny came into the hallway when she heard the commotion, then saw the state of me and went back into the study.

George said I needed a hot bath and I agreed. He asked if Jenny was okay and I said that she was, all things considered.

He paused at that, unsure what to say. I thanked him and said that I'd be fine, we both would. He left reluctantly, his eyes on the study door.

I had a shower, not a bath; a long one. I thought about the numbing cold, how I'd welcomed it. How small I'd felt at the centre of it all.

*****

Next morning I walked to Vinegar Lake. It's not much of a lake; more a deep, wide pond set against a wall of rock in the centre of our village's long-spent quarry. The water is the colour of vinegar, though. There are a couple of warning signs at the lake's edge, set in the scruffy rubble that runs down to the deceptive shallows that ring its perimeter. The water here is iodine tinted and, in summer, teems with tadpoles and caddisflies and water spiders.

Sometimes the signs are ignored. Most years someone – often young, but not always - will jump into the ugly, acidic water. They don't always come out again.

I stood at the lake's edge and thought about Jenny. Sarah would have been a more pleasant subject; the smell of her, her oddly angled, elliptical smile, but we do not always choose where our minds go. Jenny's grief had driven her further into her faith and her church. Her father would've been proud; assuming that the bitter old bastard was capable of directing such an emotion at anybody other than himself. He'd always blamed me for Jenny's initial loss of faith. In her teens, around the time we'd met at university, all those years ago. But it was nothing to do with me; she was merely growing into herself and away from her timid mother and her father's stifling doctrine.

I was, on the surface at least, deeply cynical and amoral as well as a vocal and committed atheist. It was all a front. I had my own insecurities to hide.

Somehow, Jenny found this combination attractive. I suppose I was passable physically, in those days at least. And I was everything that her father was not. That, to my gratitude and astonishment, was enough. Jenny was a catch. She was deeply pretty in an ethereal and typically English way. And there was money in the family. Everybody said so. Not from the father; vicars weren't rich. But from some distant generation; something shady. Slavery perhaps? I called myself a socialist so the money shouldn't have mattered. But it did, of course.

Once, we were laid together on Jenny's bed, in her room on campus, sharing a joint. This brief and mild flirtation with soft drugs was an act of wild rebellion on Jenny's part. I noticed that she barely inhaled, however, and left most of the intake to me.

"I shouldn't be here," she said, gazing at the ceiling, arms splayed loosely above her head.

"I didn't force you."

She gave my head a lazy cuff. "I don't mean that." She took a tiny puff of the joint and passed it back to me. "Dad. He hated the idea of this." She stretched her arms wide, towards the bare, slate-grey walls of her room and the campus beyond. "His precious girl at a common little Uni. The very thought of it."

I shifted on the bed and my hip bumped against hers. A thin patina of blue smoke coated the ceiling. "All part of the appeal, I suppose. You bad girl, you."

"He doesn't really believe that girls need an education. Apart from religious studies."

"Get thee to a nunnery."

"Something like that. Or maybe marry a vicar. Do a little light breeding. An heir and a spare. Try not to think, though. No good will become of women thinking."

Her voice had become small and bitter. I barely noticed. I was pretty stoned and I'd heard it all before.

I walked the long way home, past the village hall and Jenny's church. Sunlight splashed across the 17th century stonework with its clinging wisteria and the neat, clinical graveyard. I paused at the heavy oak gate. Two young men were working on the guttering to the side of the church's entrance. One was on a ladder, the other stood with his foot on the bottom rung, looking up. They were shirtless and silent. The one on the ground was smoking. The man on the ladder had thick black hair. He looked a little like Ben. They noticed my presence eventually and they turned their heads in my direction. I nodded and walked away. I felt awkward, a little embarrassed. I wasn't sure why.

I walked for another hour or so and saw nobody else; not in the copse or by the wheat fields or in the narrow, sun-flooded streets. Sometimes, living here, I wonder if there has been an apocalypse, some disaster of which I am unaware. More often than not, I find I don't particularly care if there has.

Back home I realised Sarah was there before I saw her. Her perfume was heavy in the hallway and kitchen. Jenny's disembodied voice drifted through from the conservatory. There was a sudden pause in the conversation then I heard Jenny say something about houseplants; watering, feeding. Sarah's voice cut in; lower than Jenny's, the words indistinguishable. Her laughter followed; loud and coarse, drowning out Jenny completely. The timbre of it made something quiver inside me. I am a shallow man. I sometimes wonder if this self-knowledge provides some kind of mitigation. I suspect that it does not.

I reached the conservatory's white-framed doorway. The gaze of both women fixed on me simultaneously. They were sat close together on the long beige sofa, in identical poses; knees together, leant faintly forward, hands linked determinedly in their laps.

"It's you," Jenny said. She sounded affronted.

"I do live here."

Sunlight lapped onto the tiled floor and played itself out into odd shapes across the sofa, the chairs, a tile-topped table.

Sarah said nothing. Like Jenny she wore a sleeveless top. Jenny's was plain navy, Sarah's raspberry coloured and dotted with tiny flowers. The light invading the room seemed to bounce off Sarah. When it hit Jenny it died. It was as though she was absorbing it, holding it greedily within herself. From another room, Jenny's grandfather clock, a family heirloom, struck the hour, ponderous and sardonic.

A little later Sarah made her excuses and left. After another half hour I could no longer bear the stultifying silence so I changed into jogging bottoms and a sweatshirt, then said I was going for a run.

I turned left out of our gate and had barely broken out of a brisk walk when I saw Sarah standing by the entrance to a wild meadow; her eyes were fixed on her phone and she was smoking a cigarette. When she saw me she dropped it guiltily to the pavement and ground it out beneath an immaculate kitten heel.

"Busted," I said as I approached her.

"Don't tell Richard. He'd kill me. "

"I didn't take you for a smoker."

"Old habits," she said. She closed the screen on her phone and tucked it into her bag. "Very old habits, actually."

There was an odd, small silence. Behind Jenny the meadow was a jumble of ragged, tumbling colour. A pair of Red Admiral's floated drunkenly from flower to flower. The air was sweet and not too hot.

"Were you waiting for me?"

"You wish." Her smile was crooked. Her voice was different – deeper, less mannered.

"This is the first time we've been alone." I wasn't sure why I said that, but it earned a laugh, although it was hard-edged and mocking.

"How romantic." She fetched another cigarette, lit it and took a long pull. "You know my secret now," she said through a long stream of smoke. "No point denying myself."

"My lips are sealed."

"What a sweetheart." She turned to face me. When she spoke again her voice was stripped of all mockery or artifice.

"Look, cards on the table, I *was* waiting for you."

"Okay."

"I didn't really see Jenny to get hot tips about caring for my spider plant, useful though that was."

"She certainly knows her houseplants."

"She really does. Talking to Jenny… it's so…"

"Frustrating?"

"Tiring. She's so relentlessly nice." She tapped ash onto the pavement. "Well, to everyone except you, of course."

"Of course."

"She's so vanilla. So damned soft. So…" she struggled for the right word. "…pillowy."

"Pillowy?"

"I think you know what I mean."

"Actually, I do."

"She only ever says precisely what people want to hear. As long as it is not outside her comfort zone. Anything difficult, she just ignores. It's why everyone at the church adores her. She's so warm and lovely. On the face of it. And that's all that matters there, isn't it? Appearances."

"You tell me."

"Not really your thing, is it?"

"You could say that."

"Your absences are noted. Frowned upon."

"Colour me astonished."

She had a tattoo of a butterfly on her left wrist. It was faded, indistinct. She ran a finger across it. The fine hairs on her forearm were silver and erect in the clear light. "Why don't you just come along? For Jenny's sake, if nothing else. It's not as though I believe and Richard certainly doesn't."

"Why bother then?"

"Contacts, dear boy." She shrugged. "And where Richard goes there go I."

"Fair enough. What did you want to talk to Jenny about?"

She dropped her cigarette, stamped it out, examined its corpse alongside the first. "Jesus."

"I would have thought she'd have enjoyed that."

"No. Not… him." She exhaled firmly and I smelled the nicotine on her breath. "This is difficult." She said. "Can we go somewhere?"

I felt a jolt in the pit of my stomach. "Go somewhere?"

"I feel a bit exposed, standing here like this. This village, you know?"

I did.

*****

I drove to Nottingham on my own the day that Ben died. Jenny couldn't face it. For a while she could barely function at all. A woman from the church stepped in at short notice to look after her. She stayed a week. I remember thinking how kind it was of her. I haven't seen her since and I can no longer recall her name.

The drive was nightmarish. At the time it seemed endless, but now I wonder if it actually happened at all. I suppose it must have because at some point I was required to identify Ben's body. The room they took me to was small and white-tiled and reeked of cleansing fluid. I don't know what building it was in or how I got there. I had intended to visit Ben's room at the University and to speak to some of his friends. I did neither. I found a nondescript B & B where I stayed for three nights. I walked long, pointless loops through an unfamiliar city. It was mid-winter and daylight barely registered; the streetlights were on all day. They cast an appropriately baleful penumbra of sepulchral light. Back in my room I lay on a bed that smelled faintly of semen. I stared up at a water-stained ceiling and thought of Ben's face; cleansed of expression, bone-white, pure, blameless. My thoughts became toxic, boxed in. I barely ate or slept. I was constantly blindsided by the sheer weight of my grief. It seemed demonic, obsessive; intent solely on clinically and systematically hacking away any semblance of light or hope or warmth from my consciousness.

Eventually I drove home. Back in our kitchen, a December evening, outside now rimed with frost, I found my wife and her friend praying to a God in which I could never believe.

*****

Sarah and I walked eastwards, cutting past the village green to a small copse and a clearing beyond. A couple of tree trunks had been hewn into rough seats. The area was shaded and cool. We sat, closer together than was entirely comfortable. Sarah brushed an imaginary something from the top of her thighs.

"Bugs," she said. "I don't really like this. There's such a thing as *too* much nature."

I shifted on my makeshift seat. "What are you doing here?"

"Sorry?"

I held my arms wide. "Here. This village."

"This fucking village."

"Precisely."

She took a long breath and began to fish in her bag for another cigarette but changed her mind.

"The thing is, we couldn't stay where we were. Things were… difficult. To be honest, it's become something of a pattern since I've been with Richard."

"I don't understand."

She remained quiet for a moment, her head still, her eyes fixed on a point somewhere past my left shoulder. "Actually…" she began. She paused again almost instantly. "Look, I'm not Sarah."

"What?"

"And Richard isn't Richard."

"I really don't …"

"Please," she said, her smile not fitting at all. "Just let me explain."

I raised my hands in mock surrender. "Be my guest," I said. "Fire away."

"We're hustlers, Stephen. Grifters. Richard and I. As good as, anyway."

"I thought you said …"

"I'm not telling you our real names. It's confusing enough as it is." She moved her head languorously from side to side and smoothed the material of her jeans flat against her thighs. "I can't believe I'm doing this. Trusting you. I barely know you. This isn't me. It isn't me at all."

Instead of asking the same questions myself, like a normal

person, I relished the quiet thrill of being taken into the confidence of an attractive woman. "It's not too late, Sarah. You can stop if you like."

"Can I?" Her grey eyes were wide open. Her gaze caught onto mine, reeling me in. "Do you want me to?"

"It's up to you. You can trust me, though." My voice tailed off. It sounded weak, pathetic.

She slid her hand across and squeezed the top of my leg. The skin there tingled long after she'd pulled her fingers away.

"We met in Soho, Richard and I. Years ago. Too many bloody years." This time she did light another cigarette. "I was a waitress." A brief silence. "And a dancer." Another. "An *exotic* dancer, actually. Make of that what you will."

Wordlessly, I did.

"He was good looking, well dressed. Well connected, by all accounts. I was between men, as they say. So I thought, why not? I hitched myself to his star, if you'll permit me to mix a metaphor or two."

"You said you're hustlers. I thought Richard dealt in real estate."

"Oh, he does. We do. Have done all over the world. The thing is the land in question doesn't always belong to us. It doesn't always actually exist."

"Christ."

"The trick is to keep moving. Don't get *too* greedy. We've been good at that. So far."

"So that stuff about Richard's father. The inheritance …?"

"All rubbish. A cover story. He *is* a self-made man, though."

An arch look, cigarette smoke drifting across her face. "Of sorts."

"You had me fooled. Jenny too."

"Years of practice." She started counting on her fingers. "Richard and Sarah. This is our… seventh iteration. And probably the last."

"Why?"

She laughed unexpectedly and leant into me. I smelled her scent again and something else underneath. "It's all gone tits up, mate. Richard's fault. He bites off more than he can chew. And he thinks he's being followed. Our past catching up with us. *One* of our pasts. Could be paranoia. He does do a lot of coke." Her shoulder was still pressed against mine. "Poor us, huh?"

"Poor you." I realised suddenly that it had been ages since I'd thought of Ben. I felt drained and empty and ashamed. "Look, I'd better go."

She stood quickly, discarding the cigarette. "Really? Just like that?" She faced me, hands on hips, head tipped to one side. "I'm spilling my guts here and that's all the reaction I get?"

"I'm sorry."

"Sorry? Jesus, Stephen. No wonder your marriage is fucked."

"What? I really don't think …"

"Oh, come on. You know it. She knows it. The whole world knows it. That house of yours? I mean, it's beautiful, but it's like Ice Station Zebra in there. If it wasn't for her precious God, her *vows*, she'd have dropped you years ago."

I was stunned into silence; both by her choice of words and by the unmistakeable truth of them.

"You want to know what I wanted with Jenny?" She was pacing the clearing, more animated than I'd ever known her. "She was a mark, Stephen. I thought she'd be a soft touch. I mean, she's minted right? That house. And there's a holiday home, isn't there? Italy, somewhere like that?" I nodded dumbly. "And she doesn't work. She's very proud of that." She stood still for a moment and looked at me appraisingly. "Where does it come from? The money? I mean, it's inherited, obviously, but the old man was a vicar. There must be more to it than that?"

"I don't know."

"Of course you don't."

I tried to say something but she cut me off again.

"Thing is, I had a sob story all lined up. Thought she'd be an easy mark. Soft old Jenny. But there's no way in, is there? Not with her." She stood over me, ran her fingers across the top of my scalp. Her voice became gentler. "Well, look who I'm telling."

"Bloody hell, Sarah."

She crouched in front of me and took my hands in hers. "The thing is, Stephen; I'm fucked, you're fucked." She kissed me lightly on the mouth then on the side of my face. "I figured we may as well be fucked together."

*****

The instant that Ben died time broke. It atomised, in the same way that both my heart and soul had. I'm sure Jenny felt the same and perhaps we could have found some common

83

ground, some comfort, if only we'd been able to talk, to share our experiences like two normal, adult human beings. Instead Jenny hid behind her solid, unyielding God and I found what solace I could by exposing myself to what passed for extreme weather in our part of Norfolk. Not that there was much; the odd hailstorm or downpour or brief, violent storm. I craved a tsunami, a tornado; something localised, brutal, and focused entirely on me.

Jenny only said the words once, out loud at least. I mean she thought them, and lived them. She may as well have had them framed in needlepoint in every room in the house. But she only vocalised them the one time, at breakfast, while she was buttering toast.

"It's your fault." Her voice was light and conversational. She was looking at her toast, which was slightly burnt. "You wanted him to go to Nottingham. You agreed. If he hadn't, he'd still be alive." She took a tiny bite of her breakfast and chewed it slowly. She spared me the merest glance. A millisecond. It burned. It burns still.

Her words were reductive, absurdly so.

She was also entirely correct.

*****

When I returned to the house Jenny had gone. I felt lighter than usual, giddy and a little sick. I walked around the house, through its myriad rooms, all spotless, immaculate and shredded with sunlight. It seemed that Sarah's scent was everywhere; the kitchen, the study in my bedroom and the room where Jenny slept. The covers, white and pristine, and the faintly rumpled pillowcase carried no trace of Jenny. It was all Sarah, the sense of her emanating from me, I supposed. It was buried deep inside me; not by love – I wasn't quite that stupid – but by some dreadful, hallucinatory need.

I hesitated by the door to Ben's old room. I ran my fingers along the grain of the stripped pine. I didn't enter.

I took a shower and by the time I'd dressed Jenny was home. We ate dinner together. Pasta with some rich ragu; salad, red wine. It was probably excellent, Jenny's cooking usually was, but I couldn't taste anything.

Jenny was strangely skittish; she had her phone on the table, by the side of her plate and kept glancing at it and touching the screen.

"Expecting someone?"

She shrugged. "Church stuff."

"Hotline to God?"

"Something like that."

After a moment I said, "Have you been with Richard?"

She pushed her phone to one side and appraised me coolly. "Why on earth would you say that?"

"No reason." That, at least, was true. I had no idea where the words had come from.

She took a miniscule sip of Rioja, her eyes still fixed on mine.

*****

The funeral passed, then the autopsy. Misadventure. They never found out who put the drug in Ben's drink; his so called friends and acquaintances quietly and implacably closed ranks. These were grim, chilly way stations along grief's endless path.

I segued from full time work in a bustling Norwich office to home-working, hours to suit, no pressure, none at all. It was ostensibly very kind of my employer – kitchen design, it's all computerised now – but at our last meeting I could not help but note the relief in my boss's eyes when I confirmed that I would no longer be attending the office. I didn't blame him. Who needed a broken husk of a thing haunting their workplace, pulling everybody down?

I worked fewer and fewer hours. I'm not sure why I bothered at all. Appearances perhaps. I didn't need the money. We didn't need the money. Jenny's father had left her wealthy enough to support both of us without blinking. I suppose I realised deep down – perhaps not so deep, it was pretty bloody obvious – that I needed to keep my options open. Our marriage was as dead and cold as Ben. We both knew this, both knew that the stasis within which we were trapped could not last much longer.

*****

I reached out my left hand and ran my fingers down Sarah's spine. She didn't react. She remained sat up in bed, smoking quietly.

"Well, that's a first for me. I've never cheated before."

"That's a good line," Sarah said.

"It's not a line."

"I'm not quite sure what you expect me to say, Stephen."

"I don't expect you to say anything." I'm not sure that was entirely true. But then again I wasn't really sure of anything anymore.

We'd met in Norwich for coffee, a couple of days after Sarah had waited for me by the meadow. It was her idea. The café was in a side street near the Guildhall. The day was brutally hot so we found a cool, isolated spot deep in the shop's interior. It was decked out like a library; walls of rich, mahogany shelves crammed with books. We were in an alcove. A ceiling fan churned listlessly above us.

Sarah sat opposite me. She placed her sunglasses carefully in front of her. She wore very little; a strappy top and a pair of tiny, lemon-coloured shorts. I couldn't stop looking at her. My son was still dead; would always be dead. My marriage was torn and broken beyond repair. And yet…I couldn't stop looking at her. I knew it was wrong. My self-judgement didn't stop exactly; even then that particular meter was running, still ticking deep in my blood, tucked far enough away that I could only really see Sarah's cool grey eyes and her mouth and the faint sheen of sweat that coated her throat and neck.

A bored looking teenager sporting a nose ring and a tattoo of a blue dragon on her exposed midriff took our order. We both had coffee, despite the heat.

"I've booked us a room," Sarah said, after the girl had gone.

"A room?"

"Yes, Stephen. I assume you are familiar with the concept?" I could see the strain hidden behind the smile. She was trying to sound playful, seductive. I could have told her that she didn't need to work so hard. I was hooked anyway, despite the thread of dark energy that ran behind her eyes and words; despite the fact that I had no real idea of who this woman was.

"It's just around the corner. Very discreet."

"Are you a regular?"

There was a flash of real anger then, cutting through the faux-coquettishness, but she tamped it down quickly enough. "Funny man."

The girl brought our coffees and dumped them gracelessly on the table. Sarah gave her a smile as well, which was all over the place. She didn't get one in return and when the girl had left us Sarah braced her arms on the table and stared down at the dark, stained wood. It was as though she was setting herself for something.

"Are you okay?"

"Yes. A little nervous perhaps. Despite your implications I don't tend to make a habit of this."

"I'm sorry." I extended my hand towards hers and she took it. Her skin was cool and dry. "It was a joke. A poor one."

She looked at the coffees in front us. "Look, I don't want these. Shall we go?"

I tried to say something but I didn't want to seem too eager so I just nodded and she squeezed my hand. We both stood and I followed her out onto the baking street.

*****

Ben's funeral was grotesque. It was held at the local church on a bright and severely cold January afternoon. I was outnumbered by people I barely knew. This was Jenny's flock; middle aged, well groomed, smug amid their obvious affluence and their cosy, unchallenged beliefs. I felt as though I was from a different species. I uttered not a single word of dissent. I let them have their way with me. I was engulfed by their thin, platitudinous sympathy; by their damp, endless handshakes and perfume-drenched hugs.

The vicar said a few words, then Jenny stepped forward. This wasn't planned, not to my knowledge, at least. But I sat in silence and while I listened I burned with shame and a curious flat, cold fury.

Jenny's voice was remarkably clear in the chilled air. She leant against the dais; her face tilted upwards, eyes cast towards her God. I could have been proud of her then, of her unexpected strength and her austere beauty. Perhaps I could've even loved her again. It was the words that she spoke that were the problem.

Her speech was a paean to God and to her late father. When she mentioned Ben it was not a version of our son that I recognised at all. Her Ben was a devout Christian and had he not been taken so tragically early he would surely have followed in her beloved father's footsteps. There were more words – so many more – all devoted to a remoulding of Ben's existence. I looked around at all the pink, adoring faces, glowing in the cold light that angled in through the stained glass windows.

She glanced at me once, briefly, as she finished speaking. Her face was expressionless but there was a message there and it was for me and for me alone. It said; I win, you lose.

Later, much later, when the whole benighted thing was finally over, a hard, insistent rain fell. I stood out in it for an hour or more. I think I screamed or cried or both. I'm not sure it matters either way. There was no one to hear me.

We did what grownups do. As during the walk to the coffee shop Sarah led and I followed. Her mouth and hands were soft and warm and eager enough and she appeared to enjoy herself. She also made sure that it didn't take too long. For my part, I didn't do anything obviously wrong and everything worked as it should. This was something of a relief; it had been a while.

When she'd finished her cigarette she lay back again. It was a king size bed so we weren't touching. I glanced at her breasts then looked quickly away again.

"It's a little late to be coy, Stephen."

"I suppose it is."

There was sweat on my arms and chest. Her skin was dry.

"I need your help." She was staring at the ceiling. I had a flashback to Jenny and me on her bed at Uni all those years ago. I drove the thought away.

"I don't have my own money. Not much, at least." As I spoke I was calculating; how much did I have? And was it worth it?

"It's not money. Not yet."

"Okay."

She turned on her side. A hand snaked onto to my thigh, my stomach, my groin. "I need to get away, Stephen. *We* need to get away." Her voice, which had fallen into a robotic drone, came alive again. She looked into my face. Her lips were slightly parted. I could see the tip of her tongue.

"Just like that?"

"He's gone too far. Richard. He'll be the death of me. Of

both of us."

"That's a little bit melodramatic." My voice was not entirely steady. Her fingers worked slowly and skilfully. I thought it would be too soon. It wasn't.

"I know how it sounds." She sat suddenly, releasing her grip. She leant over the side of the bed and fished something out of her handbag. It sat in the palm of her hand. It took a moment to register what it was. A gun. A revolver, I think; small, metallic blue, utterly incongruous.

"Jesus Christ, Sarah."

"A present from Richard. For protection."

"Put it away. Please." I sat up, erection gone.

"It's perfectly safe. I know what I'm doing." She placed it gently back in her bag. "Which is more than I can say for Richard."

I pulled the covers over my waist, as though for protection. "I'm out of my depth."

"You and me both." Her voice was casual now, almost wry. "Things have… taken a turn. He *is* being followed. Richard. I've seen them. They're driving some big, black thing. Tinted windows. Not very original. It wasn't paranoia. I mean, he *is* paranoid. Richard. You know how he drinks and I mentioned the coke. He really loves that stuff."

"Do you …"

"Coke? No." She lit a cigarette and folded her arms across her breasts. She seemed comfortable now. Relaxed. She blew smoke away from me. "These are my only vice. Well, apart from fraud, I suppose."

"Where are they from? The guys in the black car?"

"Not sure. London, probably. We were there for a while a few years back. Had an office on the South Bank. We screwed over some pretty shady sorts. I mean, we didn't know they were shady, not until later. But that was a while back and we were careful. Perhaps we weren't careful enough." She tipped ash onto the top of her bedside cabinet. "Maybe it always catches up with you in the end."

"Why don't you just move on? You and Richard? Become… someone else? Again."

"The money's gone. We're running on fumes. And anyway, I'm sick of him." She moved her shoulder against mine. "Just now, with you? It was nice. You were… gentle." She could have been talking about a fruit scone, a slice of cake, for all the passion in her voice, but still, I lapped it up. "Richard just takes what he wants."

We'd drawn the blinds, of course. The air was grey and cool. The smoke from her cigarette rose and gathered at the ceiling. "What do you want me to do?"

*****

Jenny changed when her dad became ill. They'd been estranged for years, but when Ben was born he softened; he wanted to see his grandson, he said, wanted to be part of his life. He chipped away and Jenny weakened. We were living in a semi-detached in Norwich, happily enough. Her father was in the vicarage, the house we now occupy, just him and a housekeeper, rattling around in far too many rooms.

I didn't think he was ill at first. I thought it was a ploy. Jenny visited frequently; weekends, occasionally for days at a time.

She took Ben with her, more often than not. He didn't mind. He was a happy little soul, content to do whatever mummy and daddy wanted. The old man doted on him, by all accounts, although I found it hard to imagine. Still, he didn't infect Ben, at least. Jenny though… I lost her in increments; it seemed as though she left a little more of herself at the vicarage each time she returned home.

When he finally died – and he took his sweet time, the bitter old bastard – Jenny insisted that we sell up and move to the village. We had the old house stripped and re-modelled. We made it modern and open and full of light. It made no difference; the old man still haunts the darker corners of our house. He haunts the shadows at the end of the garden. He haunts his daughter.

*****

We'd both parked in the multi-storey at St Andrew's. When we reached her car she kissed my mouth and told me to follow her. When I hesitated she kissed me again and said, "Trust me. Please?"

It was ridiculous, of course. But I did.

She drove quickly, cutting corners on the narrow country roads that led to our village. The drive took half an hour; I had time to think, to weigh up my options. I did neither. My mind kept replaying our time in the hotel room on a fevered, febrile loop. I could still taste her kisses and feel the touch of her fingers on my skin.

Sarah drove to her house, on the outskirts of the village. As she pulled her burgundy hatchback into their wide drive I parked at the road's edge, my engine running. She hurried to my car, impatient, signalling for me to wind the window down.

"Leave it here. It's fine. I need you to come in."

"But Richard …"

"Richard's not here. You can see that." She smiled to smooth the edge from her voice. It was still stupidly hot. The air was damp and suffocating.

I got out of the car, locked it and followed her into the house.

It was detached, big enough, modern.

"We're renting," she said as she worked the key into the front door. "Overdue, of course."

All the curtains were drawn. The atmosphere was ripe and fetid and dominated by the scent of spoiled food. When we entered the living room she turned the light on. Half-empty takeaway containers crowded the surfaces of a coffee table and large leather sofa. A pyramid of empty beer cans sat next to the large screen TV. There was an over-flowing ashtray on the small glass table by the sofa. The glass itself was smeared with a whitish residue.

"Do you like what we've done with the place?" I said nothing. "We tend not to entertain much."

"How do you live like this?"

"We don't settle. I told you."

"You've been here six months."

Her voice hardened. "We're not exactly putting down roots. And stop fucking judging me. Remember what we were doing an hour ago. I was good enough for you then."

"I didn't mean …"

She came to my side. Her breathing was ragged and irregular. "Who cares about this? It doesn't matter. It isn't real."

"What do you want, Sarah?"

She pressed against me. I could smell her sweat and her breath. "What do you think I want?"

I was trying to formulate a response when I heard the front door open.

Richard's voice. "Sarah?"

"In here, sweetheart." Her eyes were wide open. She looked, briefly, utterly deranged.

"Fuck," I said.

Richard entered the room. He said my name once, then stood very still. Beside me, I was aware of Sarah reaching for her bag.

"Look," I said.

Sarah extended her arm.

Richard's expression changed and he raised both hands to shoulder height.

Before he could speak Sarah shot him twice in the chest.

*****

We reached an impasse of sorts, I suppose, Jenny and I, in the years after Ben's death. All warmth and affection had fled but we kept up appearances, attended some village events together, held dinner parties for Jenny's ever changing cast of church related friends. I played my part, if a little grudgingly at times.

The rules were simple enough; we never touched, we never

kissed, we never talked about Ben.

I considered a trip, on my own, of course, to somewhere tropical and wild; to try and find some genuinely extreme weather. I don't think Jenny would have minded. It would have suited her, I think, if I'd simply gone off somewhere and died without fuss. It would have made things easier all round.

I never took the trip. Some crippling, yawning sense of inertia held me back. I made do with minor winds and indifferent squalls.

Perhaps I thought if I stood out for long enough, in the cold, in the rain, that Ben would eventually join me. I'd feel his presence beside me. He'd take my hand.

*****

There was surprisingly little blood.

"I need your help," Sarah said. She tucked the gun back into her bag. She was all business now. She saw the expression on my face. "Come on. We can't leave him here."

He was a big man and death hadn't rendered him particularly helpful. It took both of us to drag him into the hallway. Sarah backed his estate car up to the front door. Somehow we manhandled him into the rear of the car. We had to roll him over the tow bar and he ended up face down, arms twisted towards his spine, shirt and trousers askew. At least I could no longer see his face. When we'd finished we were breathing heavily and drenched with sweat.

"Jesus," Sarah said.

I couldn't speak. I was pretty sure I'd put my back out but I was glad of the physical pain as it distracted from the horror show playing on a Technicolor loop in what passed for my mind.

"Where shall we put him?" She looked down on her husband's corpse as though he was an old sofa that needed to be dumped. "Any ideas?"

My brain flooded with an unexpected cold clarity. "Actually, I do." Something in the tone of my voice made her look up. "Do you have anything thing heavy? And some rope?"

There were some breeze blocks in the garage and Sarah found a length of washing line. We loaded them up then I drove my car back to mine and Sarah followed in Richard's. There was no sign of Jenny or her VW Beetle so I parked up and walked back to the Richard's car. Sarah was in the passenger seat, checking her phone.

"You can drive. I don't know where we're going." She put the phone between her legs. Her expression was clear and innocent. I did as I was told. I drove us to Vinegar Lake.

The light was beginning to fade and a meaty haunch of cloud was gathering, occluding the sky's eastern edge. It was still as hot as hell.

As I drove my stomach roiled with a sudden cramp. "What the fuck have we done?"

Sarah sucked her lip thoughtfully. "I assume that it if anything happened to Jenny, you'd inherit?"

"What?"

"Just wondering, sweetheart. No need to stress."

I glanced at her as I drove. There was nothing real about her; not in her words, her voice, her expression. I'd sought oblivion in extreme weather and I'd found it instead in the woman next to me. I still didn't know her real name.

I drove up to the edge of the lake, as close as I could. Dark water, still and deep; the flint outcrop beyond, looming.

Sarah jumped out of the car. "I love this place. Why didn't you tell me about it?"

I opened the boot and started unfurling the clothes line.

"Actually, don't bother with that. We'll just roll the car in."

"Roll it in?"

"Richard and all. Easy peasy." Her expression was taking on the same demonic cast as when she'd shot her husband. She stood loose-limbed, at ease. Behind her the sky was cherry-black and thick with cloud.

"What have we done?" I said again. Every atom of me ached. I wanted to sink to my knees.

"What have *you* done, I think you mean? You naughty boy. Poor Richard. You never did like him. Everybody knew." Her phone beeped and she studied it. "That's my ride," she said. "Right on time."

"Your ride?" I heard a car approach, the engine sound oddly familiar.

Headlights scissored across Sarah's face as the vehicle crested the small rise that lead to the bank of the lake. She squinted then rummaged in her bag and brought out the gun. She looked at it for a moment as though she wasn't entirely sure what it was. "Turns out your wife is quite the dark horse."

Jenny's Beetle pulled into the clearing. She got out of the car, leaving the door open and the engine running. The glare of the headlights illuminated us all. She went to Sarah's side and slid her arm around her waist. Sarah raised the gun.

I could smell the flat, mineral stench of the lake. The air was cooler here, by the water, as the light died. There was a storm coming. I could sense it. I reached my arm out to the side, my hand open.

Training Crows
Joan Leotta

A free place to live for the summer was the offer I accepted from Professor Fonet last year. All I had to do was house sit for him in his wonderful modern town house on the top of Pittsburgh's Mount Washington while he was off in France.

His balcony overlooked the place where the Monongahela and Allegheny Rivers combined to form the Ohio--Pittsburgh's Point. The neighborhood's view of the three rivers was not its only charm.

"Only some occasional thefts, no real crime," Fonet assured me when he handed over the keys. "And friendly neighbors—especially the people who lived in the two townhouses identical to this one." He shook my hand, as professors do, adding, "I really can't thank you enough, <Insert Name>." Then he disappeared into his waiting taxi, off to the airport.

The townhouse trio was new housing built on the property of a grand old house. The front lawns of his house and the neighbors were touching of course, and in the back the three balconies were so close, you could reach across and borrow a cup of sugar from either should necessity call for it. Backyards were not meant as play areas—they were steep rocky slopes.

His neighbors had both perched sheds on their respective areas.

I planned to take Pittsburgh's answer to an urban ski lift, *The Incline*, down to the first level street to ride the bus for downtown and wander the old city streets to the 'Strip District', an historical commercial food zone, to buy fresh fruits and veggies. My summer job at the Heinz History Museum, was also in the Strip. And, I could easily hop a bus to the Oakland cultural district to catch a museum exhibit and schmooze with friends and check in with the history department—especially to keep up with the assistants to the professors who would be on my PhD committee in the fall.

Once I'd moved in I began sipping my morning coffee on the balcony overlooking the rivers. In the evening, I enjoyed the sunset with a glass of wine on that same balcony.

My balcony reveries were almost derailed by my prof's neighbor, two doors down in house number three. This man had made his home a center for crows--large black, shiny, raucous crows.

On the second day, as I was about to retreat back into the house, I noticed that the older woman who lived in house two, between bird man's and the Prof's, was not bothered by the crows. Mrs. Phineas, (aka Mrs. P) a retired librarian, waved at me.

"Introduce yourself to the crows. They won't bother you if they know you. Especially if you offer them a little something on your balcony railing."

She told me that Wilson, the bird man, had been working with crows for two years.

"The people across the street called the police when he first started, claiming he was encouraging a nuisance. Then he had the animal rights folks claim that the crows of Mt Washington were special and should be protected."

I went back inside, got another cup of coffee and two cookies. One for me and one to break up and put on the railing for the crows as Mrs. P suggested. I sat down. The birds circled me.

"Smile at them. Say hello," she advised. I complied. The birds moved over to my railing and raucously proclaimed their approval for my cookie offering.

Keeping one protective hand on my coffee and a napkin over my cookie, I looked over at Mrs. P and asked, "Why does Wilson like crows so much?"

"Well, they're one of nature's smartest creatures. Wilson was with Pittsburgh Zoo's bird department before he retired. He teaches his crow visitors tricks. I don't know how that fits in with the animal rights folks, but…

"Anyway, we don't have to be afraid to have coffee on the balcony. A few small offerings and soon the crows will even bring you flowers or seeds to thank you. They sometimes even try to talk to me, now that they know me.

"Watch this. I've taught them a trick of my own." She took the cover off the sugar bowl on her little table and pushed her coffee cup toward it.

One of the birds left the railing. He gave what could only be described as a querying caw.

Mrs. P answered. "Yes, I know you've already put some in for me, but the new neighbor wants to see you do it. Please repeat."

The bird threw back his head and cawed again. Laughing? Then he dipped his beak into her sugar bowl, daintily scooped up a sugar cube and carefully transferred it to her cup. He repeated the trick and then flew back to the railing.

"Good boy! Thank you," Mrs. P called out. "I'm going to miss them doing this trick for me. They do it for Wilson too. My doctor told me to switch to an artificial sweetener." She held up a little bottle. "I have to squeeze in two drops of this."

So, I continued to have my coffee outside, and by the end of the first week the crows had started to come closer to me. Rather politely, they landed not on my table but on the chair across from me, moving their heads to one side and then the other, as if waiting for me to speak or teach them a new trick.

I started talking to them. "I've put some treats on my railing for you, guys."

To my surprise, they seemed to understand and scooped up the proffered treats from the railing, just as Mrs. P had told me they would.

The first rainy Saturday, I pulled back the curtains on the deck sliders and four of the birds were lined up as if waiting for me. I had not planned to go out. However, instead of shooing them away, I cut a piece of toast into four pieces, buttered it, and set it out on a plate. Each crow daintily took one piece and nodded at me as they flew away.

I waited for the rain to stop before checking the mail and caught Mrs. P and Wilson in an unpleasant conversation— one might say an argument. She was her waving hands and he was shouting and waving his hands. He stomped off as I approached.

"Mrs. P, what's wrong?" I put my arm around her instinctively.

"Oh that man! He wants to buy my townhouse—thinks I should move to an old folks' place. Says I'm not capable of caring for myself. Told me he was going to buy it after I die anyway, so why not sell it to me now. I know I'm old, I'm 85. My reflexes are not the best. I don't drive—I use taxis or uber to the market. My niece, Amanda, gets me audiobooks on CDs at the library, since I don't see that well anymore and takes me out to lunch once a week. I have my walk here memorized and I enjoy the river view, even though it is blurry. I even like his crows."

"Why does he need another townhouse? Rental?"

"No, he wants to tear it down and build some kind of giant structure for his crows. He once told me he has visions of a grand corvid, that's crows and others like them, study and training center. It just makes me upset that he gets so *aggressive* about my house. When he talks to me, he waves those huge arms of his around as if he were a large crow flapping his wings in my face. It's bad enough that he is over six feet tall and I'm only five foot one."

As a fellow short person (five foot two in bare feet), I sympathized with her. "I should think he'd be happy to have you as a neighbor. You don't complain about his crows. What about the neighbor on the other side of him, the older house with the big yard? Or does that copse of trees between the two properties give them enough buffer, so they don't complain?"

Mrs. P smiled. "Those trees belong to the city—and so does

the house on the other side of them. The city plans to make it into a George Washington museum. The trees are a great roosting place for the crows. He claims it's their historic home."

I was impressed. When I next went to the history center to work on my thesis, I poked around on some websites. |Eventually I came up with a couple of articles from local papers, along with some in zoo society magazines. One was written by Mr. Wilson, extolling the attractive qualities of crows.

My own daily encounters further convinced me. About twenty birds were regular visitors to Mrs. P. Four became regulars on my balcony. One was exceptionally large crow who also visited Mrs. P and plunked sugar cubes into her morning coffee.

After the toast incident by the door on the rainy day, he and his three companions began leaving me little gifts of flowers— ok, yard-plucked weeds, but pretty ones – on the railing where I usually left their treats.

I began to be able to discern differences among the birds although I could not distinguish male from female. I made up names for them. I called the big one, *Gigantor* and named the other three, Uno, Due, and Tre. Not very imaginative but….

I also noticed that the birds did not restrict themselves to our three backyards. Besides roosting in the trees on the other side of Wilson's house, they swooped about the neighborhood, though not in large gatherings. It seemed they were trained or had trained themselves to break into small groups of two or three when outside the realm of the townhouse trio yards.

I was able to pick out Gigantor quite easily no matter where he was. I began to ascribe human-like motives to the birds, suspecting their roaming about in small groups was done so as not to discomfit human neighbors. One group of birds hung out by the corner grocery, probably hoping for treats. I passed by the spot on my way home from The Incline stop every weekday.

It was during one of these journeys that I realized Gigantor and my three other pals also *knew who I was*—even when I was not feeding them from the balcony.

A week or so later, while walking home, I must have put my hand into the coat pocket to put in my change and when I pulled my hand back out, I dislodged an old bus pass. The pass fluttered to the ground without my realizing it had fallen. Gigantor noticed. Before I took two more steps from the stop toward the house, Gigantor swooped in front of me with the pass in his mouth. I held out my hand, instinctively and he dropped it expertly into my awaiting palm. Impressive!

The next morning, Mrs. P called over. I looked up and shouted a greeting. Before I could tell her about Gigantor's trick, she began to speak: "Watch this. To make up for the way he treated me at the mailbox, Wilson's taught the birds a new trick. They've learned how to squeeze the sugar substitute into my coffee."

As if on cue, Gigantor, hopped onto her table, picked up her bottle of liquid sweetener in his beak and dutifully squeezed two drops into the cup. Then he flew off with the sweetener bottle.

"Good trick, eh?" She saluted me with her cup before sipping. "Don't worry about the sweetener. He'll bring it back tomorrow. He puts it back on the shelf at Wilson's where it was during his training."

I told her about Gigantor picking up my dropped bus pass and returning it to me.

She laughed. "Yes, crows look out for those who look out for them."

That was the last time I saw her laughing. The last time I saw her alive.

The next few days were too busy for me to spend time lounging on the balcony in the morning with Mrs. P and our bird friends. The professor had called and wanted me to do some additional research at the history museum for him. That meant I had to get to the museum early, and leave late, in order to accommodate his request and do my own work. I did remember to put out a few treats for my friends and waved at Mrs. P, but no lounging on the deck for me.

On the following Saturday morning, when I usually try to rest in bed as long as I can, the sound of a siren sliced through my dream. I jumped out of bed. Wrapping my bathrobe around my flower print nightie, I headed for the front door. EMTs were carrying a fully covered body out of Mrs. P's house. An obviously distraught younger version of my elderly neighbor—her niece, Amanda – followed them out. I padded over in my slippers. "Is there anything I can do to help?"

"No, no. My aunt, she passed away. I'm not sure exactly when. She didn't answer the phone this morning when I called to remind her, we were going to go shopping after lunch today. Did you see her yesterday?"

I shook my head. I hadn't seen her the previous day. Or the

few days before that. It saddened me that I hadn't said a proper good-by to the dear lady.

In the days following Mrs P's death, I saw Amanda often. One afternoon by the mailbox, she invited me to the funeral and to read a scripture at the service.

One of the crows, I think it was Tre, flew by as we were talking. Amanda looked up. "I wish there were some way I could invite the crows. She had really grown fond of them." I nodded in agreement.

Mr. Wilson walked over. He started to talk to Amanda, pointedly ignoring me, so I excused myself. I wondered, if he were going to be crass enough to talk about buying the house already.

Along with a couple of Amanda's friends and a few ladies who knew Mrs. P from her library days, I went back over to the house after the funeral reception to help Amanda with the task of cleaning. We started upstairs. I agreed to do the bathroom. There was a faint, unpleasant odor.

Amanda told me that evidently her aunt had suffered some bouts of nausea. "The doctor told me she'd called him about it. Evidently what he prescribed didn't work. He said she probably went into a coma from the dehydration of throwing up, compounded by her sugar and heart issues, and that led to her death. Probably the day before I discovered her. If only I had come over a day earlier."

I worked until late that night and came back the next day to help Amanda sort her Aunt's belongings, deciding what would go to charity, what she would take, and what would go to the dump. We set aside a collection of leftover cleaning chemicals for hazmat disposal.

The day after that, I decided to go into work a couple of hours late, so I wandered out to breakfast out on the balcony. It seemed a bit lonely without Mrs. P calling out from across. Gigantor approached Mrs. P's little table with a bottle of sweetener in his beak. Suddenly I began to cry. The poor crow didn't seem to know his friend was gone.

"Come back here Lucifer, you idiot." The harshness of Mr. Wilson's voice shouting from his window, startled me. I'd never heard him yell at the birds. Almost as shocking was to hear the name he had given poor Gigantor. Lucifer, Prince of Evil. The bird dropped the bottle on Mrs. P's balcony deck before flying back to Wilson's house. The bottle bounced off into the yard below.

Later that day, after I came back from work, I decided to do the last chore I had promised Amanda — empty Mrs. P's garden shed to see what could be given away or tossed. It wasn't locked.

A lawn service cut Mrs. P's grass, so her shed contained only a few flowerpots and some hand gardening tools. There was also a bag of potting soil and a container of a cyanide based pest removal product. I shuddered, thinking about gentle Mrs. P killing anything.

I put a note on the poisons for the gardener to take the soil and dispose of the poison properly. Then I made a pile of "donate" and put the rest into a black garbage bag. As I dragged the bag across the lawn to put it out with my own garbage, I noticed the bottle Gigantor had dropped. It had landed in Mrs. P's flower bed. I picked it up and put it in my pants pocket.

Uno and Due came flapping by me. Due clipped himself onto my sweater sleeve with his beak and pulled me toward Wilson's shed. All three sheds were alike—small door, one window. Mr. Wilson's had one big difference. An odd sort of cage had been fitted around the window of his shed.

I watched one of the crows lift the cage to allow a second crow to slip under. Another crow stood guard until his friend came back out, and closed the cage. Gigantor was watching from the roof of the shed.

What was that all about? Curiosity and cats don't mix but I never thought that applied to humans. I turned my head up to the balcony area. Mr. Wilson was not home, or at least not near the balcony. The crows continued flapping about. I thought about looking in the shed but then decided to hurry back before Wilson came out and saw me snooping about.

As I walked back through Mrs. P's garden to my own place, I noticed something glittering on the ground. A ring with a green stone. I picked it up and when I got back, I called Amanda and read her the list of what I thought should be disposed of from the shed. She agreed with my decisions on give and keep. Then I told her about the ring.

"That's not my Aunt's, "Amanda told me. "I don't know who it belongs to. "

When I hung up, I stuck the ring back in my pants pocket. My fingers brushed the bottle of sweetener Gigantor/Lucifer had dropped. I decided to take the ring to local police station lost and found. Maybe one of the people who came to help after the funeral lunch had dropped the ring in the yard.

The sweetener, well, that made me think so much of Mrs.

P, I pulled it out, sat it on the table and stared at it. Aspartame. Aspartame gives me migraines, so I was not inclined to try it. But I was curious. I wondered if it smelled sweet. I took the top off and – Whoa! It smelled more salty than sweet.

I put the bottle on my kitchen table and forgot about it. The next day I took the ring to the police station. They were very interested in it. More than I thought they would be. Turns out, the ring was a real emerald and was part of a group of heirloom jewelry that had been stolen from a house only a few blocks away from our townhouse trio. The police theorized that the thief had run through the back yards making his escape. I shivered to think about a criminal having come so close to where I was living.

A couple of days later, I was back out on the porch at breakfast and spotted Wilson. He was talking to the crows. He looked up, saw me, frowned, and then tried to cover his annoyance with a smile and a wave. The crows dispersed. He sat down to sip coffee on his own back deck. He used sugar in his coffee, I noticed. Cubes.

Three days in a row I watched as he brought out his sugar bowl, the creamer, and his coffee cup on a neat metal tray. He sweetened his coffee before downing it in two giant gulps. Then he packed everything back on the tray and went back into his house. I noticed he had trained Uno to put the sugar cubes in his coffee.

The crows had been ignoring me but, on that day, Uno, Due, and Tre came swooping down. I spoke gently to them, reminding them that Mrs. P would not be out. Gigantor was nowhere to be seen. In fact, he did not come around the rest of that week. As it was, I only had three more weeks left in the townhouse. I hoped to see Gigantor at least one more time. I looked for him whenever I went out. But he never showed up.

On the Monday before I was supposed to vacate, I stayed home to clean. Mr. Wilson came to the door before I'd even finished my coffee.

"I've got to go away for two days. I've left food for the crows. They can fend for themselves but keep an eye out please so that no one comes around to bother them, OK? I know you're fond of them too." He smiled. His smile was even creepier than his frowns, but he was right about my caring for his winged friends. I watched Mr. Wilson get into a cab carrying a suitcase. I went out on the back deck. Several crows came swooping over right away. I recognized Uno and Due. Gigantor was still missing.

"No treats right now, fellas. Maybe I'll have something for you at lunch." But when I tried to go back into the house, they blocked my way, flying between me and the slider and flapping wildly. One even got behind me and nudged me forward with his beak—toward Wilson's house.

I was intrigued. I trotted down the steps. The crows went into a leading formation and I followed them across Mrs. P's plot, into Wilson's yard. The crows began to peck at a blueberry bush — a new one, just planted.

Mrs. P once told me Wilson was going to plant more natural food sources for his birds. But this plant looked scraggly and uncared for. How would it grow, I wondered?

Then, two crows I did not recognize, flew over with piece of bark in their mouths and began to shovel at the base of the bush. When the bush was sufficiently loose, Uno and Due pulled it out of the ground. They moved aside when I bent over to investigate.

I saw a black feathered head. A big one. Gigantor!

I ran back over to the shed at my rental and grabbed a small trowel. Carefully, I scraped away the dirt around the crow's body. Then I saw that he was not alone in the makeshift grave. Two bottles of eye drops and a bottle of aspartame lay next to him.

I went back for the big garden spade and carefully lifted Gigantor's body out of that hidden grave. He was trussed like a chicken for roasting—wings tied; feet bound. His beak was chipped, as though something had been forced into his mouth. I carried him over to Mrs. P's flowers. All the while the other crows flew in circles around me. Silently.

I ran into my unit and came back out with some scissors, a bath towel, and gloves. I put on the gloves, cut the ropes holding the poor dead bird and wrapped him in the soft, pink bath towel. The bird's head flopped about. Broken neck. I buried him beside Mrs. P's prized lilac bush. I stood over the grave and shed some tears—for the bird and for Mrs. P.

All the while, the rest of the crows watched in silence, shaking their heads in apparent approval of my respectful actions. Then I picked up the two bottles of eye drops and the other bottle of aspartame.

I took the bottles into the house with me and looked up the contents on the Internet where I learned that eye drops were poisonous if ingested. I picked up the bottle of aspartame and squeezed out a drop onto a paper kitchen towel. Then beside that a drop from each of the bottles. In comparison it looked as if the aspartame bottle I had on the table was really filled with eyedrops. The bottle buried with the bird was the real thing—of course only a chemical test would tell for sure. If anyone would even bother.

I knew then that Wilson had used Gigantor to poison Mrs. P. He had trained the bird to squeeze drops of the phony aspartame into her coffee. Even if the eyedrops only made her sick, Wilson knew that with her other health conditions, a long bout of anything that would dehydrate her could lead to her death.

But why? For her house? That seemed unlikely. Then I remembered the ring and the covered window in the shed. When night finally brought darkness to the back yards, I went out back again. The crows were still moving around.

With binoculars, I watched the shed in Wilson's yard until I dozed off. A light drizzle woke me up. The moon was full. I saw a crow fly toward the shed in Wilson's yard.

I walked across the lawns—quietly, in case Mr. Wilson had returned early. I watched a crow lift the cage over the darkened window, lift the shade and enter Wilson's shed.

I walked over. The crows did not seem to mind me. In fact, the "guard crow" lifted the cage for me. I pulled the shade aside and turned on my cell phone flashlight.

The moon and my phone lit the space enough for me to see that pieces of jewelry were scattered around the shed's interior. It didn't take a genius to realize that Wilson had trained the crows as thieves. Had Mrs. P had discovered the truth about thieving habits of her friends the crows and had threated Wilson about it?

But who would believe me? Oh yes, the police probably would buy the theft idea, but Mrs. P's health was bad. Proving that he had trained Gigantor to murder her was not going to happen. As for Gigantor's murder, I didn't think the justice system would really care much about a crow.

Then I remembered that Wilson used sugar in cube form. I stepped back carefully, waved to the crows and walked slowly back to my house. Should I call the police about the jewelry?

I fretted and researched all night on my computer. One of the things I had found in Mrs. P's shed was the cyanide-based gopher killer. The packaging was old and the chemicals so powerful it was now banned from sale in Pennsylvania, amongst other States.

The next day I bought some cube sugar in a supermarket in Oakland where no one would remember me and wearing gloves, I crushed the gopher pellets and rolled the cubes in cyanide. I dumped the treated cubes onto a paper plate and took them out onto the deck with a plastic spoon.

I didn't have much time. I called Uno, Due, and Tre over. Gave them their usual treats, showed them little stack cubes and the spoon. I demonstrated using the spoon to pick up the cubes. All the while I kept explaining that Wilson had killed their friend, Mrs. P. They already knew he was Gigantor's executioner. Did they understand me? I watched Uno manipulate the spoon—just as the other crows had used the bark as shovels.

Two days later, it was time for me to leave. That morning, I cut up a slice of toast into three pieces and put them on the deck railing. Along with a bag of treated sugar cubes. Then I went inside, finished my cleaning and called an uber to take me and my suitcase all the way downtown to the bus station.

By the end of that week I was back in my appartment and the Professor had returned home. He called me.

"Did you meet that awful Mr. Wilson when you were living here?"

"I did."

"Well, when I went out on my deck this morning, I looked over and saw Wilson—he was slumped in one of his chairs. I called 911, but he was already dead."

The professor didn't mention anything about the sugar cubes. I'm guessing the crows carried the rest off down the steep rocky hillside after they and I avenged the deaths of Mrs. P and Gigantor. Days later, the professor called again to tell me that Wilson had been poisoned but no one knew how.

The Prof also related the news about the discovery of stolen jewelry in Wilson's shed. Then he added, "It's the oddest thing. With Wilson gone, the crows have stopped coming around. They don't even roost in the park area. They've disappeared. So much for this being their historic home. Wilson thought he knew so much."

We both laughed. I continued laughing even after we hung up. Wilson may have gotten away with murder, but he hadn't escaped justice. Wilson knew so much about crows, but the crows were smarter than he knew and there was one small thing he had forgotten – a group of crows is called a murder.

Deadly Harvest
Gary Thomson

"The oil levels in the storage room are perilously low," grumbled Kimon the gymnasiarch. "And I tell you, Eleon, with the olive harvest looking to come in scant, you'll be treating our athletes' cuts and bruises with goat fat or millet paste. Hermes himself won't be able to appease their anger – nor relieve their foul smell."

Eleon the physician grimaced at this looming affront to custom and hygiene. "Can your supplier not find reserves in any coastal cities?"

"Inaros's agents are scouring every market from Miletos to Mytilene. Expensive to ship it here to Cos. His pool of workers are straggling home from their campaigns in this recent Spartan war. Still, he has recruited a few household slaves and pressed some able war orphans off the streets."

The two men eased alongside the arena colonnade to let three cadets pass them on their way to the gymnasion archery yard. Their lithe, naked bodies gleamed under a fresh application of oil; they were jesting about a meaningful wager among themselves. Kimon said, "Let me ration their lotions and they'd riddle me with their arrows."

Eleon tried to soothe his friend's agitation. "Inaros won't

take advantage. Isn't he always first to donate amphoras of oil as prizes for religious and sporting festivals?"

"To worsen matters, he's contracted to supply the autumn festival of Demeter of the Golden Barley, in Chios. Heavy fine if he shorts his delivery."

Eleon was about to ask in regard to emergency sources from area farmers when a slave lad hurriedly approached them, sweat dripping from his chin. He gasped to Kimon. "Sire, searching you everywhere. Come now. We're shifting jars in oil room. Behind one… find dead man."

*****

The body lay curled against the base of a storage vessel. Momentarily Eleon was riveted by a fierce scene painted over the amphora's side: brave Theseus clubbing the Lion of Kithaeron's gaping jaw. The king's free arm angled toward the dead man's face, hovering over his left eye and a mat of blood soaked hair. A woollen cloak covered his upper body.

Eleon pressed the victim's throat, in vain.

Kimon groaned. "By Zeus's holy beard, this shows as a prophecy fulfilled. Inaros… alive and active for us a moment ago; now, cold as the high winds on Olympos. All his wealth and soldier's valour could not stay the assassin's cudgel." He stood up, grappling with the unthinkable: closing the gymnasion for lack of crucial oil.

Eleon said, "Perhaps the attendants saw someone loitering about?"

"I was chatting with him yesterday, near closing, He'd finished his running exercises, and was heading toward the baths. He'd often come from there to here to check the levels, it worried him so. He was still stewing over a row with Theron the olive merchant at a recent symposium at his house."

"Heated debates over too much wine. Add a few beautiful women companions… What happened?"

"Late it was, Theron overstepped himself and berated Inaros for his vile treatments of Chrysis, his hetaira. Inaros dismissed Theron as a crusty old fool who wouldn't know female comeliness to ever again warm his blood. But soberer heads prevailed, got them to quiet."

"Hardly a dispute to prompt murder."

"Help us find the assassin, Eleon, and restore sanctity here in Hermes's precinct." Kimon pulled the cloak over Inaros's face. "If the attacker was wounded in this brawl, he will come to you, or the Healing Temple, for treatment."

"One among hundreds of patients, you mean?" Eleon looked beyond the shadows, said softly, "Remove the body in quiet to the Asklepion where Master Hippocrates will perform *autopsia* for Magistrate."

"You may want to chat with Inaros's associate, Nikomedes. He's a former Games pentathlete, who still spends a lot of time in the arena."

"Does he have business ties with Inaros?"

"Not in the oil trade. Rather, the entertainment side."

*****

Next day Eleon completed a tidying of medicines and case notes in his gymnasion Treatment Room. He then went walkabout in the training yards. "Where is this renowned athlete, Nikomedes?" he asked among the grunting javelin and diskos throwers. "Who can tell me of his glorious victories, won while you were still beardless boys?" His queries brought offhand silence or ribald comments.

One long jumper guffawed. "He's off with his fancy girl,

lucky man. Would I had similar sweet diversion."

Eleon left the arena and walked the pathway over the slopes of Mount Dikion to the Healing Temple of Asklepios. He found Hippocrates in a treatment room on the second terrace. The Master Physician stood before his patient, a muscled, sober-faced lad of about sixteen, who sat on a cedar wood table. He continued applying a poultice of silphium, honey and olive oil to a cheek laceration, greeting Eleon: "Euthymos here paid the price. Looking at a pretty woman when he should be watching his direction." Euthymos coloured and avoided Eleon's gaze at his wound.

Hippocrates packaged the remainder of the medicine in a leather purse, and sent Euthymos on his way. "Clean the cut with warm water twice daily, apply the salve lightly. Back here in a week for checkup. You'll have a scar to show your future wife."

Hippocrates gestured toward his departed patient. "The lad's a success story, thanks to his mistress. Learning a tumbler's skills – the hard way." To Eleon's puzzled expression he added, "The hetaira, Chrysis. I haven't met her, but she's known for her reclamation projects. She provids these war orphans with food and shelter, even finding work for some." He gathered his medicine flasks and linen bandages. "This one, to his credit, is studying mathematics and rhetoric at the Academy."

"Have you confirmed the cause of Inaros's death, sir?"

"Severe head trauma, as you could see. Slight bruising on his hands and arms. However, there is one thing I want to show you." Hippocrates summoned a slave attendant, instructed him to hurry now and fetch a linen bag from the Archives Room.

Meantime, Hippocrates led Eleon through highlights of his physicians' experimental treatment of battle stressed soldiers by shared readings of modern tragic literature. "We're partial to Sophocles's Ajax," he said. "These men can readily see the torments of one of their own. By leading them to talk about it without shame or guilt, our hope is for them to confront and tame their demons of nightmare and violence." His summary of success rates was interrupted by the slave's return.

From the bag he unwrapped a folded cloth, then held forth a slender strip of wood, shaped like the flange of an arrow head. "This was in the victim's hair. We washed it with vinegar and water."

Eleon stroked the grey, beady surface. "Slice of tree bark…"

*****

Eleon returned to the gymnasion Treatment Room. Telines the *rhizotomos* was there waiting for him, slouched along a stone bench, half asleep and grumbly. The root cutter stood up at Eleon's approach and gripped a roughspun sack beside him. "Have fetched the plants you requested, guv'nor." His face was sun darkened and ageless. There was a slight smell about him of the loam he turned and sifted in shadowy valleys or on sunny upland slopes in his search for medicinal herbs. Callused hands swung the sack onto his right shoulder and he shambled into the room behind Eleon.

Carefully he pulled stalks of herbs and unwashed roots from his sack and arranged them over the patients' bench:

"Wild carrot… yarrow … wild onion…"

To staunch the bloody wounds of the boxers, Eleon thought.

"Here's yer mint, parsley too."

In potion, pain relief for deep bruises.

Telines set a block of pine resin alongside the herbs.

Hippocrates himself wrote of its efficacy as an antiseptic for cuts and abrasions.

When he had emptied his bag Telines fiddled with the tie string. "Was poking around Theron's groves for some myrtle leaves. His workers're getting antsy."

He watched idly as Eleon assembled a drying rack. "Can't say I blame them none." Eleon hung a spray of yellow leafed yarrow over the wooden spindle. He heard this disclosure with half an ear. It was part of Telines's foraging to uncover a shard of rumour and packing it in the back of his mind for later show. "Why would that be?"

"Inaros has been buying first right of use for all the oil presses hereabout. They claim he was out to corner the processing market, and throw his competitors to the dogs."

Telines crumpled his empty sack. Then he extended his palm for his silver payment.

*****

From his bench overlooking the boxing pit Eleon watched two young fighters slam each other's face and arms with heavy blows. A trainer studied their movements. It distressed him how this pounding to the head ruined a man for his natural functioning. Soon these battered hulks would be in front of him, begging a salve for blurred vision or dizziness. A short, thickset man was approaching him along the aisle, eyeing the boxers, dancing the fighters' shuffle, jabbing at the air. Smiling.

The man slipped into the adjoining seat. "I hear you've been asking about poor Inaros. He was my shipmate, and friend. His death has shaken my world topsy-turvy." He extended a thick, scarred hand "Nikomedes of Thasos, sir. The lads said you were looking for me."

Eleon gazed on a face that embodied his present worries:

oft broken nose skewed right; ridges of scar tissue above the eyebrows, remnants of cuts inflicted from fists wrapped in leather thongs. Yet his dark eyes held a flash of excitement, nurtured by an athlete's commitment to hard training and competition. The victor's wreath sat lightly over this callused forehead.

Eleon introduced himself. "Magistrate wants this turmoil sorted. I believe maybe you can help." He scanned the boxer's hands for recent abrasions, but saw only heavy knuckles, like slinger's stones. "You campaigned with Inaros in these hostilities?"

Nikomedes flashed a crooked grin. "Aboard the triaconter *Eunike*: the lady of sweet victory. We were part of the Hellespont Fleet, patrol ships to keep the grain routes to Athens clear of pirates, and reinforce major engagements in northern waters. Inaros was our *paradros*, guardian of the helmsman during enemy assault." Nikomedes grimaced as one boxer landed a blow to his opponent's throat. "He was a warrior, first grade."

"And you, Nikomedes?"

"Marine archer. I sent a goodly number of rebels to a watery grave. Still, I'm glad now for the peace. I prefer sparring in the arena to firing arrows from a heaving foredeck."

"Can you tell me of your connection with Chrysis?"

Nikomedes's scarred face softened. "We found her in the slave market at Mounichia, same day we were demobbed. A splendid offering: Thracian, educated, beautiful. Inaros and I thought alike – here was a hetaira worth the small fortune her owner was asking. We couldn't afford her singly – so we pooled our payout wages and bought her, fifty-fifty."

"Were you able to share her pleasures equally?"

Lighthearted.

Nikomedes smiled languidly. "We installed her in her own house, in the Street of Bakers. Sadly, I needed some cash to forestall a hostile money lender, so I sold my half ownership to Inaros. Our symposia guests loved her. Witty, charming. She turned the men to adoring puppies. But their appreciation wasn't enough for Inaros. He started to suffer bad dreams and violent outbursts. Turned his cruelty onto Chrysis, berating her, doling her sexual delights among his wine soaked company with the liberality of a Persian prince. Often threatening to turn her onto the streets."

"And you wanted to purchase her for yourself. Save her from the wretchedness of common harlotry."

Nikomedes's shoulders sagged. "How many times did I curse myself and my empty purse."

"Can you account for your whereabouts two days ago, between noon and dusk?"

"I was training here most of late afternoon." He stood up. "Tell you what, physician. Come by tonight to my symposium. You are *astakles*, my special guest. Meet Chrysis, enjoy her charms for an evening. Maybe she can help in your search."

Eleon thanked the shaggy boxer, then asked, "Are you in love with her?"

Nikomedes grumbled. Too softly, Eleon thought. "A man cannot hold women companions dear. It complicates his life." He shuffled away along the aisle.

*****

Eleon was recumbent on a divan in the assembly room, sharing it with Kallistos the rhetorician. A lecturer at the Academy, he was a pale pinched man who now had given over any discussion of his craft and who rose to converse with one of the four hetairae in close attendance. Three similar divans flanked the other walls, occupied by prominent men of the city, including a shipowner, an ex-army general, a horse breeder, and a poet from Melos.

The earlier, serious discussions had played out: Spartan naval tactics in the recent fighting; city responsibilities to street orphans; subsidies to Sacred Games athletes. Now Dionysos's revelry usurped Apollo's thoughtful sobriety. The men called for larger draughts of wine. Eagerly they shared bawdy jokes, guffawing at punch lines. Their world would spin over to a new day without philosophy to guide it.

Eleon watched Chrysis glide among the guests. Easy, graceful, perceptive. She sat alongside the poet and offered him an opening line for his next lyric poem on the fragile loyalties of virgins. From the shipowner she begged an account of his most harrowing encounter with pirates. She had no awe of this accomplished company, she who had held in her confident hands the hearts of magistrates, philosphers and tycoons.

Always she kept a light gaze on the other women, measuring their comfort levels with the guests. Experience and intuition alerted her to displays of drunken tempers or thwarted desires. In the background a kithara player accompanied a tumbler who wore only a loin cloth and a red linen headband. Eleon recognized him as Euthymos. The lad moved gracefully through his routine, supple and captivating.

The horse breeder and a companion paired off and heeding Eros's summons, drifted away to a quieter room. Eleon set his wine cup on the table. Chrysis sat lightly on the edge of the divan, facing him. Her flushed cheeks heightened her natural beauty. She thanked him for Euthymos's prompt treatment at the Asklepion.

"Did he hurt himself during one of his performances?" Eleon said.

Chrysis's face clouded. "He told me he tripped over a tree stump, during his work in my late master's olive grove." Pause. "But I suspect Inaros directed his fist at the lad. He was impatient when the younger ones didn't work as fast as he thought they should." She recounted similar examples of Inaros driving his child laborers with physical assault. Eleon hesitated. "Did he beat you on any occasion?"

"He was war wounded, physician. Deep in his mind. I kept alert to his sudden mood changes and threats of violence, and so escaped many thrashings. Still, the gods may yet be planning a new bout of suffering for me."

A shriek of laughter from one of the hetairae erupted across the room. Nikomedes and the army commander were in heated contest, spitting mouthfuls of wine into a goblet on the floor.

Eleon turned back to her. "Surely some of your clients will provide living quarters and expense money?"

"Nikomedes wishes he were able, dear man. But his fondness for gambling makes him an unreliable savior." She looked toward Euthymos. Protective, tender. "If I lose my children that will be the worse outrage. For myself…" She let the thought drift into the room. She excused herself, and laughing lightly, laid her hand over the poet's arm. In the centre of the room Euthymos was taking his bow while the shipowner snored deeply on silk cushions in the corner. Eleon stood up from the divan. Before leaving he wanted a quick word with Kallistos, who was now swaying behind a companion, snuggling his head against her neck.

*****

The following day, Eleon hastened from the Healing Temple down the walkway to the gymnasion. At the treatment room he whispered a prayer of thanks that no injured athletes were waiting for his attention to their aches or bruises. Then, subdued and hopeful, he strode past the boxing arena, toward the oil storage room. The thumping of body blows and boxers' harsh grunts barely registered with him.

Shortly he stood before the painted Lion. Slashing teeth gleamed in the slanting light. A stain ribbed the stone flag. He tipped the amphora toward him, then eased his arm inside and felt along the curved surface.

He withdrew his arm. In his fist he held a stout wooden club. Wisps of hair clung to the bark. A spray of blood darkened the wood. A sliver of outer bark had clipped away to reveal a cut of pale, moist inner bark in the shape of an arrow head.

*****

Eleon stood by the wellhead in the forecourt of Chrysis's ample home, held by the quiet discipline over her foster children gathered for their rehearsals. In one corner three intent flautists played under the watchful eye of their tutor; beyond them, Chrysis directed two girls in the art of pouring wine from decorated kraters. Along the west wall Euthymos practiced short-step back flips. He adjusted his bandage impatiently.

Chrysis set the girls to tidying a table and work space, then approached Eleon. "Were you looking to hire some capable help, physician? Perhaps some hospitality work at the Asklepion. Maybe greeting weary pilgrims?"

Eleon smiled. "Surely full-hearted Artemis, who protects

vulnerable children, blesses your efforts here." He hesitated at the hard news he was about to present. He called to Euthymos to approach. "Forgive me, dear lady, but I must be removing one of your charges."

Euthymos stood before them. Sweat dripped from his brow.

"What is this talk, sir?"

In response Eleon removed the wooden club from beneath his cloak. He offered it toward Euthymos. "You recognize this, do you not? Carried from Inaros's olive grove. The weapon you used to split his skull."

Chrysis stiffened; her eyes widened in alarm. "What is he saying, Euthymos? Surely you had nothing to do with this homicide?" She gripped his arm. "Tell me – us – you are not involved."

"I spoke with your teacher in the Academy." Eleon said "He told me you hurried from his lecture early the evening of the murder. You had clear vision of Inaros passing along the colonnade, and followed him to the oil room."

The lad studied Eleon's eyes for depth of resolve and awareness. Then he looked toward the practicing musicians. His face smouldered.

"I did it for them, mistress... I could stand Inaros's whippings to my own person. But not his outrages against the other lads on his farm. The slow or the sick, all those unfortunates he sold on to galley masters, or quarry owners – they had nobody to secure their safety or justice."

"Why didn't you inform Chrysis of these offenses?" Eleon said.

Euthymos looked on his benefactor with sorrow, and gratitude. "She would demand he stop at once – and he would revenge himself by selling her into slavery."

Chrysis cradled his head against her breast. "Oh, my dear boy, may Paian Apollo grant you mercy."

*****

Nikomedes entered the Treatment Room, gentling his forearm against his chest. "I caught a bad sprain, medico. Lost my footing, fell against my opponent's leg. What're you doing there?"

Eleon leaned over a wooden model of a man's head where he was fitting a makeshift leather helmet. He tucked a length of fleece between the wood and leather. "We send our soldiers into battle with bronze helms for protection. Why can't we make something similar for our boxers? Save their thick skulls for later combat? Here, let me look at that injury."

While Nikomedes held his arm for attention, he wondered aloud about Euthymos's pending trial.

"It may not come to that," Eleon said. "Chrysis spoke with Magistrate. With admirable force and clarity I might add." He flexed the injured arm. "She stressed to him this was a crime borne of compassion. A righting of wrongs that city fathers neglected to address. Reminded him these exploited youngsters were sons of soldiers who died in defence of their *polis*. He will acknowledge the circumstances, and work out a restitution. Exile, perhaps. Or better, a supervised restoration with his lady mistress".

Eleon applied a poultice to the bruise. "So what are you waiting for, you beat up old relic. Take her under your protection, give her a secure home, before it's too late and you're too ugly to look at. She's a sound woman, and even if you look far and long, I doubt you'll find another like her."

Nikomedes squinted, flexing his scars and bruises. "Would

she have a growly scoundrel like me, d'you think? If I left off punting ..." Smiling, he pointed toward the experimental helmet. "I could've used one of these, my friend. Years ago it would've kept a few straight thoughts in my head."

He departed the room, a lightness in his step.

Murder at Mulberry Mansion
Eamonn Murphy

Feeling a touch jaded, Lillian Colman left the patio party, stepped through the open glass sliding doors and found herself in a large kitchen/dining area. Raised voices were coming from the front of the house and curiosity immediately got the better of her. As she crept down the hallway the sound grew louder. There were three doors to her left and the third one along was partially open. She went to it and peeked into the room, not wishing to butt in if it was unnecessary.

There was a group of four people and just briefly she felt sorry for Janet Rutherford. The hostess stood in the middle of the room, illuminated by light from a small side window with its curtains open. Behind her were a pair of French doors with the drapes closed, probably to protect the photos, pictures and furniture from damaging sunlight while the room was not in use. However, it was in use now, as a debating chamber.

Geoffrey Glynn, Rob Parker and June Morrow were gathered around Janet, so close they appeared almost pressed up against her. Stood next to her, in what seemed a protective way, was the Duke of Bexford. All spoke at once in raised voices.

'What is it to you if I build a bungalow, you stupid…?'

'The church cleaning went quite well before you came

along…'

'You can't expect to run the parish council as your personal fiefdom, you know…'

'How dare you talk to me like that…?'

'Please, ladies and gentlemen, let us try to…'

The last voice was that of the Duke of Bexford. Suddenly there was a flurry of movement and, to be honest, Lillian couldn't quite see what happened. Somebody bumped into somebody else or pushed somebody else into another person and tempers flared. It was all very much a kind of melee, out of which Janet Rutherford staggered backwards away from the rest of them. She retreated half a dozen steps, unbalanced, and then fell heavily on her back. She was in the gloomy area of the room, in the shade from the window with the pulled drapes.

The other people looked on in horror. Then the Duke of Bexford stepped quickly over to the prostrate woman and knelt beside her. His body concealed her from their view. He spoke her name.

'Janet. Janet!'

Lillian decided it was time to intervene. She stepped into the room and moved over to the Duke.

'Has she fainted?'

'She's not moving. Call a doctor!'

'I'll do it.' Geoffrey Glynn pulled a mobile phone from his trouser pocket and dialled. He sidled over to a near corner to converse with the emergency services.

'I'm a nurse,' said Lillian. 'Let me look at her.'

'Good God!' With a loud cry, the Duke bounded to his feet and stared at the hostess in horror.

'What's wrong?' said June Morrow.

The Duke took a deep breath. 'She's dead.'

*****

To step back a little, it all started for Lillian one Sunday morning in September with a catty remark, in every sense of the word, from the murder victim to be.

'I'll have Clawdia back when you're finished with her,' said Janet Rutherford, rather archly.

There were three women of a certain 'middle' age, gathered by the cattle-grid of Little Hogbury Common. Miss Lillian Colman, ex-nurse, her old friend Mrs Brenda Corbett and Mrs Janet Rutherford, a newcomer to the village, i.e someone who had lived there fewer than twenty years. Lillian and Brenda were having their regular Sunday morning walk with Brenda's dogs. Janet, a large, forceful woman who waddled rather than walked, was returning from some mysterious errand of her own to a nearby cottage. As all three reached the cattle grid, she accosted them.

'Pardon?' Lillian was physically slightly deaf, and very deaf when it suited her. She turned her head sideways, all the better to hear.

'I said, I'll have Clawdia back when you're finished with her. My cat. Clawdia?' Her tone was as if she were talking to someone she felt was an imbecile.

'She wants Clawdia back,' Brenda said more loudly.

'Oh. Right.' Lillian flushed at the barbed remark. Clawdia was a handsome tabby cat, a rarity for a queen, as opposed to a tom, that regularly visited her at Crowleaze cottage and now often stayed overnight. The cat belonged (in so far as a cat can belong to anyone) to the aforementioned Janet Rutherford, owner of Mulberry Mansion. Mulberry Mansion was a pretentiously named huge bungalow that once belonged to a successful car dealer but was bought a year before by the

Rutherfords, a couple from London. Country life obviously didn't suit Mr Rutherford, because he left his wife soon after the move. Lillian bore this in mind. Divorce was a traumatic event and perhaps losing a cat so soon after a husband was rather like having salt rubbed in a wound.

'Right,' she said again, a little flustered. 'Well, since my old dog, Bella died Clawdia comes round more. I'm sorry. Perhaps she likes the garden.'

'*I* have a perfectly good garden,' retorted the divorcee tartly. 'Do you feed her?'

'Well, sometimes.' Lillian fed the cat often and gave her many treats as well. She missed her old dog and Clawdia was a substitute.

'She'll hang around if you feed her, *obviously*. Stop feeding her and she will come home, where she belongs.' Mrs Rutherford turned on her heel. 'Good day to you.' With that, she stalked away.

Brenda glared at her departing back. 'Nobody seems able to get on with that woman.'

'How do you mean?'

Brenda ticked off her neighbour's enemies one by one on the fingers of her left hand. 'She joined the Parish Council straight away and immediately objected to Rob Parker's plans to build a bungalow in his garden.'

'He's right next to her,' said Lillian. 'Or she's behind him rather. But there's plenty of room for it and a huge hedge in between them. Why should she object?'

Brenda shrugged. 'She says it will ruin her view.'

Lillian shrugged. 'So, that's Rob. Who else has she upset?'

'Geoffrey Glynn. You know he used to run the Parish Council. Well, she's been holding coffee mornings for some of the other ladies - very nice coffee mornings with very nice cakes - and has sort of won them over. That's how she beat him in the election for chairman, or chairwoman. Or is it Chairperson these days?'

'Yes. He mentioned that the last time I saw him, come to think of it.' Lillian shrugged again. She was not of a temperament to worry over minor matters, even if they caused other people to fret. 'Geoffrey was used to running the show but thing's change. He'll just have to accept it. Maybe the parish needs young blood.'

'I sort of agree but he's retired now and has more time on his hands. He liked to keep his mind occupied with that.

'I can see how Geoffrey would be annoyed at losing the parish council to a newcomer.'

Brenda nodded. 'He's taken Rob's side over the bungalow planning permission. Geoffrey's smart with plans and legal documents so he'll put up quite a fight against Janet Rutherford trying to block it.'

'So: me, she's falling out with over a cat. Geoffrey over control of the parish. Rob over planning permission for his bungalow. Who else?'

'Me,' said Brenda. 'And everyone else at St. Anselm's.'

Lillian raised an eyebrow. 'She's even upset the Christian's? How?'

'The darned woman just wants to take control of everything. She joined the group that helps to do the chores and we were glad to have her, at first. But she disagrees about everything from flower arranging to cleaning rotas. She wants it all done *her* way. And she gets some of the weak-willed ninnies along to her little coffee mornings and bends their ear and *gets* her own way. It's starting to annoy a lot of people.'

Lillian frowned. 'She's a lawyer isn't she?'

'A high priced one, I gather. Works in London when she works, for big fees.'

'So, she's smart, persuasive, has plenty of money behind her, and has a huge house with a swimming pool to throw impressive parties. If she set her mind to it I suppose she could take over the village.'

Brenda smiled 'She *has* set her mind to it and she is taking over the village. I wish she would just go away. Things used to be so good around here.'

Lillian nodded agreement with her old friend, but actually she found it hard to worry about these sort of things. She was something of a recluse and not very involved in local politics or the local church. However, she sympathized with her friends and neighbours and could see their point of view over the matter.

She put a reassuring hand on Brenda's shoulder. 'Things are still good around here.'

Brenda looked at the cows, the grass, the fields on the horizon and the blue sky overhead. She nodded. 'I still wish she would go away.'

But Janet Rutherford didn't go away. Instead, she invited everyone to a party.

*****

When the day of the patio party came it was sunny. There was not a cloud in the sky as the locals gathered together in Janet's extensive back garden and sat around a trio of neat wooden tables sipping tea. A nice selection of cakes was provided. Alcohol was due to come out later – some people brought bottles –and there was to be a barbecue. Lillian stood with Brenda and her carpenter husband Barry, a short, balding man of gregarious disposition with a builder's ribald wit.

As the guests arrived they were introduced to Michael. A short, slight man with a neatly trimmed grey beard and spectacles, he was Janet Rutherford's new partner.

'Michael plays in a jazz band,' she said enthusiastically to all comers.

He was modest. 'Only a little amateur combo. We do pubs and church halls sometimes on evenings and weekends just for the love of it.'

'They're *very* good,' gushed Janet.

'What do you do for a *living*?' asked Rob. A stocky fellow of medium height with a full, bushy beard, he was the man who had fallen out with their hostess over planning permission for his bungalow. Lillian was surprised to see him there and privately hoped he would not start a row. Rob was not averse to conflict, she knew, and was never one to worry about it being public.

Michael smiled. 'I'm an academic. I teach geology at the University of Westford.'

Rob thrust out his lower lip in a gesture of contempt and turned to Janet. 'Might I have a word?' He inclined his head toward the house.

'If you must.' With a sigh, she led him into the lush interior while the party carried on out in the garden. The uncomfortable silence that followed their departure (everyone knew what he wanted a word about) was broken up by the arrival of some ladies from the church association. However, it wasn't long before they were muttering about how their host tried to take over everything. The better the spread before them of cakes and treats – and it was excellent – the more ammunition they had for the case that she was trying to buy her way to control.

The most cutting remarks came from a lady named June Morrow. She was a large woman in her mid-forties with short blonde hair and a prominent lower jaw which was often thrust pugnaciously forward. She was a local celebrity because she had once arrived home early from work to find a burglar in her kitchen. She had successfully cornered the young man, then stabbed him with a Japanese ceramic tomato peeling knife from the second drawer down of one of her modern kitchen units; the one with oak doors, next to the fridge. The local magistrates let her off with a caution when she pleaded self-defence as the burglar was a big fellow before she cut him down to size (an expression and headline that the local newspaper used to some effect.)

After the incident, Barry, Brenda's husband, always referred to her as 'Stabber' Morrow. But never to her face.

'Golly!' said Lillian to Brenda, overhearing the conversation of the aforesaid lady and her allies. 'Does Janet have any friends at this party?'

Brenda shrugged. 'Michael?'

'Might as well have more cake,' said Barry cheerfully, helping himself to a slice. 'Here's Geoffrey.'

Geoffrey Glynn came round the corner of the house into the back garden. A lean, elderly gentleman with a long face, pale blue eyes and the manner of a gentle, unworldly academic. He had been a college lecturer before retiring, but his benign countenance belied a challenging disposition. Lillian knew that when opposed in matters important to him, he would bring up clever counter-arguments to support his case until the opposition wearily gave in – thus giving the possibly false impression that he was very intelligent and very shrewd debater. Looking around for a friendly face, he spotted Lillian and her company and came over.

'Is Rob here?'

'He's inside talking to Janet,' explained Lillian.

'About his bungalow planning permission, I expect,' said Brenda.

'I want to see her as well.' Geoffrey entered the house, looking determined.

'This is more fun than most Hogbury parties,' said Barry. 'There's so much ill-feeling about you don't know what'll happen next.'

'Are you enjoying this,' scolded Lillian, grinning.

He smiled. 'Yes.

Lillian was wondering why she came to such an unfriendly do when she felt a slight dig in the ribs. 'Eh? What?'

'The Duke,' hissed Brenda.

Without ceremony, the Duke of Bexford entered the back garden. He owned Hogbury Common and much of the land around with several tenant farmers under his authority. His ancestry went back to William the Conqueror. He wore tan trousers, a nice checked shirt and well shined black brogues. Casual but smart. Conversation round about died briefly but then restarted as everyone pretended not to make a fuss. Barry moved away to greet the new arrival.

'Hullo, Barry,' said the noble. Brenda's husband sometimes did work on his estate and they were on speaking terms. Barry was the kind of down-to-earth bloke who was not awed by wealth or celebrity and they got on well.

'Hello, Brian,' he said.

Lillian looked at Brenda. 'Brian,' she whispered. 'On first name terms with the nobility, are we?' This earned her a sharper dig in the ribs.

Barry came over with the Duke. 'This is my wife, Brenda; and this is our great friend Lillian. She lives in the cottage by the Baptist chapel.'

'Ah, yes. A very nice spot,' said the Duke. 'Are their services noisy?'

Lillian chuckled. 'Not at all. I try to keep quiet while they're at prayer. One must show respect.'

'It's nice to be good neighbours,' agreed the Duke. 'Neighbourliness contributes to a pleasant atmosphere in the community, I feel.' His face was bland, almost expressionless but Lillian looked into his cold blue eyes and felt there was real steel underneath his pleasant manner. He was not a man to trifle with. 'Speaking of which, where is our lovely hostess?'

'Inside,' said Brenda.

'I must see her.' The Duke hurried eagerly away.

Lillian raised her eyebrows in surprise. 'That was…interesting.'

'He knew her in London,' said Barry.

'Didn't he used to be a lawyer?' asked Brenda.

Lillian nodded. 'He worked in London for years. He's the nephew of the previous Duke but I think the son died and out of the blue, he found himself the heir. It must have come as quite a surprise.'

'A pleasant one,' said Barry. 'There's a lot of land with that title. He owns half the farms around here and a lot of property, as well as his own estate. Mind you, he's quite an ordinary bloke at heart.'

Barry saw most men as 'ordinary blokes' but Lillian wasn't so sure. The life of a Duke was certainly far different than that of most ordinary people. Lillian had once been a mental health nurse and had seen many variations on 'normal'. She wondered how becoming a Duke might affect one psychologically and imagined that he was a man used to getting what he wanted.

She smiled at her friend. 'I doubt if Duke's are as subject to the slings and arrows of outrageous fortune as the rest of us, Barry.'

'You don't think so?' He looked around. 'Come over here and I'll tell you something. Come on.' He inclined his head to indicate a quiet spot a few feet away by the as yet unlit barbeque.

Their conversation did not take long but when they re-joined the party Lillian wore a thoughtful expression.

At that moment June Morrow came over to the group.

'Hullo, all!' she said cheerfully. 'Enjoying it?'

'She lays on a good spread,' said Barry, helping himself to yet more cake.

June made a peculiar disapproving expression by pushing her lips up against her nose and squinting her eyes. 'One can buy friends, I suppose.'

'With a bit of cake?' said Lillian, suddenly annoyed. 'In Somalia, perhaps, but hardly in Little Hogbury End, June. There isn't a house here worth less than two hundred thousand and most would fetch considerably more.' Lillian seldom made barbed comments but she hated rudeness and these constant attempts to denigrate the hostess struck her as very rude indeed. 'If the cake is so distasteful to you then leave it, dear.'

June Morrow's cheeks turned red and her eyes widened. She took a deep breath. Unable to think of any response she turned on her heel and walked into the house.

Brenda giggled. 'Well done, Lillian!'

'I was keeping an eye on the cake knife,' said Barry. 'In case she grabbed it.'

'My hero,' said Brenda sardonically. Then her tone changed. 'Oh, dear.'

Suddenly there were several loud voices coming from inside the house. Lillian put down her coffee cup. 'I'll go see what's happening. Perhaps I can calm them all down.'

She stepped through the glass patio doors.

*****

'She's dead, I'm afraid,' said the paramedic. He was speaking to a uniformed policeman who arrived on the scene at the same time as the ambulance, ten minutes after the Duke's astonished cry.

Lillian and the rest of the party were still there as the police demanded that nobody leave. The individuals involved in the argument stood around in the front room, well-lit now by the late afternoon sun as all the curtains were pulled back. The body of their late hostess lay on the carpet.

'What killed her?' asked the policeman.

'Now here's a strange thing. There's what looks like the head and a short piece of the shaft of what I think could be a hat pin. Whatever it is, it's topped by an enamelled silver thistle, and it's protruding from her chest. I'd hazard a guess and say it's pierced her heart. But no doubt they'll know more once the body's been autopsied.'

The paramedic sighed. He was a large man with a big beard and a bigger stomach. He wore spectacles with thick black frames and the brown eyes behind them looked weary. 'Got to admit I've not seen one used as a murder weapon this side of Am-Dram, or Agatha Christie.'

'She was stabbed!' exclaimed Rob, standing nearby.

The medical man nodded.

Lillian could almost feel the several pairs of eyes in the room swivelling to stare at June Morrow. She turned to look at the Duke of Bexford. He sat on the large, comfortable sofa, his gaze fixed on the intricate floral patterns of the carpet. She moved over to him and sat down on the settee by his side.

'You knew her well, didn't you?'

He nodded. 'I loved her, once. No, I loved her always.'

Lillian put her hand on his gently.

'Tell me about it.'

He gave her a sideways, measuring look then nodded. Lillian was a good listener. People naturally opened up to her. It had once made her an excellent nurse.

'I finished school with excellent A level results and was looking for a career,' he said. The Dukedom wasn't a prospect back then but my family were well off. I decided on the law and went to study it at Oxford. That's where I met Janet and fell in love. We took our exams at the same time and got jobs in the same barrister's chambers. Then she met John Rutherford and fell madly in love with him. It's an old story, I suppose, the jilted male. I joined the army – a death wish, perhaps – and served ten years before word came that the Dukedom was mine. I left, moved here and got on with it.'

Lillian nodded sympathetically. 'When did you learn that your old flame was here in the village?'

'A few weeks ago. The name Rutherford was mentioned by some ladies from the church. Obviously, I remembered that John Rutherford was the bounder who took my woman from me, but the name is a common one. Then I saw her on the high street. You could have knocked me down with a feather!'

Lillian nodded understandingly. 'Was Mister Rutherford

gone by then?'

'Yes.'

'What did you say?' Lillian watched his face carefully. 'What did you do?'

'I suggested we get back together again. She said no. That it was all over between us.' He shrugged, not without effort. 'I guess that was it. Nothing a chap can do when a woman says no, but I came here today when invited to show there were no hard feelings.'

'No hard feelings,' repeated Lillian.

The loud voice of the policeman interrupted them. 'Detective Inspector Cooper,' he said as a man of medium height in a smart suit entered the room. 'I'm glad it's you, sir. A bit of a mystery, this one.'

DI Cooper's face was clean-shaven, wrinkled by age, tanned by the sun, weary-looking from the strains of his job. He took in the room's inhabitants with a glance. 'Bring me up to date, Sergeant.'

The uniform did so.

Once finished the Detective Inspector came over to Lillian. 'Miss Colman,'

She remained seated. 'Yes?'

'It seems you were the only witness to this tragedy, at least the only one not involved in the argument and the melee that followed. Can you tell me what you saw?'

She replied evenly: 'There was a melee, as you say. Everyone was shouting at Janet Rutherford, for their various reasons - except the Duke here – and then there was a scuffle. Whether it was deliberate or accidental I couldn't say. Someone pushed someone else and they all took umbrage and started shoving. Janet staggered backwards and landed where she now lies. The

Duke went over to pick her up and found her dead, stabbed in the heart, it seems.'

'You're very calm, Miss,' said Cooper, looking at her curiously.

'I was a nurse all my life. I've seen death before.'

He nodded. 'This is a tricky case.'

'How so?'

Cooper sat next to her on the sofa. 'Well, from what I can gather, Miss Colman, they all have motive and opportunity. They were all in the group together, and they all bore some grudge against the lady – all except the Duke here.' He leaned forward to nod at the nobleman. 'Excuse me, your Grace.'

'You do know it was the Duke who killed her?' said Lillian.

'What!'

*****

The comment aroused much noise from the assemblage and it took quite a while for the policeman to calm them all down. When he'd done it, DI Cooper stood over Lillian and looked at her sternly.

'That's a serious accusation. Are you prepared to back it up with facts?'

She sighed. 'He did it.' She looked Cooper straight in the eye. 'I was a nurse my whole life. I am a farmer's daughter. I respect those who work for their living and earn their daily bread, not those who inherit titles. As a nurse, I know that all flesh is equal. The Royals, the nobles, the rich and the poor are all constructed of the same fragile stuff, both mentally and physically. I am not blinded by rank and privilege. The Duke did it.'

'He didn't have any motive,' said Geoffrey Glynn, more confused than annoyed.

Lillian shrugged. 'He did. The oldest motive in the world: unrequited love. He loved her and she left him for another man in London. He joined the army and inherited a Dukedom and then found her again, divorced and free. How could she not want him now? But she didn't. She preferred a quiet little professor who plays in a jazz combo.' She looked up at the Duke of Bexford who returned her gaze with no expression on his face. 'It was more than he could stand.'

'Now look here, Lillian,' said Rob, stepping forward. 'I hold no brief for the aristocracy, as you know, but he didn't stab her. I was stood right beside him, for heaven's sake!'

Lillian smiled faintly. 'He didn't stab her in the chaos. He stabbed her in the dark part of the room when he went over to her after she fell. Perhaps she fainted but she was not dead at that point. While his body shielded her from view he slipped the hat pin from his tie, then rammed it between her ribs, expertly; I might add.' She turned to look at the Duke again. 'Were you ever a Royal Marine Commando?'

'The Special Air Service.'.

'You admit you're a trained killer?' Cooper was looking a trifle concerned.

'It is a matter of record,' said the Duke.

'And…did…' he could hardly ask the question. 'Did you kill Mrs Rutherford?'

'I most certainly did not,' said the Duke.

DI Cooper was silent for a moment. 'Well, you'll all have to come down to the station for questioning, I'm afraid. It's murder, whoever did it.' He sighed and turned to the uniform PC. 'Lead on, constable.'

The confused crowd followed the policemen out of the room, though Lillian lingered behind, as did the Duke.

She turned to him in the doorway. 'I'm right. I know I am. You killed her, didn't you?'

'I most certainly did not,' he said loudly for all to hear.

Then, so that only she could see, he winked.

Luck

Matias Travieso-Diaz

O Fortune, like the moon you are changeable, ever waxing, ever waning; hateful life first oppresses and then soothes as fancy takes it; poverty and power it melts them like ice.
Songs from Benediktbeuern (Carmina Burana).

1

The cheap purse dangled, like fruit from the Garden of Eden, from the old lady's left shoulder as she walked laboriously up the hill. She was carrying a bulging grocery bag in the right hand and made her way up the steep sidewalk with mincing steps, a determined grimace on her face.

Had Angus Murphy been compassionate, he would have offered to relieve the old coot of the heavy burden she carried. But being a career petty thief, he focused his attention on the purse. He approached the woman in quick, noiseless steps, grabbed the purse strap, and yanked. It came off her shoulder easily and, in one practiced motion, Angus flipped it off her arm, turned around, and ran downhill.

Trailing him were the old woman's cry of surprise, followed by screams of helpless rage: "Thief! Catch the thief! Help! Catch the bastard! Help!!"

Angus turned left into the first side street he crossed, ran a block away from the cries, and turned right at the next intersection. Soon the woman's outraged cries were lost in the town's afternoon hubbub. There were no signs of pursuit, and Angus entered an alley to catch his breath and examine the takings.

The purse contained four dollars and change, an embroidered handkerchief, a compact, a comb, and a ticket for the 29 November 1986 Gold Lotto, to be drawn two days hence.

What a waste, reckoned Angus. *She must have spent a good chunk of her pension getting this ticket.* He wasn't a gambler and was not sure how much such a ticket would cost, but it was probably more than a pensioner should be laying out.

Well, at least I got enough to buy me a pint, decided Angus, tossing the purse into a dustbin on his way to O'Leary's Old Irish Pub.

2

It was not until the following Tuesday, when thumbing through an old copy of *The Courier-Mail*, that Angus saw the small column listing the winners of the previous Saturday's Gold Lotto drawing. He rummaged through his coat's inner pocket and extracted the lottery ticket, the sole remainder of his purse snatching. He compared his ticket to the winning jackpot number:

"08 18 19 25 26 29" – Supplementary numbers: 23 34." His ticket read: "08 18 19 25 26 34."

A wave of excitement went up his spine. The ticket hadn't won the jackpot, but matching five numbers and one supplementary number, was close enough to have won *something.*

He went to the nearest newsagent's that sold Gold Lotto tickets and approached the cashier to present his ticket. The ticket consisted of an original and a carbon copy; the cashier validated both copies of the ticket by inserting the ticket into a designated cash register; the copy was returned to Angus and the original would be kept by the cashier and sent to Merrysall's, the company that ran the lotteries for the Australian States. The man scanned the ticket and looked on the screen of his brand-new computer. Instantly, there was a loud, emphatic sound and a picture flashed up on the screen: "Sounds like a winner!"

The cashier then said, not a trace of excitement in his voice: "The prize for the 5+bonus this week is 216,734 dollars. Congratulations."

Angus was excited enough for the two of them: "Fantastic!! How do I collect?"

"Prizes in excess of 500 dollars cannot be paid by a retailer. I will give you a 'win receipt' that validates your winning. You must contact Merrysall's by phone or mail to make arrangements to receive the prize. Here is a printout with all the information you need." He handed to Angus a printed page and a win receipt that showed him to be the winner of *$216,734.*

Angus was taken aback by his inability to get hold of his winnings immediately. He had already decided that with upwards of 200,000 dollars in his pocket he could move to a nice place and live off his winnings without having to lift a finger to do any more work, legal or not, for some, if not most of the rest of his life.

3

The number he was given was for an office in Melbourne. He called and a man answered in a controlled, cheerful voice: "Good afternoon, Merrysall's Customer Care, my name is

Frank. How can I assist you?"

Angus answered, trying to sound like a cultured man himself: "Yes, sir. I won a prize in last week's Queensland's Gold Lotto drawing and would like to make arrangements to collect it."

"Oh, how wonderful. Congratulations. May I have the ticket number?"

"08 18 19 25 26 34."

There was a brief silence on the line and then: "Sir, you are a 5+bonus prize winner! May I please have your account number?"

"Account number?"

"Do you have an account with Merrysall's into which deposits can be made?"

"No."

"How did you purchase your ticket?"

"From a vending machine at the grocer."

"Do you have a win receipt?"

"Yes."

"You need to mail the win receipt to the Merrysall's address shown on the receipt. You must put your name and address on the back of the receipt. The prize will be paid by check and mailed to you, providing the validation requirements have been met."

"Can I bring the receipt in person to one of your offices and collect it there?"

"Only the main office in Melbourne is authorized to make a prize payment on the amount you have won. Where are you located?"

"I'm in Brisbane. I would need to fly or take a train to get to Melbourne."

"You are welcome to do so, but I would advise you to save the cost and inconvenience of such a trip. If you send your receipt registered mail it will be sure to arrive here safely."

"Thank you." Angus said skeptically and hung up.

4

Angus would have greatly preferred to travel to Melbourne to personally collect his prize. However, he was broke and his income from petty thievery was fluctuating and highly unreliable at best. It could be weeks before he raised enough cash to make such a trip, and he was in no mood to wait. Having decided what to do with his winnings, he was eager to get started on his new life.

The mail option was full of perils. Not only could his receipt get lost in the mail, but he didn't know where the check should be sent to. He lived in an unattractive group house, whose residents were not even vaguely respectable, and any official letter addressed to him could well be purloined before reaching his hands. Plus, he had no living relatives or friends who could serve as fronts for his transaction.

As a last resort, he paid a visit to O'Leary's. It was two in the afternoon and the bar was deserted. Angus saw the proprietor and bartender, Cillian Doyle, busily setting up for the after-work rush. Cillian was by no means Angus' friend, but at least they were both Irish and on a first name basis. Angus thought of Doyle as a straightforward fellow and probably as honest as any Irishman Angus knew. He approached the counter with some trepidation.

"Hi, Cillian, how's it going?"

Cillian was a little surprised. "Angus. Isn't this a bit early for you?"

"Naw, Cillian, I didn't come for a drink. I just need a favor."

Cillian narrowed his eyes suspiciously. He knew of Angus' lifestyle. "What's that?"

"Nothing much. I'm expecting an important letter from the government. I don't want it to come to the dump where I live. It's nothing of value to anyone else, but someone might steal it just for the fun of it."

"So?"

"Could I have the letter addressed to me, care of the pub? You'd only need to hold it for a day or two tops. I would drop by every day to check on whether it's been delivered."

"What's in it for me?"

"I'll make you a gift. I don't know how much, it depends on the take from my next job, but I promise I'll share whatever I get with you." Despite his efforts to appear nonchalant, Angus began tapping the counter uncontrollably.

"Why don't you rent a post office box? Your mail would come in securely there."

"I checked on that. It would cost me almost two hundred dollars to set up a box, and the postal employees are known crooks."

"Then why don't you go to St. Stephen? I'm sure one of the priests there will be glad to help you."

"I've had several run-ins with them local priests. I don't expect they would receive me with open arms…"

"Sounds like it's either me or nobody."

"I'm afraid so, Cillian."

The bartender thought about it for a few seconds. "OK, I'll do it. I'll be on the lookout for your letter and hold it for you when it comes. But I want a five-dollar fee and a guarantee that nothing will happen to me on account of the letter."

"Deal."

5

The letter arrived at O'Leary's five days later. Angus tore the envelope open and extracted a small piece of typewritten paper and his win receipt. There was no check.

Dear Mr. Murphy: We note that you are requesting that your prize money be forwarded to an alcoholic beverage dispensing establishment. Regretfully, insurance regulations only allow us to send prize checks to the private address of the winner, to maintain accountability and protect from fraud. Please resubmit your win receipt identifying your home address, or present in person at our main offices.

"*If you need more information on any lottery topic, do not hesitate to call us.*

"*Thank you for being a Gold Lotto patron.*

"*Sincerely,*

Cillian watched with amusement Angus turning purple when he read the letter. As his customer began muttering under his breath, he inquired: "What's the matter, Angus? Bad news?"

"I knew the government would find a way of euchring me out of my money. They're just a bunch of thieves!"

"Come now, Angus" replied Cillian, suppressing a smile. "It can't be that bad."

Angus didn't reply, but rushed out, slamming the door behind him.

"Hey!" cried Cillian. "Where are my five dollars?"

6

There was no way Angus was going to rely on the mail again to collect his prize. He just had to raise enough money for a plane or a train ticket to Melbourne. And he had to do it quickly, because he knew there was only so long a prize could remain uncollected before the claim period expired. In another call to Merrysall's, he learned that his prize would have to be collected within six months of the draw, so he had until next May 29 to go get his money. Of course, he didn't intend to wait that long.

Angus was a diligent thief. He was always on the prowl for snatching purses, absconding with unattended packages left at the entrance of homes, pickpocketing helpless or drunken citizens, pillaging through mailboxes, or the odd bout of shoplifting. He would commit two or three of these petty crimes a day, but never quite making enough to rise above poverty. He would need to try his hand at something else to pay for his trip.

He started walking around the residential neighborhoods that circled the downtown area, looking for homes that he could break into. After a couple of weeks, his repeated early morning and mid-afternoon surveillances identified a small single story cottage bungalow with a pretty garden out front. Every weekday, a foreign-looking man wearing a suit and carrying a briefcase would leave the house, saying goodbye to nobody. He would return in the late afternoon, again greeted by nobody, and stay indoors the rest of the day.

The third week of his surveillance, Angus drew enough courage to approach the house around noontime and look into the living room through a large side window whose curtains were only partly drawn. The house was dark, quiet and empty.

He went round the back of the house and peered through a gap in the wooden fence. Still no sign of anyone. A scrabble up and a jump down, and he was in the back garden. Carefully up the path to the back door, he picked up a large rock from the garden and smashed the small window by the door handle, cringing at the thought of a burglar alarm going off and alerting the neighbors or the police. The only sound he heard was that the shattering of broken glass. He carefully removed the glass shards, turned the Yale lock door knob and quickly entered the back kitchen.

He walked softly down the hallway and looked around the living room. The furniture was nice but bulky. There was a large television set resting on a table in a corner. Again, too heavy to carry. Prints on the walls and knickknacks in an etagere were uninteresting.

He moved on to the next room, across the hall – a combination bedroom and office with an adjoining bathroom. This was clearly the part of the house that saw most use, judging from its disarray. The bed was unmade, with pillows, sheets and blankets jumbled together as if the owner did not have the time or disposition to tidy up. On top of the bed there were random clothes: a shirt, socks, underwear, a pair of gray trousers. Slippers protruded from under the bed, as did a pair of dress shoes.

After a second, Angus' attention was drawn to a desk and chair that sat in a corner of the room. Unlike the bed, the desk was clean and orderly. An Apple computer occupied the center of the desk, with most of the rest taken up by a large table lamp and an elaborate inbox overflowing with papers. Angus sat in front of the desk and proceeded to search its three drawers. In the second drawer there was something he'd not dared hope for: a fake alligator skin wallet bulging with bank notes.

With that in his pocket he was starting to rifle through the rest of the desk when he heard a heavy knocking at the front door and a loud, commanding voice: "Police!"

He jumped to his feet, feeling his adrenaline make his heart beat faster. Should he stay quiet in the hope they would just go away?

Again, the call: "Police! Open up!"

Fear took over, which was not helped by the rug in the hallway almost tripping him up as he headed back into the kitchen. Even with the back door unlocked, he still had trouble getting it open – his panic making his fingers fumble and slip – but within seconds he was out of the house and in the back garden.

As the front door finally yielded to the policemen's attack, Angus raced down the garden path, threw himself against the high back fence, pulled himself up and took one last look behind him. Through the open kitchen door he could see the police entering the front of the house. That was all the motivation he needed. Pushing himself backwards over the fence he felt his clothing catch and tear, and the next thing he knew he was lying flat on his back on the access road at the back of the bungalow.

He got on his feet, realising he ached and hurt everywhere, but his fear was greater than the physical pain. He limped for a couple of steps and then took off, running as fast as his bruised legs would carry him. He was making his way down the access road to the street adjacent the cottage when a chorus of angry voices erupted:

"There he goes! Catch him!" In the back of his mind, Angus was surprised that so many people would be out of their homes in the middle of a working day, but the only effect of the outcry was to make him run faster. Onto the side street he went, but realized that the only thing that would save him was to find some place to hide up.

Angus ran aimlessly, getting further and further away from the suburbs and into the countryside, but was running out of steam, the adrenaline rush being replaced by fatigue.

Angus slowed down to consider his situation. He was hurt, exhausted, and suffering from severe stress. He stank of sweat. His clothes were ripped and caked with mud. He felt faint and on the verge of passing out. Yet, inside the pocket of his thin coat, he could feel the wallet that had been the prize from his adventure.

Still heading out of town, he came across a group of allotments – one had a dilapidated shack with a large sign painted crudely on its side in white letters: *STRAWBERRIES*. He stumbled towards the shack, intending to force his way inside and get some rest. The door to the shack was open, hanging at an odd angle; it was dark and dank within, smelling of decay and old age. Angus found some hay on the floor, removed his coat to serve as an improvised pillow, dropped on the ground and sank into a stupor.

He was awakened later by a chorus of approaching barks. Instantly awake, he ran out the door and into the field. Too late, though. Dogs and police handlers were approaching and caught up to him barely twenty yards from the shack.

As he was being taken away, Angus started to shiver. He thought he was having a nervous breakdown, but then he realized he had left his coat behind in the shack.

7

One of the first questions Angus asked of the public defender assigned to his case was: "How come they sent a full squad of police, dogs and all, to track me down? I'm just a petty thief and didn't even get to steal anything!"

The young lawyer was surprised. "Haven't they told you?

They want you as a witness."

"Witness to what?"

"When the police arrived at the house they tried to identify the owner so they could notify him of the break-in. None of the neighbors knew the guy, so the police went through the papers on his desk and found his name: Mete Veziroglu. Further investigation revealed that Mr. Veziroglu runs a drug-smuggling ring and is on INTERPOL's most wanted list. They arrested him and are putting together a case to send him away for life. They want you to corroborate some aspects of the matter."

The attorney leaned back in his chair. "I'm talking to the prosecution, trying to cut a deal for you. You have two prior convictions, so they are unwilling to let you get off Scot free, but they may settle for a few months sentence and probation."

"That's good news, but please try to keep my jail time to a minimum. I've been there already and don't much enjoy it."

8

For a rookie, Angus' assigned defender did a creditable job negotiating a plea bargain. In a closed-door hearing, Angus appeared before a stern judge who questioned him on why he should be let off with only a four-month sentence, at the end of which he was likely to return to a life of crime. Angus appeared contrite, and swore with feigned sincerity that this last experience had cured him of any desire to break the law even in the slightest bit. The judge retorted:

"Well, Mr. Murphy, I will approve the settlement, but if I see you in this court again, I'll lock you up and throw away the key. You are sentenced to four months imprisonment and one-year probation under the supervision of the Parole Board Queensland."

Angus appeared as a witness in Mr. Veziroglu's trial and testified that, in the course of his burglary, he had occasion to read certain compromising documents (which he had memorized, as instructed by the prosecuting counsel). On cross-examination, he was questioned by the defense lawyer about a wallet containing over three hundred dollars in cash. Angus was surprised at the amount in the wallet, which he never had time to ascertain, but avowed complete ignorance of its whereabouts. He felt no guilt at uttering such a lie, because stealing from a sleazebag like Veziroglu was not stealing at all.

9

Angus was released from jail on May 4, 1987, barely three weeks before his prize expired. He was wearing the same clothes he had on when arrested; a pocket in his pants still held the win receipt.

He was out of options. Stealing again was out of the question, since the parole office kept tabs on him and any attempts at purse snatching or mailbox tampering was likely to land him in jail again. He also felt reluctant to resume his former life, out of fear that the luck which had protected him so far would eventually run out.

He had no money. His room in the group home had been ransacked, and the landlady had kept only the few items of his clothing she had not been able to sell. She insisted on keeping those against the rent he still owed. Finally, Angus borrowed some money from Cillian (who was not particularly happy to see him) and went to a charity shop where he got used pants, a shirt and a light jacket. He then started to retrace his failed escape route.

What with his hazy memory of the events, after some difficulty, he found he relocated the shack with a fading

STRAWBERRIES sign on the side. He rushed to it.

The door still hung precariously from one hinge; the rank smell of age and decay filled his nostrils. He moved to the back of the room, where a dark lump rested on a bed of long decayed hay.

Angus picked up the abandoned coat and shook it. There was a squeak and one or two small creatures fell to the ground. Angus held the coat gingerly and took it outside into the light. The coat was ruined – the sleeves and collar had been gnawed and were now full of ragged holes. Angus, fearing an attack from hidden vermin, turned the garment inside out and felt the inner pocket. The wallet was still there.

Well, not quite. The wallet had also been attacked by the energetic mice. Portions of the material had been bitten off; what remained exhibited many tiny tooth marks. But what about inside?

Some of the bank notes had been eaten away, others were torn or had pieces missing. Angus took out what was left and did a melancholic inventory. About $200 or so were sufficiently complete that they could perhaps be traded in a bank for new money. The rest were gone or had been reduced to a disgusting pulp. Angus sighed and pocketed what could be salvaged, hoping that what he had would be enough to get him to Melbourne.

10

The cheapest air fare available was over $90; travelling by train cost as little as $65. He opted for the train, since he would need some extra cash to stay in the city and travel to Merrysall's offices. It would be tight, but he expected he would be a rich man on his return home.

Angus spent the next two days going to bank after bank to

trade the damaged bills for fresh ones, eating a frugal meal or two, and sleeping outdoors. At the end he had $183 dollars in fairly new notes. He walked to the train station and purchased a one-way ticket. The next train didn't leave until 4:30 AM the following day, so he curled up under a banyan tree in the Roma Street Parkland near the terminal.

He woke up with a start. He did not own a watch, but it was starting to get light. He ran to the station and arrived as they were boarding the train. He checked in, found himself a seat in a quiet corner of a carriage and fell asleep again.

Many, many hours later, after changing trains in Sydney, he was shaken awake by a conductor. "Time to wake up, mate. We've arrived." A clock on the wall read 7:30 AM of May 28, 24 hours after his departure.

11

Angus arrived in Melbourne too tired to get any business done. The following day was the deadline for cashing his prize, six months after the draw.

He spent $25 getting a room in a cheap boardinghouse. He figured he needed to be fresh and ready for whatever the next day might bring. The following morning, he showered, shaved and had breakfast. He then splurged by taking a cab that transported him to the building that housed Merrysall's offices.

He arrived as the offices were opening and asked for the department in charge of paying out prizes. He was ushered to a small, pleasantly appointed room with plump chairs circling a mahogany table, decorated soothingly in green wallpaper and sporting Victorian prints in fancy gilded frames.

He sat in that office for almost half an hour before an official made his entrance. The man was in his fifties, impeccably dressed in a gray suit, blindingly white shirt, and a silver necktie. He proffered a limp hand to Angus and introduced himself:

"Good morning. Sorry to keep you waiting, but you know how busy things can get on Fridays. I am Alistair Granville. How do you do?"

"Angus Murphy," he responded with a trace of hesitation in his voice.

"Well, Mr. Murphy, I take it that you've come to claim your prize. May I please see your win receipt?"

Angus extracted the receipt and Granville looked at the date, got up, and went to a bookcase at the back of the room that contained a series of identical black binders with titles and dates on their spines. He looked for one, found it, and returned to the table with it. He opened it and ran his finger down the third page, comparing the entries in the book against the ticket. He turned to Angus and smiled.

"This ticket is good for a prize of \$216,734."

"Correct," responded Angus, getting a little impatient.

"But…" Mr. Granville paused for a moment.

"But what?"

"Under the Gold Lotto Terms and Conditions, a person may file a report within thirty days of the draw in question, asserting that he or she is the rightful owner of a winning ticket and that the ticket had been stolen. One such a report, concerning this ticket, was filed by a Mrs. Gertrude Wallis a day after her ticket was allegedly purloined. The report was supported by an affidavit from one Eugene Morris, the manager of a Jack the Slasher Food Barn supermarket where the ticket was allegedly purchased. Mr. Morris states that he knows Mrs. Wallis well, since she is a frequent customer at that establishment, and that two days before the draw she purchased this ticket. The store keeps duplicate copies of the lottery tickets it sells, so Mr. Morris was able to reconstruct the transaction and allow Mrs. Wallis to file her stolen ticket claim." He paused for a second and crossed his hands over his lap.

"Mr. Murphy, we have a dispute here. Under the Terms and Conditions of the Gold Lotto, we are required to investigate the dispute and determine whether you or Mrs. Wallis is the rightful owner of this ticket. Since she claims that the ticket was stolen from her by you, the police will be a part of the investigation. My secretary will be calling them presently."

Angus turned very pale. "So, you won't be paying me my prize?"

"Not today. However, since both you and Mrs. Wallis have asserted your rights in a timely manner in accordance with the Terms and Conditions of the Gold Lotto, once the investigation is completed one or the other will be disbursed the prize amount."

"How long will this investigation take?"

"It's all in the hands of the police. If you can provide evidence that you obtained this ticket legally, the matter might be resolved in a day or two and you will be able to leave with your prize money."

That was the end of the road for Angus, and he knew it. The moment the police started looking into the dispute his past record and the three convictions would be spotted. "So. what do I need to do now?"

"For the moment, just let me have your local address so that you can be contacted by the police. I would advise you to stay in town, because if you were to leave without clearing this matter up that could be construed as an admission of guilt."

12

Angus returned to the boarding house, dejectedly, trying to think through his predicament. In a day or two, he would be out of money, unable to stay in Melbourne and unable to leave. He bought a half bottle of cheap whiskey and downed it in less than thirty minutes. He fell asleep with his clothes still on.

In the morning, he received a call from Mr. Granville asking him to present himself as soon as possible at Merrysall's offices. Angus knew this was his death sentence, but could think of no alternative but to attend. This time he walked the couple of miles to the Merrysall's building. On arrival, he was bathed in cold sweat, but his mind was made. He would turn himself in.

Granville was as impeccably dressed as the day before, but seemed less composed. He sat across the table from Angus and, without preamble, dove into the matter at hand. "Mr. Murphy, we did some work yesterday."

Angus readied to make a fully confession, but Granville went on. "We ran a background check on you and learned of your previous problems with the law, including a house break-in several months ago." Angus bowed his head and said nothing.

"We also tried to reach Mrs. Wallis but the telephone number listed in the stolen ticket report has been disconnected. As a backup, we contacted Mr. Morris, who advised that Mrs. Wallis had a heart attack and passed away last month. When we inquired as to the next of kin, Mr. Morris indicated that Mrs. Wallis was a widow who lived alone and had no known relatives. So here we are. We have every reason to believe that you stole Mrs. Wallis' lottery ticket but have nobody to whom we can award the prize she won. And we are unwilling to reward you for your crime. We will fight you in court if necessary, but you won't get the two hundred thousand dollars."

There was a momentary pause and Granville went on: "The Merrysall's Board of Directors has authorized me to offer you a lump sum payment of five hundred dollars in exchange for your signing a full waiver of any rights to compensation you might feel you have in connection with this prize." He produced from his briefcase a typewritten document and placed before Angus. "Take it or leave it" he advised curtly.

Angus sighed. He'd known all along that the government would find a way of euchring him out of the prize. But five hundred dollars was still better than nothing.

"Where do I sign?" he asked.

Liquor is Quicker
Madeline McEwen

With hindsight, Mildred Herringbone conceded that Philip had turned out like his father, a bully. Had Philip sprung from bad seed? She wasn't entirely blameless. Had Philip grown from a bad egg? As his mother, Mildred could not decide.

*****

Mildred fumbled with her reading glasses. She reread the flight details for the umpteenth time: first class return departing from Heathrow, London. San Jose, California in less than forty-eight hours. It was all so effortless and easy. Too easy?

Philip, her only son, had paid all her holiday expenses: the flight ticket, a brand new set of matching suitcases, and a taxi to the airport, to say nothing of the painstaking passport renewal application. The man was a saint despite his numerous foibles.

The only irritant for Mildred was the purpose of her visit: the graduation of her grandson, Henry, from The Waldo E Hyde Private Pre-Kindergarten School. She couldn't wait to meet Henry, at last. However, she was baffled by the concept of a formal ceremony for five-year-olds.

The telephone rang. Mildred braced herself and cleared her

throat.

"Hello, is that you dear?"

"Of course it's me. Nobody else phones you."

Mildred gazed at her birthday gift, the life-sized family portrait, a photo-cum-oil-painting next to the slender table in her narrow hallway. Philip, portly and graying at the temples. His wife, Pari Chopra, a breathtakingly beautiful, Bollywood superstar. And, young Henry, an unknown. How she longed to meet that dark-eyed little rascal with his mother's gorgeous eyes. Did he have her personality too, or Philip's?

"All packed?"

"Indeed." His mid-Atlantic accent, recently acquired, always caught Mildred off guard.

"Got your meds? Did that new doctor gave you the right ones?"

Philip didn't care for Doctor Das who insisted on annual physicals, what Philip called, "a waste of bloody time." But Mildred liked her doctor. "Trust me," he had said pouring the little white pills into an empty container. "These palpitation pills are infinitely superior to Cardiac Glycoside." He was a man with a soft voice, gentle hands, and listening ears.

"Remember," Philip said, "vacation insurance doesn't cover prescription refills, and they have different names out here."

"Yes, you've told me, several times. However, I won't need a refill for such a short trip, silly."

Rampant diabetes cost Philip a fortune with all those insulin injections and other paraphernalia. He hadn't eaten candy since his diagnoses and yet he piled on the pounds.

"Are you absolutely ready? I sent you a list. Have you checked off everything?"

"I'm as ready as I'll ever be." She kept her tone pleasant. Ever since she was widowed, and kindly Dr. Das had taken her under his wing, Philip had treated her like a dimwitted child.

"Passport?"

"Yes." She patted her purse on the telephone table. The postman had needed her signature, not on paper, but with an electronic device with a stylus—no pen, nor ink. Since then, she hadn't let it out of her sight.

"Remember, a British passport is worth its weight in gold."

"Is it? Surely, no more than a couple of ounces."

"Don't be dumb, Mom. You know what I mean. Every man and his wife wants a British passport. There's a whole damned industry behind those scams. Keep it safe. Stuff it in your knickers if you like."

She listened to his breathing, his temper rising, the same as when he was a little boy: red faced, shoulders heaving, fists clenched. Philip's rages as an adult reminded her of those rutting elephant seals on the beach during that nightmare cruise. Had that been any way to celebrate fifty years of marriage?

"Talking of gold," she said, deftly changing the subject, "should I use that credit card you sent me?"

"Yes. Use the gold card for your vacation expenses. It's linked to my account. I'll pick up the tab. Avoids the exchange rate and transaction fees. Simpler."

"You've spent too much already."

"Have you activated the card?"

"Yes, but I feel so guilty."

"Nonsense. Anyways, this is for Henry. You're his graduation gift. What's better than seeing his doting Gran?"

"Gran? Is that what he calls me?" She wanted to speak to Henry. Why wouldn't Philip allow them to chat? Why did Philip always hold the reins and crack the whip? "I prefer *Granny*."

"Don't start, *Mother!*"

"Of course. I'm so sorry." Her hand trembled, but she didn't drop the phone. Why had she ever agreed to go? Was it too late to cancel? Where had she left her palpitation pills? "Whatever you say, dear. I promise I'll be no trouble at all."

*****

Hobbling along the corridor to the kitchen, Mildred kept a firm hold on the new handrail installed by the Care for the Elderly Corporation and paid for by Philip. His generosity knew no bounds, but that's what happened when the lonely found love, and Philip had found Pari.

Mildred had planned to attend their wedding in London, but Pari Chopra, the bride-to-be, had changed her mind about the venue. Mildred should have tried harder to find a flight to Batticaloa. Sri Lanka seemed such a great distance, and as Philip had explained, the hotel was fully booked.

However, less than a week after the nuptials, a parcel had arrived from America. Tamika Smith, Mildred's carer, had brought the package in with her when she arrived.

"Hiya, Mildred." She pulled down her hood and beaded braids tumbled down her back. "Found this on the front step."

She dumped the package on the kitchen table. "Bloody heavy. What's in it, bricks?"

Mildred took a knife from the drawer. With a mixture of excitement and trepidation, she unwrapped the package and found an exquisite leather-bound, gold-embossed wedding album full of photographs of the happy couple and all their many guests.

"That's nice, he's labeled all the piccies for you. Millions of celebs."

"Yes." Mildred read the names, but they meant nothing. "Lovely. So colorful. It must have been wonderful to marry in such a picturesque place."

"Fabulous dress. Must have cost a bomb. I wonder if your Philip made her sign a prenup?"

"A prenup?"

"An agreement before you marry. If Pari cheats on him, she'll get none of his dosh."

Mildred raised her eyebrows. What a distasteful thought.

"Go on, Mildred, you've said it yourself, he's a tightfisted bastard."

"I'm sure I've never said any such thing." Besides, Philip didn't have much money. He'd already frittered away his father's inheritance.

"Glad Pari lost weight before the wedding." Tamika grabbed the loose flesh around her waist. "Those diet pills must have worked. Maybe I should try them, trim my love-handles."

Mildred, who had strong opinions about the idealization of

women's bodies, said nothing.

"Look!" Tamika stabbed a picture with her purple-polished fingernail. "That's Charisma Kapoor."

"Such a striking woman."

"Blimey, bet they had one helluva knees up. It's like a who's who of Bollywood." She made a hangdog expression. "Poor Mildred, always the bridesmaid never the bride."

Mildred twisted her wedding ring, but didn't correct her. Was there an appropriate term for an absent invitee or overlooked mother-in-law? No wonder the hotel was full, overflowing with fabulous celebrities and minor dignitaries.

"Don't be too down-hearted." Tamika flipped through the pages, "They still love you, but every guest in here is under fifty. It's an age thing, nothing personal, only the young and the beautiful."

"Well that's alright then," Mildred said, biting her tongue. "Thank you for putting my mind at rest."

*****

The phone rang in the hall.

Again? That was odd. Leaving the kitchen, she hurried, at least in spirit, toward the hall. Had Philip forgotten to tell her something? God forbid he might apologize. Those days were long gone. His current habits were cast in stone. How would they cope face-to-face if they couldn't hold a civil conversation long distance?

"Hi! Agent Frank Burns from the Federal Bureau of Cultural Affairs. This call is being recorded for training and quality control purposes. How are you doing today Ma'am?"

She recognized his accent immediately. Occasionally, Mildred caught snippets from The New Jersey Housewives on the television.

"Mrs. Herringbone? Can you confirm a few security facts?"

"What facts?" *Be careful,* Tamika warned her about personal information. Although, Tamika said, "leak" as if Mildred were a sieve incapable of staunching the flood of words flowing from her lips.

"Your first name?"

"Mildred."

"Date of birth?"

"I refuse to tell you my age, you discourteous young man."

"That's okay. I've got it here anyways. August two, 1937."

Damn! When people knew your age, they spoke in a particular tone: loud, slowly, and with exaggerated enunciation.

"Can you still hear me, Mildred?"

Yes, that was the tone. "I'm not deaf."

"Nothing to be ashamed of, Mildred. My nonna's hearing impaired too."

"I'm not your nonna, and neither am I hearing impaired. The only thing that's impaired around here are your manners."

"I'm sorry if I've caused offense, Mildred. Now, moving right along, I've got an offer for you that can't be beat. The Bureau is reaching out to help with your upcoming international flight."

"I don't need any help." *Replace the receiver.* Cut him off.

Walk away.

"Wouldn't you love the red carpet treatment? Someone to open the doors, carry your bags, and push your wheelchair through the airport."

"I don't use a wheelchair, thank you. And besides, my son has already made all my travel arrangements. I have no need for your services. Now if you'll excuse me, I have to pack."

"Wait up, Mildred. What about a green-light through the lines when you reach the States."

Mildred hesitated. She had visualized the journey; the long drive to the airport, three hours waiting after international check-in, the eight hour flight, the scramble to escape on landing—what Philip called "deplaning"—the crowds, those bleak metallic tunnels, baggage claim, finding a cart, lugging the suitcases, customs, passport and immigration control. Fatigue washed over her, but she didn't drop the phone.

Frank continued.

"Yes, that's one heck of a journey. Take this opportunity and smooth your travel experience?"

What was the catch? There was always a catch, no such thing as a free lunch. Mildred bided her time, and waited for his fall from grace.

"Mildred? For a limited time only, before the end of this call, I'm in the position to hook you into this great program. All I need is your passport details. Then, we'll draw up your visa and FedEx it to you overnight."

"But I don't need a visa. I've no plans to work. This is just a holiday." Something gnawed at her memory. When had she last applied for a visa? On her trip to Galápagos? Tamika helped her complete the on-line form at the local library. No, she didn't need a visa. But if she did, Philip would have completed the application, wouldn't he? Then again, look how the wedding plans were derailed at the last minute. Her heart began to race, a vein pulsed at her neck. Short of breath, her ribcage tightened.

"Mildred? You sound kind of weird. Are you okay? "

"Yes, give me a minute." She sat on the chair and rested her head on the telephone table, cold and firm and stable.

"Do you want me to call 911? I've access to another phone. I won't hang up on you."

911? Why hadn't he said 999? Was he calling from America? She grabbed her inhaler and took three short puffs. She pictured her lungs expanding, opening wide like butterflies wings.

"Are you an asthmatic, Mildred?"

Would asthma affect her eligibility? She didn't want to lie. Was there a health clause? She mustn't mess up her chances.

"I'm recovering from a bout of flu, nothing serious."

"Good. Wouldn't want to violate the warranty."

Mildred made no comment. Least said, soonest mended, as her mother used to say in moments of trepidation. How did one violate a warranty? Did this man, Frank, know what he was talking about?

"Right. Your application's on my screen. Passport number please?"

Opening her purse, Mildred unzipped the secret pocket and took out her precious passport. She heard Frank tapping computer keys as she gave him the details.

"Now," Frank said, "Visa, MasterCard or American Express?"

Mildred lifted the flap of her wallet. She shouldn't, should she? The gold card glinted in the low light. Temptation tickled. Philip had demanded. Wasn't this offer worthwhile?

"American Express," she said, flourishing the card, "gold."

*****

The journey, though lengthy, concluded without a hitch. By the time Mildred made her way to the Virgin Airlines arrivals lounge, she was ready to face anything. In fact, she couldn't remember when she had last felt so rested and carefree. Who would have thought she was such an international jet setter?

She looked around for Philip, but he was nowhere to be seen. No matter. Meanwhile, she perched on a bar stool at the counter and gave her order to the barista. She hadn't needed her pills for several hours, perhaps a whole day. This was the life—-the life of luxury and relaxation.

"Enjoy," the barista said placing a cup of steaming coffee on the counter next to a bowl of candy.

"Thank you." She handed him a ten dollar bill. Everyone should be this happy. "Keep the change."

"Help yourself to a Tic Tac, they're complimentary."

Mildred liked America, full of kind and generous people. She took a candy and savored the light minty flavor. They looked so similar to her palpitation pills. Had Dr. Das played a trick on her? She had never tasted her medications, always swallowing them whole, fearful of a chalky aftertaste.

The airport lounge captivated her attention: shiny floors, towering potted palms, and vast glass windows. She gazed at the panoramic view of a cloudless blue sky above the golden-yellow hills—picture postcard perfect. Surely, she must be the luckiest woman alive.

Having acknowledged that her life was too good to be true, she was improved by the arrival of a dapper man, maybe ten years her junior, wearing a light linen suit. Mildred knew that eyes did not twinkle, but his did as he smiled at her. He radiated warmth and held a placard with her name.

"Mrs. Herringbone?"

He had an accent too, but not an American one, softer and lilting.

"Yes." Her heart pounded, but not in an unpleasant manner.

"I am your escort." He extended a hand. "José Sanchez, at your service."

Mildred giggled. She could not remember when she had last if ever, giggled like a schoolgirl. Was it because he described himself as an escort? What was the difference between an escort and a gigolo? Although, nobody used those terms any more. How could they in the era of dating apps?

Mildred sipped her cooling coffee. Who was this José Sanchez? A beau or a con artist? She didn't know him from Adam. Then again, he knew her name. Could he have read her luggage labels on the carousel and then written the placard?

What if José were a white-slave trader or a pirate or a drug dealer? How exciting. She loved the attention, far more fun than fifty tyrannical years during the reign of her husband—

the bear—or the sovereign rule of her overseas son—the boar.

"You look worried, Mrs. Herringbone. Señor Philip told me you have a weak heart."

Mildred pouted. Typical. Did any other mother have such a vexatious son? Philip had ruined a moment of flirtation with his usual sangfroid.

"Did he? Well, take no notice. I'm more likely to be carried off by a Bald Eagle than die from a heart attack. That's what my doctor said."

"I like the sound of this doctor. Although, you should be careful. There are many more Bald Eagles in America than in England. Would that fact have changed his diagnosis?"

Mildred relaxed and clambered off the stool.

"Right this way." Jose pushed the cart toward the revolving door. "We're in short-stay parking. I'll leave your bags on the bench if you'll wait, and bring the car around. Okay?"

José persuaded her to take the passenger seat next to him. He drove the white Lincoln Town Car at a steady sixty-five miles per hour along the four, and sometimes six, lane freeway. They chatted freely like two old pals at a reunion. During the hour and ten minute journey, Mildred learned about his life.

"What can I say?" José flashed her a grin. "I love to drive. This isn't work, is it? Not with such a splendid vehicle, more like a boat than a car."

"I must say it's a remarkably smooth ride. How long have you driven for my son?"

"I am Señora Chopra's driver. I've traveled all over the world with her Bollywood superstardom."

"Of course. Tell me, what is she like to work for? Is she a good employer?"

"The best. I love her like a daughter."

"Good." Mildred found herself nodding in agreement even though she had never met her daughter-in-law. "Is that why she kept her last name because of her career?"

"Name recognition is vital."

"I can't wait to see her, although if I'm honest, I'm nervous about meeting such a glamorous person."

José sighed. "Hasn't Señor Philip told you? Señora Chopra is sick, very sick."

"Oh dear! Oh no! What seems to be the matter?"

"The doctors, they don't know. Tests, tests, tests, still don't know. Headaches, fever, and heart palpitations. Me, I think it is Lyme disease."

"I've heard of that."

"She likes to walk with Hector."

"Who is Hector?"

"The dog, a big Redbone Coonhound."

They had a dog? Wasn't that the kind of thing one told relatives abroad? How many other things had Philip failed to mention, like his wife's failing health?

"That must be lovely for little, Henry," she said, "the dog not the illness." Philip hated dogs, always had, so why had he allowed one in the house? "What boy doesn't want a dog as his best friend? Sorry, José, you were telling me about Pari."

"Yes, they go hiking. I think Hector picked up a flea and that flea bit Pari, I mean, Señora Chopra and that's how she contracted Lyme disease. Please don't think me disrespectful, using her first name, but when I think of her suffering, I feel such frustration. She needs a proper doctor, maybe your Doctor Das instead of all these crazies."

"Crazies?"

"Holistic practitioners: snake massage, psychic surgery, and herbal smoothies."

"Does anyone?"

"My point exactly. Don't be surprised if she's too sick to see you. Señor Philip wants her to rest and recover."

*****

"Gosh! Those gates must be ten-feet high." Is this what Philip spent his money on? "Those spikes look lethal."

José drove under a massive sign, which read, "Hyde House," and turned onto an impressive driveway lined with squat pineapple palms.

"My! It's even more magnificent than in the brochure Philip sent me." Mildred imagined her own home dwarfed next to their triple garage. "So this is what a designer, custom-built house looks like."

"Nothing but the best for Señor Philip. After you've freshened up, I'll give you a tour before I take you to the graduation ceremony." He pointed toward a lush patch of green, "Over there, The Warren E Hyde Park."

"Today? I thought it was tomorrow."

"You've lost a day because of your flight. Don't worry."

He opened the front door.

"Señor Philip texted me. He is nursing Pari and asked me

to take you to your room.”

“Three people live in this mansion?” Her voice echoed around the vaulted ceiling as they climbed the staircase.

“No, no, no. Señor Philip has staff to run the house, but they all have the day off.”

*****

In the palatial ensuite bathroom, Mildred unpacked her toiletries and lined up her medications on the shelf. Dr. Das had given her extras, five more pill bottles because he understood her fear of displeasing Philip. Standing at the double sink unit in front of a wall-to-wall mirror, she could not avoid her reflection: pale and sallow, weary and worn out.

Someone hammered on the door. She recognized Philip’s distinctive pattern immediately before he burst into the bedroom. He looked right and left.

“There you are, Mom!” He marched into the bathroom. “Why are you hiding?”

“I’m not hiding.” She took a calming breath. “How wonderful to see you Philip.” She hugged him and gave him a peck on the cheek, but he stiffened and patted her hair.

“You change in the bedroom,” he rested a hand on her toiletry bag, “and I’ll tidy your things in here?”

“No need. They’re far easier to find on the counter than stuffed in a drawer, but I do need my comfy shoes.” She hobbled toward her suitcase and sat on the bed. “My feet are killing me.” She untied her laces, slipped off her shoes, and grabbed a pair of open-toed sandals. Philip had his back to her. Should she take off her pantyhose too? No, he was too close. “What are you doing in there?”

"Nothing."

What had he slipped into his pocket? The bulge was all too obvious, ruining the smooth line of his suit. "If you want to borrow something, you only have to ask."

"Don't start, *Mother!*" He strode across the thick bedroom carpet, and paused at the door. "I have to check up on Pari."

"Is she okay?"

"She's taken a turn for the worse. I'll meet you at the ceremony. José will accompany you."

"Wait! Let me come too. I must meet Pari."

"*Mother!* Enough."

He slammed the door as he left. What had she done wrong this time? How extraordinary, and yet, entirely predictable. Another of his monosyllabic moods. What a pity he hadn't mellowed with age.

*****

Half an hour later, José tapped on her door, "I have iced-tea for you downstairs."

"Be with you in a few minutes." Mildred gathered her emotions in readiness to meet Henry. She would not allow Philip to ruin this momentous occasion. She picked up her purse, grabbed her sunglasses, and headed downstairs.

Her sandals slapped against the flagstone floor and echoed around the cavernous kitchen.

José stood next to a sliding glass door leading to a shaded patio.

"I've never visited such a stunning home. Pari must adore this."

"I think she prefers something more traditional from home. This is American colonial. Pari has modest tastes, more asymmetrical, casual, and irregular, you know, Pakistani style."

Mildred paused at the cluttered island. "What's all this mess?"

"The aftermath of Señor Philip's herbal smoothie preparations."

Mildred glanced at the liquidizer and ran a finger through the gritty, green sludge.

"Wheatgrass, kiwi, kale, spinach and ginger." José rolled his eyes. "Cleansing."

"It sounds revolting."

"Philip swears it's the secret weapon for Pari's recovery, guaranteed."

Mildred kept her thoughts to herself. She shouldn't disparage Philip in front of José. Instead, she washed off the green slime with soap from a dispenser on the wall. The box next to it whirred and a paper towel spooled forward. Philip loved his gadgets and gizmos. Perhaps this house was more a reflection of him than her. She pursed her lips. Had Pari paid for this house?

She reached over to the trash, not surprised that the lid rose automatically, and there she saw her empty pill bottle. She knew he'd taken something, but why had he stolen her heart medication? Was he trying to prove her incompetence or was he trying to kill her?

*****

José's tea gave Mildred a new lease on life. They left the house

187

and sauntered over to the park. Children, mainly boys—maybe thirty of them—sat on three rows of white chairs, the spindly chair legs sinking into the verdant lawn.

Mildred glanced at her sandal-clad feet. "This grass is like a waterlogged sponge."

"Sprinklers," José said. "California is a desert."

"Tell me about Henry. What does he like, other than dogs?"

"He's a good boy under the circumstances, but shy like his mother, doesn't like shouting."

Mildred hesitated. What was he trying to say, but before she could ask, José touched his nose and made a curt bow. Maybe it was the jet lag, perhaps she was imagining things.

She spotted Philip's shiny bald head in the front row and joined him on the next seat.

"Which one is Henry?" She examined each face. Philip ignored her, and scowled at his phone. "Is that him? Yes, it must be. Doesn't he look smart in that purple uniform?"

"Not purple, *Mother,* plum."

"His mortar board hat is too big."

"It's a graduation cap."

Mildred waved at Henry, shaking a hanky above her head, "Hello, Henry!" She glanced at Philip expecting disapproval. But no, Philip wore a smile, a genuine smile which reached his eyes, and he bestowed it upon all the people around him. Where had Mr. Congenial come from? How long would he stay?

*****

After about an hour and a half, Mildred couldn't read her

watch without her glasses, the Principal dismissed the children. They scattered like birds to their respective families.

"Well done," Philip boomed. "You did a great job, Henry."

Was he praising his little boy or broadcasting a public announcement? Mildred waited. Philip didn't introduce her. Henry, slight for his age, squirmed the toe of his shoe into a puddle by a sprinkler head. Mildred did likewise, mud oozing between her toes. A smile spread across Henry's face.

"Are you Gran?"

"Yes. Also, your number one fan."

Philip checked his phone for the umpteenth time. "Right." He took hold of Henry's hand. "Bad news. Let's go."

Startled, Mildred hurried after them, Philip striding across the park and Henry hanging on for dear life.

*****

Back at the house, Mildred dropped her muddy shoes on the mat and padded indoors barefoot.

Facing Philip in the majestic hall, she put her hands on her hips. "Why the bloodthirsty rush?"

"Someone's cleaned out my bank account, haven't got a penny in the world." He shoved his phone in her face. "Look at that balance. I'm completely skint, busted, bankrupt. Give me that Gold American Express card, now. Have you lost it?"

She fumbled in her purse and tuned out his tirade. "Here." She handed it over to him.

"I can't understand it." He stared at the card for several seconds. "Made any online purchases?"

"No."

"When you activated the account, what did you buy?"

"Nothing. I activated it by phone. It said call this number, and I did."

"Okay. What have you bought with this card?"

"Nothing." It was true, she hadn't spent a penny, apart from the coffee and…

"You've remembered?"

"I had a call from this nice young man, Frank."

"Who?"

"Frank from the Federal Bureau of something-or-other."

"I swear you're dead from the neck up." Philip closed his eyes and his chin dropped to his chest. "Why are you always such a bloody victim." He sighed. "Right! Can't deal with that now, I'm off to check on Pari." He put a hand on the banister and a foot on the first stair. "She's been left alone for two hours and five minutes."

"You make it sound as if she's at death's door."

"Don't follow me. Wait here."

"Why? Let me meet Pari, please?"

Philip vaulted ahead of her, calling over his shoulder, "No! Don't!"

Waiting until he disappeared from view, Mildred tiptoed after him. She crept toward the double doors to the master bedroom and peered inside.

Philip leaned over a woman in the bed, measuring her pulse. "Shit!" Philip thumped the bedpost, picked up a dirty glass and hurled it at the wall. Splashes of green slime spattered the wall and carpet.

Mildred darted toward the bed and smiled at the occupant. "Pari?" She stuck out her hand, "I'm Mildred."

"I don't understand." Philip paced the room raking his remaining hair follicles. "Should be all over by now." He took a pill bottle, another one of Mildred's pill bottles from his pocket, and examined the label. "Enough to kill a bloody horse."

"Oh, no! You didn't put my pills in Pari's smoothie, did you? Is that what you wanted them for? They're no good for Lyme disease."

"Shut up, Mother."

"You should never take other people's medications." Mildred shook her head. "That's a dangerous thing to do."

"You know nothing about Lyme disease. Don't interfere. I'm trying to help Pari, not hurt her."

"Good because those pills wouldn't hurt a fly." Mildred sat on the edge of the bed. "Although they might improve the smoothie's flavor."

"What?" Philip blinked.

Pari glanced at Mildred, and then spoke to Philip. "I thought that smoothie tasted weird today, far too sweet and ever so slightly minty. Almost refreshing."

"I worked it out at the airport." Mildred smiled at Pari. "Dr. Das must have switched out my palpitation pills, and given me a placebo instead. You're a lucky man, Philip. You may not have a penny to your name, but you have a wonderful, healthy and wealthy wife. Let's hope she forgiving too."

"A placebo," Philip roared. "Your prescription's not a genuine Cardiac Glycoside tablet? It's a generic?"

Liquor is Quicker

"I don't know if it's generic, but it's a genuine Tic Tac, one-hundred-percent pure."

(Candy is dandy, But liquor is quicker—Ogden Nash)

Hallway Odours
Lyn Fraser

I ask the police officer if she'd wait just five more minutes while I take off my shoes and go barefoot. One of the things I miss most is going barefoot in ryegrass. Sergeant Swanson speaks into a gadget on her shoulder that crackles back. We're on our way to the station, and I've watched enough police procedurals to know what happens there--the fingerprinting, the mouth swab for DNA, unflattering photographs, and the one phone call. I'd probably call Jerome.

He visits his mother at Sun Glo. Sun Glo Care Home. But I can tell you the closest thing to care is provided by Heather, Jerome's dog. Heather pulls at the leash and comes right up to me in the hallway as if she didn't know any better. That's what we need more of around here, indiscriminate friendliness.

People don't know how relate to us, but that dog does. Nuzzles on over to old legless Toby in his wheel chair and sniffs him right in the crotch. And Gladys. She's so humped over she can hardly look up, but she can see Heather and reach down to her. They both dangle strings of slobber while she rubs the dog's neck.

On Tuesdays I take the Sun Glo bus to the Shopping Triangle, which is how I've gotten to know Natalie because she sometimes goes with us. It's her volunteer project. She rides along and chats and offers to help us in the stores if we need any assistance, which I don't. I don't even need help from the bus driver Ted, although I indulge him by letting him hold my arm while I go up the bus steps. That way he avoids any potential legal liability, something he has in common with all the other staff at Sun Glo. That and halitosis.

At TESCO I shop for my intimate products and necessities like toilet roll. You wouldn't believe the quality of what they stock at Sun Glo. Natalie does things like pull a credit card sized calculator out of her pocket and tells me the cost per square inch for Andrex Gentle Clean relative to Cheeky Panda Ultra Sustainable.

I'd never pursued that line of inquiry with anyone, but Natalie seemed to be quite sharp about financial issues generally. Her financial savvy especially appealed to me because of my house. Well, our house. My husband Fred didn't want to sell it. He's still planning on moving back into the house after his health improves. Good luck on that.

Natalie's an estate agent, it turned out. She gave me her card on our second bus ride together after she found out I was a property owner:

Natalie P. Denson Estate Agent
Denson Real Estate Agency
Commercial* Residential * Orchards
My Clients Get the "Real" Deal

That opened up quite a line of ongoing conversation between us as she elbowed me to make sure I got the 'real' deal connection. We've talked about my house every week since, either on the bus or in the shampoo aisle or back at what they call the snack bar at Sun Glo that offers one food item—popcorn--and a choice of red or orange punch. Apparently, Natalie wasn't all that busy getting her customers the 'real' deals because she seemed to have plenty of time for me. Natalie explained that this was her slow season.

Fred and I had lived in the detached house at 79 Meadow Way our entire married life of forty-seven years until we moved into what they call a 'couple's flat' at Sun Glo, which actually is a large room with a curtain in between and has its own bathroom. My niece Elsa insisted that we move because she decided I couldn't take care of Fred any more since he's on oxygen around the clock and frequently has an IV hookup for hydration and antibiotics to treat urinary tract infections.

Elsa figured the revenue from selling the house would be more than sufficient with our other financial resources to enjoy an upscale private senior living facility. But Fred wouldn't sell or even consider renting, so we wound up downscale at Sun Glo. Elsa lives over two hundred miles away.

He still goes out for a walk several days a week with his friend Jerry, who can manage all the apparatus, but Fred can't do much else.

Natalie was very sympathetic even though she hadn't met Fred or seen our alleged couple's flat. Yesterday after the TESCO run she offered to do an appraisal for me, not official of course, but close to it since this was her business, helping clients know the value of their properties. After she pulled up a page on her laptop computer, I could see the photo of our beige brick with the red tiled roof, along with some columns of financial information about the property.

As we looked closer, I showed Natalie the fir tree by the

corner bedroom window and described how we'd used it as our Christmas tree every year, wrapping on a string of outdoor lights, sharing wassail and carols with the neighbours. Our one Christmas at Sun Glo had been ghastly. Artificial silver tree with blinking lights and a gift for each resident. Fred got a red clip-on tie, and he doesn't even wear dress shirts. Me, a necklace with the price tag still on it. "That's what my life has come to, "I told Natalie, "blinking lights and cheap jewellery."

Natalie nodded at my input without comment and returned to her screen. She pointed to a figure underneath the photo and explained it was the Zoopia estimate for our house. It came in at £372,400.

"But to be honest," Natalie said, leaning toward me and speaking rapidly, "that's a sort of average real estate pricing, you'll find something similar on several sites. But with all my contacts and business experience and social media connections, I could easily get you a lot more than that for the house. We might be looking at least at 400K . Who's taking care of this place anyway?"

"My niece hired some company to do the gardening," I said, "and make sure the pipes don't burst."

"Thinking this whole thing through, what about just as a starting point you go ahead and put the house on the market yourself with me as the agent, and we'll see where we are?"

"Not possible. Fred has to sign off on anything about the house, it's the way the title was done. No children, sadly. We were all ready to sell it, but then Fred changed his mind."

"How is his mind?" Natalie asked.

"Fine. It hasn't changed back."

"You're saying that he thinks he'll get healthy enough to leave Sun Glo and move back into the house… and that he's mentally competent to make that decision? I mean, if you don't mind my asking, since we're talking business here."

"Sure, mentally competent. Decisional, as they say, and affirmed by the medical assessment my niece insisted on to check him out. Elsa looked into this whole thing, thinking the decision was temporary."

"Does your niece have any legal authority over your business affairs? Or medical? Again, I hope I'm not overstepping here."

"Nope, it's all ours. We have wills made up, signed and sealed, leaving everything to each other."

"Sad to even consider this, but if he died, you'd be sole owner?" Natalie asked in a low voice.

"Yep, each of us is in charge of our own destiny."

"I see."

Which I doubted, but we could fix that. "Would you like to meet Fred?" I asked. "We usually have a little toddy before dinner, and you could join us."

"Sure. Do I need to sign in or anything to be allowed into your room?"

"Nope, we're wide open here."

Natalie walked with me by the unattended nurse's station and down the hall, which smelled its distinctive combination of pee, shit, disinfectant, and dinner cooking. When we arrived at the last room on the right, I called out, "Fred," as we entered. The two beds are divided by a curtain, with equal space on either side so we can both have some privacy. "Fred, this is Natalie, she sells orchards," I said, pulling back the curtain.

Fred looked out from his bed through the maze of IV tubes and an oxygen connector. He attempted to roll toward us. "Howdy, Madam," he said, smiling at Natalie and extending a hand.

I rushed over to prevent him from pulling out of anything, which I explained to Natalie would be a disaster. "I mean, if it weren't for all these medical gadgets he has to stay hooked up to all the time I could have taken care of him at home."

"What if he uh, needs to …?"

"Diapers," I explained.

"Cherries or apples?" Fred asked.

Natalie looked confused.

I offered her a gin. "Straight or with tonic? Fred has his with Milk of Magnesia, but I find that a bit rich."

Natalie shook her head. "None for me thanks, but you two go ahead."

Just as well, because I didn't have any tonic. I'm just grateful for the wines and spirits section in TESCO, and Ted winks at me when I pop over there while he's loading everybody else on the bus.

I went into the bathroom to 'mix' our drinks, a shot of gin for me and an equal slug of Milk of Magnesia for Fred. As I poured, it occurred to me that I could put anything into Fred's cocktail, and he'd never know the difference.

What Natalie had said, if Fred died, stirred up some thoughts about how soon he might die. Sad for me to consider, but wouldn't having a gentle ending be compassionate in a way, really? Fred would never be leaving Sun Glo. But I could, if I sold the house. Senior assisted living at its finest, I'd seen the Vista brochure—casino nights, wine with dinner, trips to the theatre, dances, individual balconies.

Actually, they made it easy here at Sun Glo, in a sense. There'd be no problem with access to drugs—some nurse or another usually leaves her med cart unattended by the door of a patient's room almost every day. I could just walk by and help myself. It'd take a bit of research on what to use, but I'd read enough mystery novels to know it wasn't all that complicated. There'd be the minor issues of guilt and illegality, of course, but Fred was on so many prescription drugs, whatever showed up in his system would be irrelevant to any investigation. And as Julia Child said about the chicken she dropped on the floor before putting it back into the pot, *who's to know?*

I returned to our room carrying the two tiny paper cups with our drinks. "Salut," Fred said, lifting his, and we downed our tipples.

Mavis, a nurse's aide, came into the room and rolled a tray over to Fred's bed. "It's time to eat, sweetie." She sat down beside the bed, helped Fred sit up, uncovered a plate, and put a straw into a glass.

"I take my dinner in the so-called dining room," I told Natalie. "Food's the pits, either here or there, but at least they usually have some meat with it, or something they call meat. Don't even have to cut it up."

Fred waved a fork with something unrecognizable stuck in it.

"So sorry to leave, but I have to get back to work," Natalie said. "Good to meet you, Fred."

"Peaches, pears, and plums," Fred called to her, adding, "Grapes, cherries, and mulberries."

"Orchards," I said. "He's referring to types of orchards, so he must have understood me when I said you're an estate agent."

"Uh hum. Does that woman with the food stay with him?" She whispered to me, as if she disapproved that I was just going off and leaving him.

"No," I whispered back, "just while he eats. But Fred'll be fine. She reconnects the restraints to keep all his lines attached and puts on back-to-back episodes of "Fawlty Towers" when she leaves. Fred falls asleep after that. Gives me plenty of time for a wild evening out. I can stay down there after dinner for cards or a movie or a sing-along, whatever adventure they're having."

Natalie had no comment about my evening plans but said, "I might swing by your house. Take a look for myself."

As we walked toward the common area, Jerome passed by on the way to his mother's room. Heather trotted beside him, sniffing vigorously, after which Natalie had to rearrange her slacks, slightly damp in the seat.

She went on to the parking lot, and I went on to creamy carrot soup, parmesan pork chop, congealed potatoes, fruity green salad, marshmallow treat, and milk offered at every meal. Don't even get me started on the subject marshmallow treat.

The Tuesday night classic movie featured "Out of Africa," with two of my favourites--Meryl Streep and Robert Redford. Since I'd only seen it four times I decided to go. I especially liked the parts showing the relationship between Karen Blixen and Denys Finch-Hatten, like the one where Karen finds him asleep in a chair on the veranda. Without waking Denys up, she moves a chair next to him and sits, holding his hand, just watching him sleep. Sweet.

But when the movie reached that part of the story, I was barely managing to stay awake. So I decided to skip the rest of it and go back to our room. I wanted to hold Fred's hand and apologize for my temporary insanity about his Milk of Magnesia. He wouldn't understand, I knew, but he'd squeeze my hand.

Before I could get through our hallway, however, I encountered a full-blown commotion. At the end of the corridor, I saw several police officers and a crew of paramedics. Usually the ambulance staff just showed up when one of the residents had died. I began to hyperventilate as residents spilled out of rooms and staff flurried. Please, no, is all I could think. However and whenever, I wanted to be with him.

Jerome and Heather came through the milieu in my direction. But before they reached me, the head nurse, with whom I had spoken only twice the entire time we'd lived in Sun Glo, grabbed me by the arm. She pulled me into the office of the facility director. I knew this wouldn't be good.

*****

I was wrong. Fred's still connected and kicking. An attempt was made his life, but not by me. And that's why I'm barefoot in our Meadow Way yard now with Sergeant Swanson looking on. Sergeant Swanson said for me to go ahead and enjoy the grass, that she wished she could take her shoes off her too.

We'd finished checking the inside of the house, nothing amiss as far as I could tell. Apparently, Natalie hadn't been able to get inside, if she'd tried. Sergeant Swanson and I were going from here to the police station for my official identification of her. I wondered if Natalie would be in a line-up or if I'd watch her through some sort of two-way mirror.

No question, though, that she'd tried to murder Fred. While I was at dinner-and-a-movie, she'd maybe driven over here to our house, nobody knows for sure, but what's certain is that she did come back into Sun Glo. No witnesses saw her enter our room, not surprising given the level of inactivity that time of evening. But Heather smelled her.

Jerome said that dog raised her head, sniffed, snorted, and almost leapt out of his mother's room to get to ours. Raced through the hallway, "Nothing and no one could have impeded her," according to Jerome.

Heather's barking brought the cavalry.

Natalie had detached every one of Fred's hook ups, and he was drifting into unconsciousness as she readied a syringe to speed the process. Assumed, probably correctly, that when Fred was found, staff would believe he'd pulled out the connections himself. There would be no autopsy.

Fred's recovering. He roused enough this morning to eat a late breakfast while I told him Natalie was an imposter. She didn't sell orchards or any real estate for that matter, wasn't licensed. She'd lied on her volunteer form to get into the facility, the first of many untruths. Anything for the real deal, I guess.

"No problem," Fred said. "Elsa's taking care of it. She called while you were at that movie last night. I told her we were fine and wanted to sell the house so we could move into more gracious quarters. I'd like to try some ballroom dancing."

Diamonds for Queens
Ella Moon

"Snow is really coming down out there," Stephen Stephens announced blandly, from where he was standing looking out of the manor house's broad parlour windows. Marjorie nodded, holding her knitting up to the light of the grand chandelier, and Father James Fennock, slowly making his way through a crossword on the other side of the room, hummed in agreement. The snow was indeed coming down, great swathes of it coating the manor's acreage until no more than the occasional struggling rose bush could be seen poking its head out from underneath. They had been effectively snowed in as of last night, with no-one able to get in or out, their only link to the village, or elsewhere, the rather erratic telephone connection. Mrs. Marjorie Weston and Father Fennock had been trapped in with the family, who were gathered for the Christmas holidays. Marjorie had been meant to depart yesterday, to return to her cottage in Otter's Leap proper and allow the family to spend the rest of the holiday together, but all seven of the manor's inhabitants were now well and truly stuck.

*****

Though plenty large enough, the manor was nevertheless

struggling slightly to contain its cast of characters. Marjorie was there at the behest of Nigel Stephens, owner of the manor and an old friend of hers. He had been two years above her in school – she was a little embarrassed to admit that she'd had somewhat of a childhood crush on him, with his sleek auburn hair and high cheekbones. His hair was now white and more often than not bore a distinct resemblance to someone who had recently jammed their fingers into an electrical socket, and wrinkled skin hid his cheekbones, but he still retained his sweet charm. In any case, he had at the time borne her crush with great grace, and after she had gotten over herself they had become close friends. They had drifted apart lately, which was no doubt something he had been attempting to remedy by inviting her to stay.

He lived with his wife Charlotte – Marjorie had never gotten to know her very well, and couldn't say that the past few days had made her much regret that. Of course, she would never say such a thing out loud, but between her rather ostentatious style (she always appeared to be looking down her long and expertly powdered nose at one, and never presented at dinner without a necklace composed of diamonds that seemed specifically designed to blind her mealtime compatriots) and her overbearing attitude, Marjorie was less than charmed. She was one of those people who seemed to take delight in knowing every secret about others, for no greater reason than the power it allowed her to hold over them.

Their son Stephen was up for the holidays, he of the obvious statements – Marjorie had always been baffled as to what on earth could have induced them to name him Stephen Stephens, but she couldn't deny that, in an odd way, it suited him. He had inherited some of his father's good looks, but his hair was constantly ruffled in that way that so many young men spent hours trying to achieve, only his was clearly that way by nature's doing and somehow less compelling for it, and his light hazel eyes always seemed focused on some point just behind one's shoulder. He was a doctor in the city, and by all accounts quite skilled at it, but he had a nervous edge to him that would have made Marjorie mighty uncomfortable with him using any sort of medical instrument on her. He'd come up with his new wife, Queenie – they had been married for the better part of two years now, but despite her family knowing the Stephens of old, this was apparently the first time she was spending any significant time with them, as she had been with her own family last Christmas holidays. Marjorie had her suspicions that Nigel may also have invited her in the hopes that she would help to defuse some of the tension introduced by the family's newest arrival – she seemed a charming girl, but a little inclined towards flashy dresses and expensive perfumes in a way that the small town of Otter's Leap and its old money – such as the Stephens – tended to view with disdain. The whole situation was not helped by her age – more than ten years younger than Stephen, leading to extensive and rather unkind whispers that she had married him only for his money.

The housekeeper, Florence Kappel, was the last permanent inhabitant. Very much of the old school of domestic servants, her deportment was as tightly wrapped as her white bun and her insight no doubt as piercing as her sky-blue eyes. As was standard for such types, she refused to admit to a personal life or to use any form of address besides 'ma'am' or 'sir' in the presence of the Stephens. Apart from Marjorie, the final visitor was the Father. He had been the parish's pastor for only three or so years, since poor Father Benson's passing, but his smiling efficiency and determinedly middle-aged demeanour – he had the kind of face that would be read as '50-ish, perhaps' from when he was 35 until he was 70 – had won over the inhabitants of Otter's Leap with impressive speed. No doubt it also helped that he had immediately taken it upon himself to do such things as dropping round to each house personally to spread a little Christmas cheer. The Stephens manor was last on his list, due to its location on the far outskirts of town, away from the general village hustle and bustle, and he had arrived yesterday shortly before the snow had trapped them all inside.

*****

Nigel's head, with its shock of white hair, appeared around the doorway, interrupting Marjorie's musings. It was soon followed by the rest of him, as he took a few steps into the parlour, and Marjorie placed her knitting down beside her to smile at him.

"Ah, Marjorie, Stephen. Father. I'm off to bed – the cold has thoroughly worn me out. The old leg just does not like it." He slapped the leg in question, which bore a minor injury from the war – he always claimed to be rather grateful for it, as it had invalided him out before he saw any real action, but it had left him with a slight limp – then peered at his hand. "Wait– oh, I've put my scotch down somewhere." He turned around to leave again, presumably in pursuit of it, but before he could, Miss Kappel appeared in the doorway.

She handed him a small glass of whiskey, informing him with an air of forbearing detachment, "You left this in the library, sir."

"Thank you, Miss Kappel," he told her warmly. As she left again, he sat down in the armchair nearest the door. "I don't know what I'd do without Florence, really. You know, every year I offer her Christmas off, but she's never taken it. Well, once, but only because she was already sick that year."

"That was when I was twelve, wasn't it?" Stephen said. "I only remember because it was so odd not having her around!"

"She's very dedicated," Marjorie said.

Nigel nodded, then gave a twinkling grin and said, "Anyway, I was going to bed, wasn't I?" He stood up again, and turned to leave.

"Don't forget your glass," Marjorie called, and he stopped and turned around.

"Ah! Thank you."

Picking up his whiskey, he left the room, and Marjorie resumed her knitting as Stephen sat down.

"What are you making, Mrs. Weston?" he inquired politely.

"A sweater, for one of my goddaughters," she said, holding it up for him to see. "She just had a baby, and I always like to give the new mother a present then. The baby gets so many presents, and after all, the mother is the one who did all the work."

Stephen gave a short laugh. "True, true."

"Five-letter word for 'undercover female drink hawker', second letter g…" Father Fennock mused from the other end of the sofa.

"B-girl," Marjorie supplied.

"Ah, thank you. My education is a little lacking in such

areas."

"How do you know things like that, Mrs. Weston?" Stephen asked in amazement.

"I'm old, my dear boy, not dead," she told him, eyes twinkling.

His apology was fortuitously interrupted by the reappearance of Nigel, stumbling into the room.

"Did you forget something else, Pa?" Stephen asked. When there was no reply, Marjorie looked up at Nigel properly. He was trembling, and his eyes were wide. She dropped her knitting and rushed over to him, putting a hand under his arm.

"What's wrong, Nigel?"

"Char– Charlotte," he gasped out.

"What about her?" Father Fennock asked, as he and Stephen both rose to their feet.

"Charlotte's dead. She's been killed!"

*****

Nigel led them up the stairs at a considerably slower pace than Marjorie would have liked, hampered by his bad leg. At the doorway to their bedroom, he paled even further, and Marjorie gently took control.

"You two stay out here," she told Nigel and Stephen. "The Father and I will make her as peaceful as we can."

Nigel nodded faintly and wrapped an arm around Stephen.

"Father?" Marjorie said.

He tilted his head at her. "Ladies first."

Giving him a small smile, she opened the door and led the way in.

The room was large, but not outlandishly so. Wallpapered in a solemn maroon stripe, with one large window that must have a very pretty view of the front gardens in daylight, but currently had thick velvet curtains drawn across it, the room exuded a rather stern air. It housed a tall oak wardrobe, a low bookshelf full of history books which must have been Nigel's – it had been his favourite subject at school – a dresser with a pretty mirror and a set of hair tools laid out across it, and two twin beds. On the floor at the bottom of the bed closest to the dresser, the body that used to be Charlotte Stephens was lying, a thick hairpin jammed into her throat and her blood soaking the plush white carpeting. Marjorie spared a thought for the poor housekeeper, who was going to have – pardon the language – a hell of a time getting that out.

Father Fennock glanced sideways at her as he kneeled next to the body. "If you don't mind my saying, you seem remarkably unruffled by all this, Mrs. Weston."

"Unfortunately, it's not the first time I've been placed in such a situation. By my age, one has usually been exposed to rather more of life's villainies than one might wish. I could say the same for you, though, Father." Marjorie peered at the dresser. The hair tools indicated that Charlotte had been preparing for bed, but she obviously hadn't gotten far, as she was still fully dressed in her dinner clothes.

"Well, the priesthood does rather lend itself to being around dead bodies. Admittedly they're usually already in coffins, but death is not unfamiliar to me. In any case," he said, gently closing her eyelids with one hand, "her soul is no longer here. She's with God now."

"Mmm." Marjorie sat carefully on the bed behind the body,

and waited for him to finish his prayer before she asked, "Have you noticed anything yet?"

He frowned at her. "What?"

"Her diamond necklace. She isn't wearing it, and it's not on her dresser. And look there, next to your knee."

He looked down where she had indicated. "The blood is disturbed."

"And there's a strand of Mrs. Stephens' hair. Someone unclasped the necklace after she had died, yanking a few pieces of hair out with it, and took the diamonds."

"Well, I suppose that is a motive," Father Fennock said faintly.

"There is another motive evident in this room as well," Marjorie said, patting the evidence in question with one hand.

"The beds," he said, still looking slightly shaken, but quick on the uptake nonetheless.

"Indeed. Nigel and Charlotte were, apparently, separated, but had informed no-one of this fact."

"When you say you've been in such situations before…"

"A lady doesn't like to toot her own horn."

"Very well." He stood up, and extended a hand, which Marjorie took gratefully. Getting up and down wasn't quite as easy as it had once been. "I suppose all we know for sure is that neither of us did it."

"Yes, it can't have been more than two hours since she retired after dinner, and we've been in the parlour the entire time."

"I'll get poor Stephen to help me move her."

She nodded. Stephen and Nigel were still standing with each other just outside the room, and as the Father gently took Stephen by the arm, Marjorie laid a hand on Nigel's shoulder.

"Marjorie…" He blinked at her, and she steered him to an armchair on the other side of the hallway. After a moment sitting down, he seemed to regain some kind of equilibrium.

"How did it happen?" he asked her. "How could…" He trailed off again.

"I don't know, dear, but you don't need to think about that right now," she told him softly.

His eyes focused on hers. "Will you find out for me? I have to know, Marjorie."

She nodded. "Of course, Nigel. I'll figure it out."

He patted her hand weakly in thanks.

*****

Making her way downstairs, Marjorie almost ran straight into Miss Kappel, who was holding a linen basket full of clean clothes that partially obscured her from view.

"Oh, sorry, ma'am!" she exclaimed, peering around the basket and stepping aside.

"It's no problem, dear. My fault, I wasn't looking where I was going."

"No, ma'am, it was my fault."

"Actually, Florence, I wanted to ask you something – do you mind if I call you Florence?"

"Miss Kappel is more appropriate, ma'am," she replied stoutly.

"Of course, my apologies. I was just wondering if Mr. and

Mrs. Stephens – the elder – were having any trouble? In their marriage, that is. I do want to be there for Nigel, but you know he doesn't like to talk about these things." She felt a little guilty about probing Miss Kappel for information before she was told of Charlotte's death, but she was the most likely person to know – outside of Nigel himself, who could perhaps not be trusted to answer honestly – and these questions would be simply too awkward in the wake of that information being revealed.

"It's not proper to be talking about the master's personal life," she hedged.

"I completely understand. I just didn't want to misinterpret anything in front of Nigel, you see."

Miss Kappel nodded slowly. "Yes. Well, they have been having some troubles. More than some, actually."

"Oh?"

She frowned at Marjorie, who simply waited expectantly, trusting in that old reliable instinct for gossip shared by every person over 40 in Otter's Leap and all skilled domestic servants everywhere. After a moment, the frown cleared and she leant in. "There was a lawyer here only a few weeks ago, talking about divorce. And not only that, but Mrs. Stephens was asking about changing her will after the divorce, to cut Mr. Stephens out!" She blushed immediately. "I shouldn't have told you that. Forgive me." She lifted the basket of clothes back up in front of her and hurried past Marjorie, up the stairs.

*****

Stephen was standing in front of the library fireplace, staring vacantly into the fire. Leaping sparks came perilously close to his linen pants, but he didn't seem to notice.

"Stephen."

He jumped and turned around, and Marjorie waved a hand at him. "I'm sorry, Stephen. I didn't mean to alarm you."

"No, no, it's fine, Mrs. Weston. It's good to have someone else around. Queenie was with me, but she went off to… I'm not sure. To do something." He arranged himself into a low armchair, long legs drawn up into rather a comedic figure. "It seems like we only just saw her, you know?"

"I'm sure. And we were in the parlour together for so much of that time."

The attempt to draw out an explanation of his activities in the short time between Charlotte's last appearance and his entry into the parlour was unsuccessful, as he just muttered a faint agreement and drew further into himself. Marjorie took the matched armchair across from him, much better suited for her stature than his.

"I'm sorry, Stephen. There really are no proper words for this situation."

He nodded, staring down at his empty hands. "Thank you, Mrs. Weston."

Leaning towards him, she took one of his hands in her own. "I do apologise for this, Stephen, but I'm afraid I have to ask." She debated telling him his father's request, but really, the less information fed out the better. "What were you doing before you joined us in the parlour?"

He looked up at her, frowning. "What- you don't think *I* could have killed her? She was my mother, I loved her!"

"Love is so often involved in these things," Marjorie replied opaquely. "But no, I'm sure you didn't, but you understand that one must check such things."

He sighed. "Father did tell me about your reputation with mysteries. I– I was on the telephone. With a medical colleague back in the city."

"Would you mind terribly if I asked for his phone number? Only to clear you entirely, you understand."

Stephen blanched and sat back, ripping his hands from hers and crossing his arms across his chest, and Marjorie cursed herself. She knew better than to be so forthright, but being locked in a house with a murderer was enough to throw anyone slightly off balance.

"No! I won't be distrusted like this in my own home!"

She smiled at him, and pushed gently. That reaction *had* been a little melodramatic. "I do apologise, Stephen. Of course I don't distrust you."

"Well, good," he muttered.

"If there's anything you want to talk about, just call on me. I'm a very good listener."

He looked back at her with a slightly desperate expression. "I–"

She smiled encouragingly, and he seemed to come to a decision.

"You won't tell Pa?"

"On my mother's grave, God rest her soul."

He sighed. "I wasn't calling a colleague. I was– I was calling my bookie. I'm in trouble, Mrs. Weston. The horses just haven't been going my way, and I love Queenie but she does like expensive things, and Father keeps such a tight hold on my trust fund, and I just- I don't know what to do."

"I'm sorry, Stephen," Marjorie said softly.

"I'll give you the number. Queenie was with me, though – I've been trying to keep it from her, but last week she told me she'd known for months. About the gambling, at least."

"Thank you, dear. You'll work it out."

"Thanks, Mrs. Weston." He sighed again, and dropped his head down to rest on his folded arms. Marjorie rested a gentle hand on his back as she left the library.

*****

"Oh, Father, good."

Father Fennock gestured into the small sitting room to their left, and they slipped into it, taking two armchairs.

"After you left, Mr. Stephens told me, quite unprompted, that he was in the library for the entire time between Mrs. Stephens going upstairs and him coming into the parlour to say he was following her," he said. "Not that that's much of an alibi, I suppose, since he would have been alone other than when Miss Kappel brought him his scotch."

"Well, the younger Mr. Stephens seems to have motive galore, unfortunately," Marjorie told him with a mild grimace. "He is in deep gambling debts, and apparently Mrs. Stephens was planning to write Nigel out of her will after the divorce – oh yes, they were getting a divorce – which would presumably have left Stephen as the sole benefactor. And he may have stolen the diamonds as a quicker way to get cash, if there are people looking to collect on debts from him. He did give me the number of his bookie, though, who he claims he was on the phone to between Charlotte's retiring and his coming into the parlour."

"Didn't you hear? The phone lines just went down completely. We won't be confirming it that way."

Marjorie sighed. "That is unfortunate. He did say his wife was with him at the time, but a spouse is never the most reliable of witnesses."

Father Fennock's reply was cut off by a yawn, which Marjorie immediately felt overtake her as well.

"Let's go to bed, Father. We won't accomplish anything more tonight, and I believe the whole household could do with a good sleep." She was fairly certain they wouldn't be murdered in their beds tonight, and sleep deprivation wasn't going to help anyone, detective or murderer.

"Yes, let's. We'll pick this up tomorrow. After you, dear lady."

*****

The following morning, Miss Kappel had set out a modest breakfast in the smaller dining room for the inhabitants to pick at as they pleased, accurately predicting that no-one would be in a particularly appetitive mood. Fortuitously, Marjorie happened to be composing a small fruit plate for herself – she always detected better on a light breakfast – when Queenie Stephens came in.

"Hullo, Mrs. Weston," she greeted, perhaps a trifle more cheerfully than the situation called for – but then, it wasn't as if she had been close to the elder Mrs. Stephens. "How are you doing? Terrible thing, isn't it?"

"Indeed it is, Mrs. Stephens," Marjorie agreed.

"Oh, please, call me Queenie. Mrs. Stephens was her name. Not that my real name is Queenie either, did you know that?"

"I suspected," Marjorie replied. "What were you christened, then?"

"Flora! Flora Fairchild, that was me. I was very glad to trade that name in. I love my parents, but Flora never suited me."

Marjorie was inclined to agree. "How is your husband holding up?"

She shook her head, piling a gratuitous amount of butter and strawberry jam upon a slightly struggling bread roll. "Poor Stephen. First the money troubles, now this – he told me he talked to you about those."

"Yes, he said that you found out not long ago."

"Oh, I've known for ages, I just didn't realise the gambling had gotten *quite* so bad. But then I realised I had to do something, so I made him call his bookie and cancel all of his accounts – that's what we were doing last night, in fact – maybe even right when she was being killed! Oh, it's all too terrible."

She did indeed look a little shaken by that realisation, but it didn't prevent her from taking a large bite of her roll, which was now trembling under its load of conserves.

"At least Nigel and Stephen have each other to lean on," Marjorie pronounced, adding a slice of melon to her plate.

"Yes. Although I must say– I don't like to speak ill of the dead, you understand?"

"Of course not."

"But she really could be very unfeeling towards Nigel. I'm

sure you know that they were separated, you seem like the sort of old lady who knows things – no offence meant!"

"And none is taken." In fact, Marjorie was rather flattered.

"Oh, good. But yes, I'm sure Nigel was still in love with her, you could see it in his eyes, but she was constantly flirting with boys down in the village – she boasted about it to me, and told me half of them flirted back! I can believe it, she was very beautiful even at her age, but still, it seemed a little cruel while they were still married. Everyone says my mother was like that, an outrageous flirt, but she stopped as soon as she married my father. Not that men necessarily stopped flirting with *her*, you know? But she never reciprocated."

"I'm sure they didn't, if she looked anything like you," Marjorie told her. A little flattery never went astray – and it was true, she was very pretty, with shining blue eyes and a short blonde bob with a slight wave in it – a style that Marjorie was aware was now rather old-fashioned, but Queenie was clearly not the type to let that dissuade her from something which suited her so well.

Queenie giggled. "Thank you! She doesn't, actually – she's beautiful, but she looks nothing like me, she's all dark-haired and angular. So are my two younger siblings, I'm the odd one out – I'm afraid I'm rather that in this family as well. They're all so close, and seem to know exactly what… what role they play, you know? I feel rather like a pencil that's been jammed into the gears of the Stephens." She sighed. "And I'm afraid that didn't make a lot of sense, did it?"

"Oh no, dear, I understand what you mean, but you'll find your place." Marjorie smiled at her. "You're just shaped a little differently, and you have to figure out how you fit in. But

Stephen loves you, and that is the most important thing."

"Yes, that's true. And I love him."

Marjorie patted Queenie on the arm, then took a fork from the sideboard. "So you'll be fine. Have a nice breakfast, dear."

"You too, Mrs. Weston," Queenie called as Marjorie left the room, mind churning.

*****

Marjorie wandered into the parlour, where Father Fennock was already sitting with his crossword abandoned in front of him, staring into space and twirling his pencil between his fingers. He nodded at her in greeting as she sat down in the armchair.

"Hello, Father," she said. "I just had a very interesting conversation with Queenie Stephens. Apparently, Charlotte Stephens was not above stoking jealousy in her husband, and the separation was at her behest rather than Nigel's. I must admit, I can't easily picture him flying off the handle in such a disastrous way – or acting out his shock quite so well – but people have done stranger things when confronted with the loss of a love. He did ask me to investigate, but I suppose he could have been covering himself there." She sighed, and speared a piece of apple. "In better news, Queenie did corroborate Stephen's alibi, unasked, which is a point in their favour. But of course, she is just as affected by their current financial situation as Stephen is – and substantially less attached to Charlotte – so they may very well be covering for each other."

"I was just thinking about that, actually," he said, putting the pencil down on top of the crossword. "Shouldn't Miss

Kappel have seen Mr. and Mrs. Stephens last night? The telephone is on the way from the kitchen to the library, and she brought the elder Mr. Stephens his scotch just after Mrs. Stephens went upstairs."

She pointed at him with her fork, still holding the slice of apple. "You're right, Father, very good. Would you mind ringing for her?"

Father Fennock leant over and pulled the bell, and after only a couple of minutes, pleasantly spent by Marjorie in finishing off her fruit and watching the sunlight glint off the chandelier, Florence Kappel appeared.

"Miss Kappel!" Marjorie greeted. "Could I, perchance, get some tea? Also, I believe the Father had a question for you."

She nodded smartly at Marjorie, then turned to Father Fennock.

"Yes, I was just wondering," he began. "Did you happen to see Stephen Stephens on the telephone last night, with Mrs. Queenie Stephens?"

She frowned, then nodded. "Yes, Father. On the way to give Master Stephens his nightcap in the library."

"Thank you, Miss Kappel."

"Of course, Father. I'll go get that tea now, ma'am."

A strand of hair had slipped out of her tidy bun, and now curled around the back of her ear. Marjorie watched it bob slightly as she walked out of the room, and hummed thoughtfully. "Father, this may seem a strange request, but would you mind terribly asking Queenie Stephens to come in here? And then I may have two more requests of you."

Father Fennock raised his eyebrows at her, but nodded and

got up.

*****

Nigel was the last to enter the parlour, where, already seated, were Stephen, Queenie, and Miss Kappel on the sofa; and Marjorie, who was still sitting in the armchair opposite them, working on her knitting. Nigel looked around the room and barked out a short laugh. "What the devil is the Father up to?"

"I'm afraid I'm the one who asked him to invite you here," Marjorie told him.

"Ah." He nodded, and lowered himself down to sit between Miss Kappel and Queenie, rubbing his bad leg. "Well then, what are you up to?" he asked, his tone distinctly less surprised. "And where has the Father gone to now?"

"He'll be back shortly, he's just fetching one more thing for me. And as to the reason–" She set aside her knitting, and focused all her attention on the inhabitants of the sofa opposite. "I know who killed Charlotte Stephens."

There was a collective intake of breath from all four. Stephen pulled Queenie closer into his side, and Nigel gestured at her. "Well, do go on, old girl."

She nodded, and did as bade. "Initially, it seemed that anyone but myself and the Father could have committed the crime – there was a period of roughly two hours between the last time Mrs. Stephens was seen alive and the time when her body was found, for the entirety of which, Father Fennock and I were together in this very room. But Stephen only joined us after a period of half an hour, which would have been plenty of time to commit the murder; Nigel was ensconced by himself in the library for the entire time, bar a brief period in which

Miss Kappel brought him his whiskey; and Queenie and Miss Kappel herself spent most of the time moving around the house, entirely out of sight of anyone else."

Nigel raised his eyebrows, and Miss Kappel, seated on the very edge of the sofa with her hands folded in her lap, frowned at Marjorie.

She stood up and began to pace the room in short laps as she expounded. "Motivations, too, seemed only to grow in abundance: the deceased was in the process of divorcing Nigel, who still loves her, and was not shy about flirting with other men in front of him – not only that, but she was planning to cut him out of her will."

Nigel gasped. "What? She didn't tell me that!"

Marjorie nodded thoughtfully. "I believe you, dear, but it did produce another possible motive – Stephen would, presumably, be left as the sole benefactor. As it stood, she had not yet changed it, I don't believe, but he may not have known that. And he is sorely in need of money."

"You are, son? Why?" Nigel asked Stephen, who waved a nervous hand in the air.

"It's nothing, Father. I'm working it out."

"Indeed you are," Marjorie continued. "But there was another thing that pointed in the direction of money being the motive – Charlotte's diamond necklace was missing. It seemed entirely plausible that it had been taken by Stephen, in need of a quick monetary boost. However, Stephen's alibi was solid – for the period in which he was not with me and the Father, he was seen by both Queenie and Miss Kappel. Of course, it was possible that Queenie could have orchestrated it, as she would have benefited as much from the inheritance as Stephen."

"Mrs. Weston!" Queenie exclaimed, rising slightly, and Marjorie raised a placating hand.

"However, earlier today, having breakfast in this room, I noticed something which cleared both Queenie and Nigel."

Queenie settled back, lips pursed, as Father Fennock entered right on cue, holding a stepladder acquired from the pantry. "Where did you want this, Marjorie?" he asked.

She indicated a spot in front of the coffee table, underneath the chandelier. "Would you do this part for me, Father? I'm afraid I don't quite have the agility. If you climb to the top of the stepladder–"

He did as instructed, and she continued. "If you could just stretch up to the chandelier, and just grab– no, a little to the left– yes, those."

He grasped the crystals in question, and they came off the chandelier and into his hand. A ripple spread through the inhabitants of the sofa.

"Mrs. Stephens's diamond necklace," Marjorie said. "Thank you, Father, you can come down now."

He stepped down, and went to sit on the armchair nearest the door, still holding the necklace. "Now, anyone looking for money would never have risked leaving the diamonds out here, and quite frankly I couldn't see Queenie attempting such a task as to hide them in the chandelier – which after all, would have required even more agility than retrieving them. This also, naturally, ruled out Nigel, whose leg would never have let him get up there. And with Stephen already being cleared, this only left one suspect."

All eyes turned to Miss Kappel, who drew a sharp breath and exclaimed huffily, "But I've served Mrs. Stephens for decades! I have no reason to have killed her!"

"That's what I thought at first too, which is why I had not initially considered you as a suspect," Marjorie agreed. "But then some things started to come together for me. I asked Queenie one last question before the rest of you got here, the answer to which provided the lynchpin."

"What did you ask her?" Stephen asked when Marjorie fell silent.

"When her birthday was, and she confirmed that she is indeed 'a Christmas baby' – the reason why she missed the holidays last year is because she had stayed with her parents to celebrate her birthday."

"And what is that supposed to mean?" Miss Kappel asked sharply.

"Yes, Mrs. Weston, do explain, I've been dying of curiosity ever since you asked me," Queenie said.

"Well, it meant nothing by itself, but along with the facts, revealed to me earlier, that Queenie looks nothing like her family, that her real name is Flora, and that Miss Kappel had only ever taken one Christmas off, twenty-six years ago – that was to have a child, wasn't it, Miss Kappel? Specifically, Flora, who shares your beautiful blue eyes and wavy hair. She was named in dedication of you, Florence, and given to the Fairchilds."

"What?" Queenie breathed, on a delicate gasp.

Miss Kappel shot up out of her seat and ran to the door, but was stopped by the conveniently placed Father, who held her gently by the arms until she stopped struggling.

"There really is nowhere you can go anyway, my dear," he told her.

At that, all the fight collapsed out of her. He let go of her, and she turned back, sitting down on the coffee table in a jarring display of unprofessionalism. "She made me give her up," she said softly. "I could have done my job and raised her at the same time, if only she'd let me bring her into the household. But she was out of wedlock, and Mrs. Stephens wouldn't countenance it. She told me either – either I'd give Flora up, and she'd place her with friends who hadn't been able to have a baby yet, or she'd fire me and I'd be out on the streets with the babe. I couldn't lose this job. I couldn't."

Marjorie nodded sympathetically. "You didn't realise that Stephen's new wife Queenie was Flora, did you? Not until she got here, and you saw her, and all those old emotions came back up."

"She was my baby!" Florence exclaimed, with sudden fierce strength in her voice. "She had no right – she was mine!"

"You took the diamonds as a distraction, a red herring."

She shook her head, less at Marjorie than at some hidden fact of the universe, then nodded, resigned. "I didn't mean to kill her, not really. I just went up to give her her nightcap and help with her hair, with the maid off, and I finally asked her about Flora." She cast a glance at Queenie, who was still staring at her in astonishment but had settled back into Stephen's embrace. "I knew the moment I saw her, but she'd never told me the name of the family, and I just– I needed her to tell me. I thought maybe– maybe after all these years, after Flora had become *her* child, maybe she'd apologise. And she just waved me off, as if it was nothing! As if– I didn't want Master Stephen to go to jail for it," she explained, switching tracks again. "But I knew he had money troubles, and I thought maybe if everyone was looking at him… But I didn't want to keep the diamonds on me, so I brought the pantry ladder out that night after you were all abed, and put them up there."

"Yes."

"I didn't mean to do it," she repeated, with some of her former stalwartness leaking back into her voice. "But I don't regret it."

"Florence…" Nigel murmured. Stephen seemed frozen in shock, both arms around a cogitative-looking Queenie.

"Father, would you be so kind as to tie Miss Kappel's hands together?" Marjorie said, handing him a ball of thick yarn from the armchair. "I'm sure you understand, dear, that it's a little dangerous to leave you loose after all this. I'll call the Inspector as soon as the phone lines are up again."

Father Fennock nodded, and looped the yarn around a compliant Miss Kappel's wrists.

"Why, Florence?" Nigel asked, as she stood up.

"Flora was mine," she told him in a stern monotone. "She took her away from me once, and now Flora – Queenie – was her child, when she should have been mine." Her next words were directed not at Nigel, but at Queenie herself. "I never wanted – I never want – to hurt you, but she didn't see what that meant. She refused to see what that meant. She had no right." With those final words, she fell into blank silence.

"I'll just take her to her rooms, shall I?" Father Fennock

said, and led her out.

"Well," Queenie announced, breaking the room's shocked silence. Stephen's arms were still around her, seemingly frozen in place, but she seemed entirely unruffled. Marjorie was beginning to rather like her for that.

"I suppose we'll be making our own tea until the snowstorm's over," Queenie finished.

Truth, Justice, and Junior High
Gina Grandi

Kelsey took stock. From the back, the shops along this street all looked the same, but she had scoped out the alley the week before, counting doors, and knew which was Antonia's Art and Antiques. From here, there was just the one fence to get over, and she thought they could make it. She tightened her ponytail and tucked her flashlight into her boot. "Let's go over the plan."

Jessica was staring off in the other direction, fingering the white scarf slung around her neck.

"Jess!" Kelsey hissed.

Jessica blinked. "What?"

"The plan!"

"I know the plan, Kelsey. Can I take these gloves off? My hands are getting sweaty."

"You want to get arrested when they find your fingerprints? Let's go over the plan!"

"You already made me go over it, like, a hundred times."

"So make it a hundred and one."

Jessica huffed. "We get in, we grab the bowl, we get out."

"And then?" Kelsey scanned the street. No cars. No movement. Nothing in the shadows.

"We mail it to the Smithsonian."

"With our card. Are the cards done?"

"I'm still working on our logo. I'm thinking a stiletto. Or a black cat. Maybe a cat wearing stilettos?"

Kelsey sighed. "Fine. Whatever. Let's just get going. Give me a boost."

Jessica hesitated, examining her fingernails. "I was thinking…"

Kelsey waited, tapping one foot. She was glad she had chosen boots over sneakers. Maybe a little less comfy, but definitely on the right side of vigilante chic.

"This just doesn't seem very… well, glamorous," Jessica said finally. "For a heist. Couldn't we do something with jewelry?"

Kelsey frowned. "Haven't we been over this? That's just stealing."

"Not if we're liberating ill-gotten gains."

"Do you know of any bejeweled ill-gotten gains?" Kelsey stared hard at Jessica. "No? All right then." She gripped the chain link with both hands. "Boost me."

Jessica laced her fingers together. "Don't get my scarf dirty."

"You're supposed to be in black." Kelsey stepped gingerly into Jessica's hands and pushed herself up.

"It's from Stephen Murray. He was my Secret Santa. In homeroom."

"So?" The chain link hurt Kelsey's fingers. She heaved a leg over the top of the fence.

"So I think he likes me."

Kelsey wasn't sure how to get down. Should she roll? Shimmy? Drop? She might be stuck. "He was your Secret Santa," she said. "He *had* to get you a present."

"But not a nice one! I think it's silk!"

"No way it's silk. And his mom probably picked it out." Kelsey tried to swing her other leg over, lost her grip, and landed in a painful heap in the alley. She'd have bruises in the morning, for sure. She pulled the flashlight from her boot and clicked it on; it hadn't broken in the fall.

"I think it means he likes me." Jessica was standing next to Kelsey, examining the scarf.

Kelsey stared. "How'd you get over so fast?"

Jessica shrugged. "There's a pretty big hole over there."

Kelsey gritted her teeth. "Just keep quiet."

"There's no one here. Everything closed at nine."

"Still. My mom will kill me if she knows we snuck out."

"When we get home, maybe we could call Wendy? She has math with Stephen."

"*Shhhhhhh.*"

The girls crept forward. The alley was deserted; not even a cat prowled between the overflowing garbage cans. All was still. Kelsey kept her light trained on the back door of Antonia's.

"How do you know this bowl thingy is ill-gotten anyway?" Jessica whispered.

"I told you. I recognized it from art history class. That day we talked about museum looting."

"You're sure it's the same one?"

"Of course I'm sure. I got an A in art history."

"Everyone gets an A in art history. Mrs. Crenshaw is like, a thousand years old."

"That's not true."

"It is. Craig Bilker got an A in art history and he wasn't even enrolled."

"The point is, I recognize it. And I've had, like, twenty million hours to look at it since my mom keeps dragging me in there. I even asked once, and the woman said it was from an estate sale and she *looked away* when she said it."

"So?"

"So she looked away! Haven't you watched that show? That means she's lying!"

"I just think –"

Kelsey grabbed Jessica by the shoulders. "Jessica," she said, "we are going to be in high school next year. We are no longer children. It is time to make our mark. Do you want to be ordinary?"

Jessica bit her lip. "Maybe a little ordinary," she said.

"We can do more than talk about boys and worry about the next history test." Kelsey stared into Jessica's eyes. "We can be a *force for justice*!"

Jessica shrugged. "Ok, fine. Force for justice. Whatever. Are you sure Randall unlocked the door?"

"His uncle works for some janitorial service. He said he'd

take care of it if I did his English homework for a month." Kelsey turned the knob, her heart racing. The door opened.

Sirens whooped and clanged. Kelsey stumbled backwards and fell. "There's an alarm!" she shrieked from the ground.

Jessica waved her arms. "Quick, what's the code?"

"I didn't know there would be an alarm!" Kelsey clambered to her feet and slammed the door closed. The alarm continued to blare. "What's the backup plan?"

"*What backup plan?*" Jessica was hopping from foot to foot.

"We agreed! When I said we should be underground superheroes you said you'd be the sidekick so you didn't have to do the work and I said ok but the sidekick does the backup plan!"

"I have no memory of this."

Another siren wailed in the distance.

"Oh god – the police!" Kelsey was starting to panic. "What do we do? Do we stay and fight? You take the grizzled veteran and I'll take the eager rookie!"

"*What?*"

"That's how they pair off!"

"Run. We have to run. Now!"

"But the bowl!"

"RUN!" Jessica scrambled towards the fence, yanking Kelsey by the arm. She pulled Kelsey through the gap and the two girls ran, boot heels echoing over the empty sidewalk.

"Get off the main street!" Jessica gasped, and they turned the corner. "Keep your head down!"

They dashed past the darkened houses, cutting across

lawns to silence their shoes. A dog barked and they turned again, running until, Kelsey, clutching her sides, staggered to a stop and collapsed on the sidewalk.

"I think – we're safe," Jessica panted, holding onto a parked car.

"But we failed," Kelsey moaned from the ground, trying to catch her breath. "*Failed.*"

"We did what we could," said Jessica, dropping down beside Kelsey and wiping the sweat from her forehead. "Maybe we could write the Smithsonian anyway. Let them handle it."

Kelsey brightened. "Yeah!" She sat up and brushed off her jeans. "Maybe our missions are the scouting kind." She frowned. "At least until I get my license."

"Until then," Jessica agreed. They heaved themselves to their feet and turned towards home. "Think it's too late to call Wendy?"

Death of a Village Snob
Louise Taylor

More than one lace curtain twitched when Police Officer Pete McDonall came racing through the village, siren breaking the tranquillity of a late summer day. Minutes after he flagged young Jeremy Meyer to the side of the road, pulling the boy out of a distinct pale pink Jaguar XK coupe, the news was spreading that something had happened to Cynthia Smythe. Something bad. That this news was communicated with more glee than genuine grief betrayed the general dislike of the victim.

Old Finchley was a mixed basket of social climbers, *arrivistes* and genuine old money, all co-existing uneasily in the small village. Flanked by a leafy country club on one side and an expanse of nature preserve on the other, the area was decidedly upscale. Yet Cynthia Smythe still managed to out-snob her neighbours. Her china was that much thinner, her long massaged and oiled legs that much tanner, and her sweeping emerald-coloured lawn possessed that much more square footage.

Ten days earlier, on a languid sunny morning, Lydia Larouche was admiring this very turf as she slowly passed Cynthia Smythe's property on her way to the Gump Pony Club with petulant five-year-old Cerise in the back seat. Crawling to a stop, Lydia idled the engine while she studied her map. She hadn't been in the area for years. There had been no Gump Pony Club back when she was a child.

Lydia Larouche was readjusting to life in the village after the spectacular collapse of her marriage in Paris. Jean-Pierre had traded her in for a piece of arm candy – a ten-years-younger, skinny-as-a-greyhound, French bimbo. One glimpse in the mirror confirmed Lydia's suspicions that she was no longer in the arm-candy category. Alone in the wee hours of her now single bed, an unwelcome question would intrude: *Was I ever arm-candy to begin with?* She had always been too sporty, too dishevelled, too wide in the hip, too unwilling to sacrifice comfort for beauty.

But I'm fun! I'm witty! I'm intelligent! Her inner voice protested. Yes, she was all that. But Jean-Pierre had opted for the candy.

Now Lydia was back in the exclusive enclave of Old Finchley, living in the family home, which had been shut since her mother moved across country to a Palm Springs retirement community two years earlier. Almost twenty years Lydia had been married to Jean-Pierre, traipsing after him far and wide for his work, before they finally settled in Paris. For fourteen of those years she had tried and failed to produce a child. Finally, at age 41, she had borne him an heir – but it was the wrong gender. That, Lydia sensed, was the final coffin nail on their marriage, hammered in with the amount of weight she had gained during her pregnancy – most of which she had yet to unload.

Lydia was still consulting her GPS when Cynthia Smythe swept down her driveway in her pale pink Jaguar XK coupe, almost clipping Lydia's sedan. Peeking over the top of round Gucci sunglasses, Cynthia lowered her window a fraction.

May I help you?" she asked in a tone that succeeded in conveying the unspoken but unmistakable order: *Do not linger next to my property.*

But Lydia had only too much experience with this type of attitude from her years in Paris, where French women reigned when it came to cutting remarks and frigid looks.

Looking coolly about her Lydia asked, "Is this a private road?"

"No of course not, but you *are* very close to private property," came the clipped reply.

"But we *are* on a public road?"

"Yes," Cynthia was forced to concede, shaking her silvery blonde hair behind her shoulders.

"Alright then."

But now Cynthia was scrutinising Lydia in a most uncomfortable manner. She even let her car roll forward a few feet to get a better look.

"May *I* help *you*?" Lydia did not stint on the sarcasm.

"Haven't we met?" Cynthia queried.

"I don't think so," came the cool reply.

"Oh yes, I remember now," Cynthia murmured vaguely, lost in memory. "Don't you recognise me?"

"Not at all. Should I?"

"You're Lydia Hanson."

"I was," Lydia was forced to concur, reflecting that she should probably reassume her maiden name. Lydia occupied a sprig on the prestigious Hanson-Planter genealogical tree.

"It's me, Cynthia! Cynthia Smythe! We were at Miss Martin's together!" Miss Martin's was still the *de rigeur* private girl's school in the area.

Cynthia Smythe! For a second all went black before Lydia's eyes. She didn't think such a thing really happened – but she literally could not see. Instead she felt her blood pulsing in her eardrums. She was finally brought back to the moment by the familiar whining of Cerise.

"Let's *gooooo*!"

Obeying the child's demand for once, Lydia pressed her foot to the accelerator and sped away, heading, she hoped, in the general direction of the Gump Pony Club.

*****

A few days later, Cynthia was leafing through some travel brochures, trying to decide where she would winter this year. She was hesitating between Austria for two weeks of skiing or a cruise through the Maldives. She set aside the brochures and moved on to the more mundane task of scrutinising her financial statements. She was a shrewd investor and had ridden out the last economic downturn with very few losses. Interrupted by the doorbell, she sat working for another minute until the bell chimed again and she remembered that she was alone. Rosa had the day off and Manny, who took care of the garden, had gone into the village to pick up the rose bushes Cynthia had ordered.

Cynthia swept the door open only to wish she had left it shut. Her neighbour Skip O'Neal stood there grinning like an idiot and holding, of all things, a silver cocktail shaker and two glasses.

"Yes?" Cynthia said coolly.

"It's Thursday," Skip announced.

Cynthia raised her eyebrows and closed her large made-up eyes for a minute, giving Skip the facial expression for '*What the hell are you talking about?*'

"We made a date for drinks," Skip continued, his cheerfulness becoming slightly strained.

Cynthia was going to have to cut down on her drinking! She was forever making plans for things she forgot about afterward and would never in a million years agree to with a clear head. She looked at Skip's white nubuck loafers and crisp Ralph Lauren leisure suit. He looked like he had yachted over instead of trudging 200 yards up the road.

Cynthia reluctantly stepped aside to let him enter. The last thing she wanted was him knowing that she couldn't recall their conversation, which, she assumed, had taken place during Frank and Missy Pilcher's gold plate dinner fundraiser to obtain a new building for the police station. God knew those events were hard to get through without a steady stream of gimlets. She was still kicking herself for the size of the donation she had drunkenly made that night, the evidence of which had shown up on her bank statement three days later.

Skip strolled about her reception area appraising the furniture, paintings and carpets as if he were at an auction house. He made no bones about the fact that he wanted to "merge assets" with Cynthia. He had never made clear, however, what she stood to gain from the deal. She had successfully made her own way since her parents death in the crash of their private plane fifteen years earlier and she didn't need Skip's help – financial or otherwise. Besides, she was barely over forty. Even if she did want a steady companion, she would not have to stoop to the likes of someone who made his fortune developing adult diaper products! She had enough offers – in which she occasionally indulged – for brief, uncomplicated liaisons with men of her own ilk. God, how grateful these guys were for a woman who didn't want to establish a long-term agreement, or break up their marriages, but instead was randy, well-groomed, and capable of ordering *osso bucco* from a restaurant without turning the scene into a Professor Higgins-Eliza Doolittle duet. Besides, what neither Skip nor anyone else realized was that Manny the gardener serviced Cynthia regularly and satisfactorily in the *human relations* department – an arrangement that suited him just as well as it did her, she guessed.

Skip was now unflasking the cocktail shaker and pouring them both a vodkatini. Cynthia rolled her eyes but accepted the proffered drink. She supposed now was as good a time as ever to dispossess Skip of his delusions toward her. They were not cut from the same cloth and never had been.

"Shall we sit by the pool?" Cynthia asked smoothly, leading the way to the back garden without waiting for assent from Skip. The late afternoon air was fragrant, warm and still. Cynthia poured herself into a chaise lounge and sipped her drink. Skip *did* make a good vodkatini, she had to admit. She studied his tan face, the lines around his eyes becoming pronounced as he squinted at the sun's glare on the surface of her heart-shaped pool. She could tell his tan came from a bottle. There was nothing genuine about the man. His voice still held traces of the Pittsburgh neighbourhood where he grew up despite his effort to modulate the accent. She heard he even saw a speech therapist.

Cynthia was debating how best to broach the subject when Skip raised a topic of his own.

"I saw Lydia Larouche last night."

"Who?" This was not something Cynthia was expecting.

"Oh, that's right. She was Lydia Hanson-Planter when you knew her."

"I didn't know you two knew each other," Cynthia replied for something to say. Was this his attempt at name-dropping?

"Oh, I know Lydia all right." He gave Cynthia a wink.

What – was he banging her or something?

"In fact I'm the one who convinced her to come back to our little village."

Cynthia recalled that Skip was often abroad. Apparently older Europeans needed diapering as much as their American counterparts.

"Yeah, she was going to stay in her Paris apartment, but what did she have there that was hers, really? Her husband was her whole life."

"You seem to know a lot about it," Cynthia commented.

"Oh yes. I know a lot. The *whole* story you could say."

Again she had the impression that he was implying something. She recalled the strange manner in which Lydia had fled upon hearing her name.

Manny was back with the roses. She watched him carry the plants, the root balls still swathed in burlap, to the poolside area where they were to be planted. They looked even more spectacular than they had in the catalogue.

"Yep," Skip repeated, "I know it all."

What the hell was he getting at?

"If you have something to say, Skip, just say it," Cynthia snapped.

"Don't worry about me…I would never *say* anything," Skip said. "But you should really consider the offer I made the other night."

What offer? And what the heck had Missy Pilcher put in those gimlet cocktails? She had to remember to eat something before these events!

Cynthia watched Manny take a spade and dig a hole in the ground. His firm shoulders flexed with effort under his t-shirt. She felt Skip's beady eyes watching her appraise Manny. Enough was enough. She stood up and handed Skip his cocktail shaker.

"Thank you so much for dropping by," she said firmly.

As he reached for the shaker, Skip put his hand over hers and squeezed hard. Too hard.

"Fine," he hissed. "Play it cool. But married women band together and close ranks when one of them has been wronged. Remember that. This is a small village. Lydia Larouche knows all about you and Jean-Pierre. And she's got more than a big ass – she has a big mouth too."

"Let go," Cynthia shrilled. Manny was standing, his hand resting on the spade, watching the scene.

Skip let go of her hand and headed back into the house. He flung open the front door.

"A lot of women would be thrilled to receive the offer I made you," he said harshly.

"Well, I'm not 'a lot of women', am I?" she retorted,

wondering again what that damn offer was.

"Nobody humiliates Skip O'Neal!" he proclaimed.

"Are you *threatening* me? You're no longer in some Pittsburgh slum, Skip," Cynthia's lip curled with disdain.

Skip turned purple with rage.

"If you can't act the part around here, maybe you better go back!" she flung at him, adding, "And take your adult diapers with you!"

"You'll pay for this," he spat at her.

"I'll have the police after you if you threaten me again!" Cynthia retorted.

"Who? McDonall – the village idiot? Don't make me laugh! You go to him and your news will be all over town before you can blink an eye."

Cynthia slammed the door. She turned the lock for good measure and stood watching out the window until he had trekked to the end of her driveway and back down the road toward his house. It was true –incompetent, blundering Pete McDonall would turn the skirmish into a source of gossip for weeks. The damn village didn't even need policing. Nothing ever happened. Cynthia thought again of the donation for the new police station she had made under the influence and another flash of anger shuddered through her.

*****

The next day, Cynthia was sitting in front of her computer, frustratedly manoeuvring the mouse around to get the little arrow to appear on the screen. She suspected that Rosa, her day maid, had been using it again behind her back. Rosa neglected to delete the history of her movements, and Cynthia had already seen from the sites visited that the woman was actively seeking employment elsewhere. Cynthia hadn't said a word, but she continued monitoring the dumpy woman's Internet activities. Besides the job hunt, she learned that Rosa was looking to rent a moving van and, more importantly, that she had investigated more than one tacky bail bonds website. Then all activity ceased. But the mouse had been fine yesterday and Cynthia wondered if Rosa wasn't helping herself again. Honestly, she was going to have to let the woman go. She also wondered what else Rosa might be indulging in during Cynthia's frequent absences. There seemed to be postage stamps and stationery missing, but she couldn't be certain.

Succeeding to get the little arrow back on the screen, she decided to check the history again. There it was: another bail bonds site. And what was this? A Google search for rodenticides, and another for Strychnine. How strange. She doubted Rosa could pronounce *Strychnine* let alone spell it. Wasn't that something the pool maintenance company used to get rid of the rats last summer? Were the rats back? Surely Manny, the gardener, would have said something? Just then Rosa came into the room. Once again, Cynthia noticed that she was refusing to wear the black skirt and white blouse Cynthia had specified. She looked brazenly at Cynthia, who responded by glanced pointedly at the computer then back at Rosa.

"Everything okay, Rosa?"

"Yes, Miss Cynthia."

"You finding everything you need?"

"Yes, yes, fine." Rosa continued through the room to the kitchen where she started humming as she cleaned the countertops.

She's a cool one, Cynthia mused. They were the worst kind. Better to be rid of her now. Things would only get worse.

Cynthia picked up her handbag and followed Rosa into the kitchen. She took out her check book and started scribbling. If nothing else, you could always buy your way out of a scene with these people. Two months' salary ought to be sufficient. It was too bad. Rosa was efficient – the crystal and silver had rarely gleamed so bright. More importantly, Rosa was discreet. She took it in stride when she brought Cynthia her morning coffee only to find both sides of the bed occupied, placing the porcelain coffee service on the night table without missing a beat. Poor Rosa – she had even walked in on one of Cynthia's guests when he was *al fresco*. Cynthia smiled at the memory. She had almost forgotten about that little episode. Who was that? How funny – she remembered his body (particularly a certain part) but could no longer see his face. It had been an evening *bien arrosé* with a very good champagne. He was that industrialist, no? The Frenchman. Jean-Marc? Jean-Patrice? Cynthia suddenly paled. Larouche. Jean-Somebody Larouche. So that's what all the fuss was about. She had had no idea. She thought he had no connections to the village. He said he was en route for the Business without Borders conference being held in the city. He was probably visiting that kid. Or settling the final terms for the divorce. Men. They were all selfish lying bastards at heart.

The phone rang. Rosa reached for it, but Cynthia waved her hand away. She'd been getting strange calls for over a week now and would prefer no one knew about them. Especially not her staff. She knew how these people gossiped amongst themselves. Wasn't it Rosa who told her about Dee Dee Martin's botched tummy tuck? Rosa learned about it from Dee Dee's Ines. Cynthia sighed. That was another thing she would miss about Rosa: getting the dirt on her neighbors. But, she remembered, that was a two-way street. She couldn't be certain that Rosa wasn't divulging some of Cynthia's escapades. The phone stopped ringing. Cynthia waited until the answering machine started flashing then hit the playback button and picked up the receiver to listen.

"You whore!" There followed a jumble of expletives worthy of a truck driver in rush hour traffic, all spat down the phone with violent animosity.

Cynthia quietly hung up. Whoever was calling seemed to be using one of those devices that alter the voice. Either that or the caller was sucking regularly on a helium balloon. The voice was unnaturally high-pitched. But whether it was male or female Cynthia had yet to determine. She was leaning toward female. Maybe she should get a guard dog. If only she didn't despise animals!

She should call the police. But no, she mused. Skip O'Neal was right about Pete McDonall and his big mouth. Cynthia recalled how the domestic dispute the lumbering police officer was called upon to quell last Christmas had rapidly became fodder for the village tongue-waggers. By New Year's everyone in the village knew that Chip Squire had drunkenly threatened his wife Marjory with a carving knife while slicing the Christmas goose. No, Cynthia couldn't report the obscene calls. She valued her privacy even more than her safety.

Cynthia picked up her check book and followed Rosa to the patio where the woman was brushing down the teak table.

Manny was fussing again with the rose bushes. They weren't doing well – the heavy buds drooped in the late summer heat. Cynthia finished writing the check and handed it to Rosa, who froze in mid-motion, her hand holding the little wooden brush above the table as she looked at the check and then up at Cynthia.

"What is this, Miss Cynthia?" Rosa usually received her pay in cash at the end of the month.

"It's a check. I'm including two month's severance pay plus this month's full salary."

"But why?"

"I won't need your services anymore, Rosa." Cynthia started back toward the house, but Rosa stopped her with her next words.

"I don't think so, Miss Cynthia."

Cynthia turned around. "Rosa, two month's severance is more than generous. I'm not obliged to –".

"I think I decide when I leave here," Rosa refused to meet her eyes, but she spoke with a firmness Cynthia had never before heard.

"Rosa, I hardly think the decision to let you go rests with you."

"I do," Rosa's voice was calm, but her dark eyes glinted with something – could it be menace?

Cynthia was enraged.

"What the hell are you saying? Don't you understand basic English, for Christ's sake?"

Rosa resumed brushing the table again slowly. "Maybe the

tax people like to hear about my employment with you," she said almost inaudibly.

So that was it: a clumsy, amateurish attempt at blackmail.

Cynthia pursed her lips. She had been paying Rosa cash since she engaged her almost four months ago. She meant to get around to declaring her legally, but so often these people didn't work out – case in point with Rosa – and why go through all that paperwork until she was sure?

She sensed Rosa was bluffing. Well, Cynthia also knew how to bluff.

"So? What's the worse they can throw at me? A fine?" Cynthia quickly dismissed a fleeting image of herself in prison stripes.

Cynthia once again proffered the check. Rosa ignored it.

"Or maybe," Rosa said coolly, "Mrs. Roger Pennybank would like to know what her husband was doing here last month in the middle of the night? Or maybe Mrs. Buckins-Grail be interested in a phone call from me…"

"Okay, I get it," Cynthia snapped. She could have slapped Rosa and would have done if Manny wasn't still messing with those damn roses. "What do you want?"

"Like I said – I decide when I leave – not you," and with that Rosa turned on her heel and swept past Cynthia into the house.

There was one thing in life Cynthia could not stand: insubordination. Her face turned hot with fury. She charged into the house, snatched up Rosa's shabby leather handbag, and came up behind the maid, hustling the small woman toward the front door.

"Now you listen to me. You just lost yourself two month's pay. Get out and don't ever come back. And you tell anyone anything – you even breathe my name – I'll hire someone to track you down and tear out your tongue."

"I can go to the police. You're threatening me," Rosa said, although a note of doubt was creeping into her voice.

"I dare you," Cynthia responded coolly. "You're forgetting who just donated to the fund-raiser for the new police station. I'm practically paying for the whole damn building myself."

"You think you can buy your way out of anything," Rosa protested, but tears of defeat were glittering in her eyes.

"Because I *can*!"

The two women stood glaring at each other on the front porch until Cynthia finally reached out and gave Rosa a little shove on the breastbone, pushing her backward off the step. She then turned back into the house, slamming the door so hard the hug bay window shook dangerously in its casing.

*****

Lydia Larouche had just conducted an internet image search of Cynthia Smythe. Dozens of photos popped up on the screen. There was Cynthia at a cancer charity in the city, looking tall and slim and elegant in a black sheath dress set off with red strappy Manolo Blahnik sandals. Cynthia at the opera gala opening, her long silver-blonde mane spilling down the bare back of her retro Halston halter gown. Cynthia even in bloody Egypt, squatting in front of a sarcophagus in crisp khaki shorts and blouse. What was it Jean-Pierre said during one of their final post-divorce blow-ups?

"There are many America womans who manage to be chic

– why don't you ask someone like that Cynthia Smythe woman for her diet tips?"

"How do you know Cynthia Smythe?" Lydia had queried sharply.

"Through you, *non*?" Jean-Pierre had replied coolly, but not before Lydia had seen a fleeting yet unmistakable trace of exasperation at his blunder cross his face.

Lydia's stomach churned with rage at the memory. Women like Cynthia shouldn't be allowed to live.

*****

Where the hell was Manny? Cynthia was more than a little upset and hoped that one of his "massages" might restore her nerves. The idiot must have gone into the village to get more fertiliser for the rose bushes.

*****

The members of the charity steering committee were only mildly annoyed when Cynthia failed to show up at the autumn kick-off meeting. Used to her frequent absences, they were scarcely surprised that she accepted to coordinate for upcoming fundraiser without even bothering to turn up to the planning session.

*****

When young Jeremy Meyers came to skim the growing scum off Cynthia's pool the next morning, he was stumped. After ringing the door-bell several times, Jeremy pounded vigorously on the door. When his efforts failed to get a response, Jeremy was unsure what to do. Miss Cynthia or her maid always came out front to open the side gate so he could get to the pool with his equipment. Besides, he could see Miss Cynthia's pink Jaguar glinting in the dark cavernous garage.

Maybe she was going out? Why else would the garage door be gaping wide open? A car like that should be tucked out of sight. Jeremy was still working on a plan to get Miss Cynthia to take him for a ride in it; perhaps by pulling a spark plug out of his dad's van (*Meyer's Pool Supply and Maintenance*) then asking Miss Cynthia for a ride back to the shop. Riding through the village in that car with Miss Cynthia at his side would be heaven.

Yet if Miss Cynthia wasn't home, why could he see the flickering images from her enormous flat-screen TV through the window? What if Miss Cynthia was hurt!

Jeremy crept round the side of the house and managed to scramble over the gate. He peered through a crack in the drawn curtains of the living room window. Boy it was dark in there. He clambered onto the window ledge, knocking off a terracotta planter of cherry tomatoes in the process. Uh-oh. Miss Cynthia wasn't going to like that. Perched precariously on the ledge, his pudgy body wavering back and forth, he had to grasp the window for support. But the window swung open, tumbling Jeremy into the room. Cracking his head sharply on the coffee table on his way down, tears filled Jeremy's eyes. The pain was blinding.

When he touched the spot on his forehead, blood came away, red and sticky. He pulled himself up into a crawling position. As he did, his hand touched something both clammy and bristly at the same time. He blinked his eyes, trying to adjust to the dark room. Looking down, he pulled his hand away in horror. It was resting on Miss Cynthia's naked crotch. Jeremy lurched backward, knocking a vase off the coffee table as his back smacked into it. He could feel blood pooling in his eyebrow. Was she sleeping? Was she playing a trick? His brother Henry did that – sprawling motionless until Jeremy leant over him then suddenly lurching up screaming. Jeremy didn't find it funny.

But Miss Cynthia wasn't moving. Jeremy's eyes roved curiously up her body, resting first on the furry mound he had inadvertently touched, the hair of which was trimmed into the shape of a heart. He'd never seen that – not in the magazines he had found in a shoe box at the back of his father's closet and now consulted regularly. Cynthia's legs were splayed open. Leaning his head sideways, he could just see the fissure between her thighs. He looked at her smooth stomach and large pale breasts, spilling flatly across her chest.

Stop looking! He ordered himself. But he couldn't. She was better than anything he'd seen in his dad's magazines. Finally, he forced his eyes up to her face and froze in terror. Blood blackened her mouth and leaked from her nose. He now noticed the large seeping stain spreading on the rug beneath her. Jeremy stood up and groped about for the light switch. Finally finding it, he snapped it on – then almost turned it off again. Had her hand just twitched? Was she alive? Did he just hear a noise? Was someone else still in the house? Jeremy's mind bubbled with panic.

He noticed on the sofa her open handbag, a set of keys visible inside. The keys to her Jaguar. Jeremy had a brilliant idea. He could take the Jaguar and fetch Police Chief McDonall. It would surely be quicker than his dad's van. His brother Henry said jaguars were the fastest. Or had that been the animal? No matter. He would fetch the police and they would catch whoever did this before they got away. Jeremy would be a hero. For once in his life. Miss Cynthia would still be alive and she would love him for saving her. Buoyed by the thought, he grabbed Cynthia's car keys. He better take her handbag too. Someone might come back and take her money.

After several jolting stops and starts, Jeremy finally got the car down the driveway. It sure was different from Dad's van. The slightest pressure on the accelerator and the car lurched forward. Same thing with the brakes. Super touchy. Boy, he was going to have to be careful.

*****

There was even more twitching of lace curtains as Chief McDonall clamped handcuffs on Jeremy's wrists and placed him in the backseat of the police cruiser. The police station was less than a block away, they could have walked there faster. Still, Pete McDonall reasoned, he needed to get the car back to the station somehow. He had to admit, he wasn't used to making arrests.

After inspecting Cynthia's house and calling in the coroner, Pete McDonall was back at the station, sitting behind his ample desk, trying to remain patient.

"So, you're saying she was naked when you found her?"

Poor Jeremy. He never could express himself well.

Seated on the other side of the desk, he reddened and became tongue-tied when asked about the bloody fingerprint found on Cynthia's pubis. Guilt flushed through him as he recalled how he'd leered at her nude body.

Nor could Jeremy explain how he got inside Cynthia's house or why there were signs of a scuffle (including the gash on his forehead). He became completely inarticulate when asked why he was speeding through the village in Cynthia's Jaguar with her handbag on the floor of the car.

Most damning of all was the poison found in Cynthia's coffee – Strychnine mixed with additives – the same combination that was in the brand of rodent poison Jeremy used to keep the local vermin under control. An open pint bottle of the stuff was found in his Dad's van.

As far as Pete McDonall was concerned, it was an open-and-shut affair. He called for the county sheriff to come and pick up Jeremy. He could scarcely wait to get to church Bingo that night to spill the lurid details.

*****

Throughout the village, a mild quiver of guilt accompanied the much bigger frisson of excitement created by the news of Cynthia's murder. With no true feelings of grief, the villagers were free to give full reign to their speculations. Many were more upset about young Jeremy Meyer than Cynthia's death. Okay, Jeremy was a bit odd, something of a loner. But still! He was so nice and polite! It just went to show. You just never knew anyone. Cynthia quickly came to blame. She teased him. She was a temptress. Look at the way she ran around in that pink car, flirting with other people's husbands. Was it any wonder? She drove him to it.

Certain members of the village, however, were feeling disconcerted. Rosa went to church and lit a candle for Miss Cynthia. She considered going to confession – but why push her luck? Jeremy was clearly the perpetrator, so why muddy the waters by admitting to her own murderous thoughts?

Lydia Larouche, meanwhile, worried that Pete McDonall might go through Cynthia's phone records, tracing the obscene calls she'd placed to Cynthia. How would she explain those? She was counting on his incompetence and laziness to keep her safe.

Skip regretted having badmouthed Cynthia to more than one society matron. What if his name cropped up as a suspect? Lucky thing that the evidence so clearly incriminated young Jeremy, even though Skip, like most of the villagers, could hardly imagine Jeremy doing such a thing.

Yes, three people were feeling especially culpable – not because any of them actually killed Cynthia – but because they had each one fervently wished her dead. To escape their potential implication in the murder, each one perpetuated arguments to further incriminate poor Jeremy. Rosa spread stories of how Jeremy always ogled Cynthia when he came to clean the pool. Lydia saw Jeremy trying to talk to Cerise when he came to clean her pool, which was weird, if you thought about it. Skip thought he saw the Meyer's van passing slowly by Cynthia's house late at night.

Curiously, the one person who should have felt guilty had no remorse. After using Cynthia's check book to spring his girlfriend from jail on a bail bond, he was already hundreds of miles away, driving a rental van loaded with Cynthia's best artwork, carpets, jewellery, and silver, along with a huge wad of cash from her safe. No, Manny didn't feel guilty. In fact, he felt a surge of elation as he contemplated that, from now on, the only rose bushes he'd be tending would be his own.

Live Free or Die
Judy Penz Sheluk

The first time any of us met Jack he was wearing a dark green suit. That seemed odd to me. It wasn't St. Patrick's Day, and the office attire was mostly business casual, with an emphasis on the casual. This was especially true in "cubicle hell," where an overworked staff of four plus supervisor made collection calls and routinely canceled insurance policies for non-payment.

Later, Jack would confide in me that the green suit was his only suit. "Wear a green suit and everyone assumes you must own a black one, a brown one, and a blue one," he had said, and I had to admit it made sense. But the first time I met him, my only thought was, "Green suit, can't be from around here."

I should have known Jack was going to be trouble right from the beginning. In my defense I was twenty-one to his thirty-one, and until a few months before, when I'd been dumped for a girl with the improbable name of Ankh, I'd had the same boyfriend throughout high school.

Anyway, my inexperience with men aside, there was something riveting about Jack. It was more than his stature—six-feet-two with the build of an athlete; you could imagine six-pack abs and muscled thighs—more than the penetrating stare of eyes a bluish shade of tanzanite verging on violet. It was as if he wore his charisma like a suit of armor and polished it up every morning.

Jack came to the company as an efficiency expert, imported from the U.S. Head Office in Portsmouth, New Hampshire, to the Canadian head office in Toronto. The suburb of Don Mills to be exact.

Apparently we were inefficient at collecting monies owed. I could have told them it was because we tended to empathize with the insured, if only because we were all stone broke ourselves. Thanks to our minimum wage jobs and age-rated auto insurance, most of us couldn't afford to pay the premiums, let alone own a car. Extending payment terms for a week or two, where was the harm in that?

My first mistake was agreeing to have lunch with Jack, though to be fair, he asked all five of us in the Credit Department, each on a separate day. My day of the week was Friday. Jack made me feel as though he'd saved the best for last.

He drove a midnight blue Chevy pick-up with a front bench seat and extended cab. The license plate included the message, "LIVE FREE OR DIE," which Jack informed me was the State motto of New Hampshire. I preferred Ontario's more mundane "YOURS TO DISCOVER," but I'll admit to being somewhat biased.

I suppose I was expecting a sandwich at the local deli, or maybe fish and chips from Captain Sam's, given it was Friday. Both were just south of the office, and regular hangouts for the many white-collar workers in the area. But Jack drove west on Eglinton. Clearly we were going to take more than my allotted hour for lunch.

"Molly tells me you like authentic Mexican," Jack said, not taking his eyes off the road. "I was in Toronto a few years back.

I remember a decent place on Yonge Street. Viva something-or-the-other."

Molly was my supervisor. I wondered how the subject of my food preferences had come up. "Molly told you that I like Mexican food?"

Jack grinned, his teeth flashing in the sunlight. "Let's just say I was curious about you."

The Mexican restaurant was no longer in business, but that didn't stop Jack. He navigated the truck into a tight parking spot along the street, hopped out, put change in the meter, opened my door, and led me to a British-style pub a couple of blocks down.

"It's not Mexican, but I was here a couple of nights ago," he said. "Typical pub food, but a good atmosphere, and a nice selection of draft beer."

I don't like beer, but the idea of dining out in a pub on a workday lunch hour had a certain charm. "I could go for an order of bangers and mash," I said, trying to demonstrate my worldly knowledge of tavern fare.

"So could I," Jack said, and chuckled softly. I got the distinct impression we weren't talking about the same thing, and found that I didn't necessarily mind. It had been a long time since Norbert had dumped me.

Lunch lasted a couple of hours, during which time I found myself telling Jack my life story, or at least the *Reader's Digest* version. I even told him my real name was Emerald, although everyone called me Emmy. It was only after we were headed back to the office that I realized he hadn't shared anything about himself.

"How long are you going to be in Toronto?" I asked.

"For a while. I'm starting with the Credit Department, but

there are inefficiencies in all areas of the company that need to be identified and resolved."

"So you're moving here?"

Jack nodded. "I have a one-year contract. The company found me a rental apartment near Fairview Mall. But I'll be doing surprise audits in other cities now and again. I'll also be going home to New Hampshire for a few days every three weeks or so. To be honest, I'm already homesick. It's lonely, not knowing anyone."

"You've met a few people in the office, though, haven't you? I mean, besides those of us in Credit?"

"Oh sure, but it's not like anyone's really opened up to me. Not the way you did, Emerald."

"Emmy," I said, embarrassed. "And you're just being kind. I probably bored you to tears."

"Not at all. As a matter of fact, I'd like to get to know you quite a bit better."

And that's the way it started. We spent every moment of the weekend together, walking downtown for hours, taking in the CN Tower, the Eaton's Centre, Yorkville, Yonge Street, City Hall, old and new. We made plans to visit the Royal Ontario Museum, the Art Gallery of Ontario—even the Bata Shoe Museum. Jack's thirst to see and experience everything was contagious, and I found myself being a tourist in my own hometown, and loving every minute of it.

We were driving back to his place late Saturday night when he mentioned that it might be best if we keep our friendship a secret. "Not that we have anything to hide," he said, "but why fan the flames?" I thought about my co-workers, gossips each and every one of them, and my supervisor, Molly, who didn't appear to care much for Jack—likely because she felt her job was in jeopardy—and decided he was probably right.

"Okay." I edged myself closer to the passenger door, not quite sure what else to say.

"Why don't you slide over here, Emmy," Jack said, patting the seat beside him. "Otherwise, folks might think we're married."

*****

It was about six weeks later when Molly came to my desk, carrying a card and a large brown envelope. Jack was back home in New Hampshire for a few days, returning midweek. I missed him.

"I'm collecting for the Jack and Jill shower on Wednesday," she said, handing me the card and the envelope. "Whatever you can afford."

I looked at the card, which had an image of a man and woman holding hands and standing under a white umbrella, a glittery rainbow behind them. It was the first I'd heard about a Jack and Jill shower, but then again, I'd kept pretty much to myself since getting involved with Jack. It was safer that way.

"Who's getting married?"

Molly gave me an odd look. "Well, Jack, of course, and what's totally ironic is that his fiancée's name is actually Jill. I thought he would have told you that day at lunch. You were gone long enough. Say you weren't…"

"Of course not," I said, fighting the urge to throw up.

"It's just that Jack developed a bit of a reputation as a womanizer the last time he was here. Of course, that was five years ago. He could have changed."

It was the way she said it, more than what she said, that made me realize why Molly didn't care for Jack. And it had nothing whatsoever to do with job security.

Five years ago, Molly had been me.

*****

"He slept with you, didn't he?" Jill spoke so quietly I almost convinced myself she didn't say it. I took a deviled egg from the paper plate on my lap and popped half of it in my mouth, trying to look nonchalant.

"Didn't he?" Jill said, again. Her otherwise pale cheeks had bright red splotches on them, as if someone had decided to paint a clown's face on her.

Jack was standing at the other side of the room, his back to us. He was laughing at something one of the sales guys had said. He hadn't said one word to me since he'd gotten back. Hadn't given me so much as a passing glance.

"I didn't know about you, Jill. You have to believe me. I'm not the kind … I know what it feels like…"

Jill looked over at Jack, who was still kibitzing with the sales team, then back at me. "We need to talk. Somewhere private. Tonight, when Jack's out drinking with his buddies."

I agreed to meet her for dinner at a local Italian restaurant known for its great food, good wine, and generously proportioned booths—an entirely sensible combination of public and private. After all, I had no idea what Jill wanted to discuss with me, but I was pretty sure she wasn't going to ask me to be in the wedding party.

*****

"Let me start by saying that I believe you, Emmy," Jill said.

We were sitting near the back of the Italian restaurant—our choice given it was a Wednesday night and there was plenty of available seating. We'd ordered a liter of house red and a basket of bruschetta to split as an appetizer. The whole thing felt a bit surreal.

"I appreciate that you're taking my word for it," I said, fingering a piece of bruschetta. I didn't have the appetite to bite into it.

"It's not like you were the first. And you're unlikely to be the last." Jill studied the diamond ring on her left hand. "I suppose I thought once we were engaged Jack would stop misbehaving."

"How long have you been engaged?"

"Three months. About a month longer than you've been sleeping with him, if my math is correct."

It was. "You're still willing to marry him?"

"I suppose you think that's pathetic."

I thought about my initial reaction when I found out about Norbert and Ankh. Devastation, certainly, but also a sense of determination, an irrational desire to win Norbert back, if only to be the dumper versus the dumpee. "I understand what it's like to invest years in a person. You don't want to think it was all a big waste of time."

Jill nodded. "That's exactly how I felt before we got engaged. But now I'm done. Finished. You were the last straw. No offense."

"None taken."

"Good. Now, the way I figure it, Jack owes both of us, and more than just an apology. What I'm wondering is, how would you like to get even?"

"Get even with Jack?"

Jill nodded again. "You see I have a plan and I need your help to pull it off."

*****

There are times when you have to commit a crime to prevent an even bigger one. At least, that's what I tell myself when I

263

can't sleep at night.

I'm not going to go into a lot of detail here. Suffice it to say that if we had implemented Jill's original plan we both could have done twenty-five to life. What did either of us know about guns? As much as I hated Jack in the moment, as much as I commiserated with Jill, I wasn't about to go to prison for either one of them.

Which is exactly why I came up with my own plan.

I never said it was perfect.

*****

"Live free or die." Jill and I spoke the rehearsed lines in perfect unison when Jack walked through the door. We were standing in Jack's apartment, and by the shocked look on his face, he wasn't expecting to find his fiancée and mistress waiting for him.

"What are you two talking about?"

"Live free," I began.

"Or die," Jill finished.

"Free of the cushy job that allows you to travel across North America and pick up unsuspecting women," I said. "Women who don't know that you're already spoken for."

"Free of all your money—well, actually, free of anything you own of value," Jill said. "I just wish the pick-up truck was black. I've never been a fan of midnight blue."

"You can always trade it in, Jill, maybe get a nice little sports car," I said. "A black one."

"I'm not sure I'm following," Jack said, but it was clear from the hint of perspiration forming on his forehead and upper lip that he was getting the gist of it.

"It's actually very simple," I said. "Tomorrow morning, you're going to hand in your resignation, citing personal reasons. Then you're going to go back to New Hampshire on your own dime."

"Except you won't have a dime—or a vehicle, come to that," Jill added. "Because you're going to transfer all of your money into my personal bank account. And your vehicle ownership into my name. Don't worry, we'll come with you so you don't screw it up."

"What you're asking is preposterous," Jack said, his face flushed. "Why would I do any of that?"

"Because if you don't, I'll have to tell upper management how you took advantage of your position of authority and how you coerced me into bed." I leaned back into the wall. "Perhaps I'll even hire a lawyer, file a sexual harassment suit. The company would love that."

"Maybe I wasn't completely upfront with you," Jack said, "but there was no coercion." He turned to face Jill. "As for the money and the truck, you're delusional if you think I'm just going to hand it over."

"It's called payback time, Jack, for being a liar and a cheat." Jill folded her arms in front of her. "Consider it a pre-nup, without the nuptials."

"Of course, you're perfectly free to ignore the 'live free' part of this plan," I said.

That got Jack's interest. "What happens if I decide to do that? Ignore the 'live free' part?"

"Ah," Jill said. "That's where the 'or die' part comes in."

Jack had the nerve to laugh, the smug S.O.B. "You two? You're threatening to kill me? Just how do you propose to do that?"

"Let's just say that you'd never see it coming," Jill said.

I nodded and tried to look menacing.

I'm not sure Jack believed us, but in the end he chose to live free. Who wouldn't, given the option? After all, living free had its benefits—at least you were living without the threat of death hovering like a dark shadow.

There were some negotiations, of course. I like to think we were reasonable in our demands, and the reality is that despite his philandering ways, Jill still wanted to marry Jack. Especially since she'd found out she was pregnant. I didn't pretend to understand—surely she and the baby would be better off without him—but it wasn't my place to judge.

We eventually agreed that Jack could keep his job. That Jill would move into his apartment. They'd get married earlier than planned, given Jill was now with child. And that way we could both keep an eye on him, me at work, her at home. Ultimately, it would mean more money for Jill and the baby, since his paycheck was going to be directly deposited into her personal bank account. All Jack had to do was stay on the straight and narrow.

Some men never learn.

*****

"Seriously," Molly said. "A green suit? At a funeral?"

I didn't tell her it was Jack's only suit. Maybe when they'd dated five years ago, he had other suits. Suits no longer in style, or maybe too big or too small. Maybe he'd lied to me and had a closetful, ready to pull out for a special occasion. It hardly mattered any longer.

"I don't mind the green," I said, more for something to say than anything else.

We both stared at the open casket, at Jack's hands clasped loosely together in front of his stomach. The mortician had done a good job of disguising the damage from the accident. I could have said Jack looked at peace, but I didn't believe it.

"A true tragedy," Molly said. "Jack falling into the subway tracks like that." She gave me an odd look, eyebrows raised, lips pursed. "Do you…do you think he'd been drinking?"

"I don't know." And I didn't. All I knew was that the ruling of accidental death would haunt me forever.

Jill was sitting in a pew at the side of the chapel, a black lace shawl draped loosely around her shoulders, her face bent down in prayer. For a moment, I thought she glanced my way, but I couldn't be certain. The next time I looked, her eyes were averted, a solitary teardrop finding its way down her face.

When the Curtain Fell

Joan Hall Hovey

Lanie took the letter her secretary and good friend Blake Nelson handed her, already feeling a sinking in her stomach just from the expression on his face. She wasn't wrong. It was from Tim Frawley, her old English teacher, and drama coach. God, so long ago since she had even heard his name. But she'd thought of him. She pictured him, tall and slim, glasses perched on his aquiline nose, moving around the stage like a cat as he called out notes and made constructive comments. He had so much enthusiasm for his subject, his dramatic instinct impeccable.

The familiar logo at the top of the letter, intertwined in red and silver ribbon—Port Ainsley High School—the school she'd run away from, the town she'd escaped, nearly fifteen years ago.

Mr. Frawley had heaped high praise on her in the letter, saying how proud they all were of her, complimenting her on her accomplishments over the years. "You know I've always said you were a fine actress," he'd written. "And now everyone knows."

How she'd wanted to please Mr. Frawley. How she adored him. And in the end, she'd let him down. Nancy Cole, her understudy had saved the day after she'd fled the building. The show must go on. She wanted to hate Nancy, too, but no one could hate Nancy. Perhaps she could be forgiven for not being overly happy for her.

While it warmed her to read Mr. Frawley's kind words, at the same time they took her to a place from which she couldn't seem to escape. She went back there now, an image of her mother rising to the screen of her mind. She was asleep on the living room sofa, snoring softly. The blanket Lanie (Jenny back then) had draped over her mother earlier now covered her face, showing only the top of her head, the mass of black, curly hair. Her mother had beautiful hair. Lanie's was straight and light brown, like her father's.

The smell of alcohol wafted up to her, a little less potent than when her mom came stumbling in just after 3:00 am.

Ever since daddy left and moved in with his new girlfriend three months ago, mom had sunk deeper and deeper into a dark depression coupled with wild mood swings. She'd go from cursing her, bellowing things like, *You're just like your goddamn father* to *I don't know what I'd do without you.* Sometimes she just sat staring into space, tears streaming down her face. And then the string of sleazy men came into their lives. It made Lanie feel ashamed. Especially the way a couple of them had looked at her, like they were stripping her clothes off with their eyes, sneakily of course. She felt sorry for her mother, and at other times she just felt contempt for her. Why couldn't she just pull herself together? Accept what happened and move forward in her life. Where did my sweet, funny, loving mother go? Daddy sent her away, she thought. He broke her heart. He broke her spirit.

"Where did you go, Lanie?"

Blake's voice brought her back to the present, to her apartment, softly scented with cut flowers and herbs from her window boxes. The oak floors gleamed and her eggshell walls were hung with her favorite paintings, a few nice prints, and some fine originals done by local artists. She reminded herself how very blessed she was.

She handed Blake back the letter in which her old teacher had invited her to return to play the role of Susy Hendrix in **After Dark**, a terrific thriller Audrey Hepburn had starred in on-screen. She'd played a recently blinded woman terrorized by a trio of thugs as they search for a heroin-stuffed doll they believed was in her apartment. This production was to be a fundraiser for renovations, including new, 'badly needed', stage curtains. They were needed even when she was there. "If you could see your way clear, Ms. Nichols, we'd be so honored..." They would stage it on dates to accommodate her busy career.

Ms. Nichols. She smiled almost sadly. He'd always called her Jenny. Her real name - Jenny Beddow. The name sounded strange to her as if it belonged to someone else. She was getting enough work now that she'd probably been recognized by a smattering of people in her home town. She was on Facebook and fan letters were being forwarded through her agent. It was no doubt how Mr. Frawley found her.

Sweet man, she thought. Mr. Frawley, always in her corner. He'd come to the house that night while she was packing to make her escape. He'd knocked several times and called to her through the door, but she didn't answer. Hard to answer when you're choking on tears of shame and disappointment. After a while, she heard his footsteps retreating down the stairs.

Landing the role of Shakespeare's Juliet had been a dream come true. Not that it came as a huge surprise to read her name - Jennifer Beddow - on the cast list taped on the classroom door. She'd felt good about her audition. You usually knew when you fell short. That hadn't changed. She was by nature a shy person. Yet she was at home on stage. She came alive on stage.

"It's an opportunity to finally put this behind you," Blake said, reluctantly taking the letter from her outstretched hand and setting it atop the growing pile of fan letters. Blake was younger than Lanie by eight years, boyishly handsome, and gay. He was not only her guy Friday, but her best friend and house-mate, had been for five years now. He'd come to Paul's Restaurant one afternoon where she waitressed and asked if he could put up an ad. She'd been there since she landed in Toronto; Paul Madison had a soft spot for actors and scheduled her hours around her auditions.

Blake had been looking for office work. He had a diploma in communications and time management, a course he took online. It turned out he had a natural ability to organize and people liked him. He'd been living in his car back then. Later, she learned he'd recently broken up with a long-time boyfriend and was also a struggling playwright. She knew about struggling. She looked at the ad for several days, then a few days later called him.

As for her, there'd been a couple of promising romances along the way, one that saw an impressive diamond ring on her finger, but her friendship with Blake was the only one that had endured. Blake still dated, but nothing serious. He was spending most evenings with his dad who was in a nursing home and sadly, no longer knew his son. "He never did know me," he told Lanie. "Didn't want to."

"Lanie," he said, now bringing her back to the issue at hand. "You didn't let what happened back then stop you from pursuing your dream to become an actress. Face your demons once and for all. You can do this; you should do this."

"I know you think so. But no. Please, just make my excuses. Send a generous donation on my behalf."

"Give it some thought at least. Sleep on it."

"No. There's nothing to think about. I can't go back there. And I definitely can't perform on that stage. Enough, okay, Blake."

But he wasn't ready to let it go. "You know, what happened wouldn't be that big a deal today. Times have changed. People share the most intimate things about themselves, especially over the internet. Hell, I was still in the closet back when you were in high school."

She smiled and touched his cheek with her fingertips. He had suffered too. "I'm going to bed now. I've got an audition in the morning, remember?" She was reading for a role in a new TV comedy. "Goodnight, sweet friend."

She slipped under the cool sheets, but sleep evaded her. Her thoughts returned to Port Ainsley, like the needle slipping into the familiar groove of an old phonograph record.

She was on stage and had just spoken from the balcony, the familiar line: "Romeo, Romeo, wherefore art thou, Romeo?" She was in the zone, encompassing all of Juliet within herself. Mr. Frawley had said she was perfect with her willowy frame, her long, fair hair. She, Lanie was Juliet.

And then it happened. From some part of her consciousness, she heard the commotion at the back of the theatre, tried to block it out, staying in character. Until the moment when she recognized the sound of her mother's voice, jolting her from the dream of Juliet. Horror impaled her very soul, struck her immovable. And then was looking at her mother stagger and lurch down the aisle toward the stage. "Thas my daughter," she told them all, amidst craning necks and whispers, her words thick and slurred. "Momma's here, my beautiful Jenny."

It couldn't be; it was some kind of nightmare. I must be asleep, dreaming.

But she was awake. She heard the gasps from the audience. Isolated snickers found their way to her ears. Her mother continued to make her way unsteadily up the aisle to the front of the auditorium, once nearly falling into the audience, coming nearer to her. Nearer. Grinning like a monster.

Galvanized from her frozen stance, Lanie ran off the stage, raced from the building, and later that night, the town. She ended up here, in Toronto.

Even now, lying in the bed, staring at the ceiling, that same scalding shame flooded through her, withering her heart. How she had hated her mother at that moment. She'd wanted her dead, a wish that was to be granted just two weeks later when she was struck and killed by a car. A hit-and-run, the paper said. She was crossing the street in front of her building. She never regained consciousness. She'd been drinking. There were no witnesses. Lanie didn't go to the funeral.

She turned in the bed and switched on the lamp, a sense of

panic washing over her. Her body felt clammy and she couldn't get a full breath. Stop it. It was a long time ago. Take deep breaths, she told herself. Soon, she was breathing calmly. She didn't hate her mother anymore. She never did. She'd always loved her, though it took some time to forgive her. With the passing of those same years, she began to realize how betrayed her mother must have felt. First by Lanie's father, and then by Lanie herself. Her husband and daughter. Betrayed and abandoned by them both. She hadn't deserved that. Her mother was a sensitive woman, emotionally fragile. She'd found comfort in a bottle, in the attentions of men who could only hurt her. She'd needed help.

Maybe if I'd been older, Lanie thought, by way of justification. Too late now, of course. *You can't go back and change a damn thing.*

The woman her dad had left her mother for was long out of the picture, and Evan Beddow now lived alone in a rooming house. In a weak moment, she called him one night, and they both cried on the phone. He'd made a mistake. A terrible mistake, he said. "I'm so sorry." He'd sounded old, tired. He'd not only gone to her mother's funeral, but he also took care of the arrangements. Somehow she knew he would. "I looked for you, Jenny, honey," he said hoarsely. "I didn't know where you'd gone."

No one had. How could she have done that? Yet, the longer she'd stayed away, the more impossible it seemed to change the course of her journey. She didn't like to think it was in part vengeance. But maybe it was.

She promised she'd see him soon, and she meant to. We forget sometimes that our parents aren't perfect beings. They are human, just like us. They mess up. They fall apart. We don't know that when we're kids. We think they're omniscient, like God. She'd given little thought to how devastated they both must have been when she disappeared, never knowing where she'd gone. Not even if she was alive.

I can see dad if I go home, she thought. I'll also visit mom's grave, so long overdue. And didn't she owe something to Mr. Frawley? He'd championed her, made her believe in her ability to succeed as an actress. If not for him, who knew what her life might have been like right now.

Blake was right; it was time to face her demons.

Lanie hesitated as she faced the opaque glass door with the word OFFICE stenciled on it. The rest of the cast had been rehearsing for a while now, and she had some catching up to do, although she'd been over the script every chance she got. It was a great role and thankfully she was a quick study.

"Lanie, how are you doing?" Blake said softly at her shoulder.

"Fine. At least I think I am."

He lay an encouraging hand on her shoulder. "Remember, you're Elaine Nichols, successful actor. All that crap happened years ago. People forget. They're too busy worrying about their own lives. And it wasn't your fault, anyway. You were just a little girl."

Not so little, she thought. Putting a smile on her face, she rapped lightly on the door and opened it. The woman at the desk, tall and dark-haired, looking like she was cast in a movie as the secretary, shot to her feet, clearly flustered.

"Oh, Ms. Nichols, I'm so pleased to meet you," she said,

extending her hand. "Mr. Frawley is so looking forward to seeing you again. They're all in the rehearsal hall right now. The whole cast is very excited that you're doing this. Thank you so much. I'm a big fan."

Lanie was touched and found herself relaxing. The woman asked about their flight, which had been smooth and non-eventful.

"Flowers and cards have already started arriving; I've forwarded them on to your hotel suite. Tickets are going like wildfire."

"That's great." Both excitement and fear rippled through her.

"I'm Irene Hemmings, by the way."

"Hi, Irene. And please call me Lanie for Elaine. My middle name, for my grandmother." She introduced Blake and they all headed for the rehearsal hall, the sound of their combined footsteps echoing on the hardwood floor, bringing back old memories.

Tim Frawley must have heard them because he met them halfway down the hall. "Oh, Jenn... Ms. Nichols..." He was smiling, but with a shyness she couldn't recall, and which she found endearing. He put out a hand in greeting. She ignored it and hugged him.

"Jen's fine. Though I go by Lanie now."

"You can't know how happy I am to see you," he said.

"Me too, Tim. I'm looking forward to working with you again." He looked the same, but for a smattering of grey in his hair and a few lines at the corners of his eyes. He introduced her to the rest of the cast, who welcomed her warmly.

They chatted for a half-hour or so, then he said, "We'll let you get settled into your hotel. Same time tomorrow?"

Back at the hotel, Blake took a call from the senior's home to be told his dad had fallen into a coma and was not expected to live. He booked a flight. "I'll come back for opening night if I possibly can," he told her. "Maybe sooner."

"I'm fine. Take all the time you need. You know I'd be with you if I could. I plan to go see mom's grave while I'm here, and since Saturday is the last show night, I'll go in the afternoon and fly back on Sunday."

"Sounds like a plan. You have a good show. Break a leg."

"I'll do my best."

In the morning, she accompanied him down in the elevator and waved goodbye when he got in the cab. Minutes later, the cab disappeared around the next corner, leaving her feeling oddly alone and filled with a strange sense of dread. Why couldn't she shake this feeling that something terrible awaited her?

Finally, it was opening night. It seemed to come up so quickly. Before she was ready. Lanie was more nervous than when she'd played at the Royal Alexander or Stratford in Toronto. She could hear the audience down in the auditorium, talking, laughing, settling in their seats. Her heart was racing like a trip-hammer in her chest.

Would they remember? This was a new generation. How silly she was. Of course, they'd remember. Maybe not from personal experience, but they would have heard the story and no doubt many of their parents were probably out there. *Let it go, Lanie! Let it go!* She slid her damp hands down the sides of her vintage skirt, then gripped the cane the prop girl handed her, smiling.

The house lights dimmed and the curtains whispered open with just the slightest creaking. Only up close could you see the light shining through the heavy but threadbare red velvet fabric.

The auditorium silenced and the suspenseful piano theme rose from the orchestra pit, just the softest of percussion, building, now fading out...

The curtains opened, evoking a smattering of applause, rightly so, she thought. Carl Branden was a wonderful set designer. He did the sets when she was last here.

This is a mistake. Too late to back out now. Take deep, slow breaths. You are Suzy Hendricks, a blind woman. Suzy is strong. She has courage.

Picking up her cue, Lanie unlocked the door that led onto the stair landing that descended into Suzy's apartment. The applause was immediate. It quickly swelled then faded to silence. Holding tight to the handrail, she took each step carefully, white cane tapping tentatively as she went.

At the bottom she cocked her head slightly, listening, then called out: "Sam.

From that moment, the character of Suzy, and the more than competent cast, carried her through. Beyond the footlights, the audience was riveted. She could feel it. With the final word, applause broke out and they were given a standing ovation and three curtain calls.

After they'd taken their final bows, and the last straggler had left the auditorium, she was swarmed by the cast and crew who showered with her with praise and she, in turn, returned their affection and appreciation. Many members of the audience had come backstage to congratulate them, some she remembered, all seemed delighted to meet her – for the first time, or again. She was exhausted and at the same time, she was flying.

The cast, everyone, had been so wonderful to work with, far more capable than their amateur status would suggest. Hard-working thespians, everyone. And nothing terrible had happened. It was all in her mind. She silently thanked Blake for pushing her to do this. She felt a measure of freedom she'd not realized she'd lost. As if a mountain of sludge had finally slid off her shoulders.

"You were amazing," Tim told her as she was getting into her coat. "But then that comes as no surprise to me."

"Thanks. I loved every minute of it." She gave a self-conscious chuckle. "Well, there were a few minutes there that haunted me. Thanks so much for thinking of me for this part, Tim."

"Who else? You were perfect. Perfect. You heading back to the hotel or is Blake picking you up."

"Taking a cab. Blake's in Toronto. His dad passed away yesterday."

"I'm sorry."

"Yeah. It's complicated. I'm going to fly back on Monday."

He nodded. "If you have no other plans, I'd love to take you to dinner tomorrow. Or maybe lunch if you'd prefer that. I want to hear all about everything you've been doing over the years."

"I'm planning on visiting my mother's grave tomorrow. I never have. So dinner sounds great."

"Wonderful, Jen…Lanie. I'll drive you to the airport Monday if that's okay."

"Oh, Tim, thanks, but I can just grab a cab. I…"

"Please. I'd like to."

"Well, if you're sure. It would be greatly appreciated."

Was this more than just a mentor interest? Could that be possible? She'd never thought of him that way. She respected him, sure; she was grateful to him. But more than that?

*****

Sunday dawned cool and grey with rolling dark clouds moving in. Seeing Tim's dark blue Toyota pull up at the curb, she hurried out the lobby doors. He got out and opened the door for her. "Hi. You okay?"

He was wearing slacks and a navy blazer. His usually messy hair from school, neatly combed. He'd dressed up. She wasn't sure if that was true, that she was altogether okay. But she would be. She'd bought silk flowers in the hotel gift shop to lay on the grave. They would last awhile. Unlike Lanie, her mother had never liked plants or flowers she had to take care of. "I'm good. Thanks."

"You're even more beautiful than I remember."

"Thank you," she smiled. "You're looking pretty dapper yourself."

They were quiet on the rest of the drive. The way he'd looked at her when she was coming out of the hotel lobby let her know she hadn't imagined a romantic interest in her and had to admit, she didn't find him unattractive. Had he always had a thing for her? Funny, she'd never considered him in that light, though she knew some of the girls at school had had crushes.

"I miss her," she blurted, surprising herself.

He touched her hand but said nothing. He returned it to the wheel as he turned into the cemetery and they drove up the narrow path, gravel crunching softly beneath the tires. Glancing at the paper with the directions her father had given her, she said, "It's just to your left."

He stopped the car and Lanie got out, walked a few feet ahead. There it was. Just behind a small upright gravestone embedded with angels, where a 7-year-old child name Molly Banks was buried, was her mother's grave, her name spelled out; Ellen Mary Beddow, and the dates marking her life.

Lanie knelt on the hard ground, her eyes filling with tears despite her promise not to cry and make her old teacher feel the need to comfort her. She laid the flowers on the grave and placed her palm flat on the small stone, which her father had arranged for. Despite the chill in the air, a warmth emitted from the stone. She hadn't even known if someone was taking care of the arrangements. She hadn't called to ask. How could she be so callous? So uncaring. You just assumed your father would take care of things, she told herself. Had she?

"I'm sorry, mom," she whispered, tears running down her face.

She felt the weight of Tim's hand on her shoulder. "I'm sorry, too, Jennie. But it was a terrible thing she did. You mustn't beat up on yourself."

She turned and looked up at him. "What?"

"I was broken up when you sent me away that night, Jenny – the night you left town. I knocked and knocked on your door...I could hear you crying."

"I know. I heard you." *What is he saying?* "I loved my mother."

A small gust of wind came up, blowing her hair across her face. She clawed it back as she rose to her feet.

"That's because you're a loving person, Jenny. She didn't deserve your love. She didn't care about you. She destroyed our play."

It was just a play. A damn play.

"I knew that wherever you went, she would follow you through your life. She would just hurt you again and again. You looked so beautiful standing on that stage. God, I wanted you. But you were my student. I looked for you everywhere, you know. Searched the internet for your name, but of course, you'd changed it. And then one day I was watching television, and there you were. That was cruel of you, Jenny."

A trickling of ice slid down her spinal column. She couldn't breathe. Couldn't reconcile what she was hearing from this man she'd known for so long. The man she admired and respected. *Crazy. Crazy.*

"I was getting ready to drive away when I saw her come out of your building. Oddly, I was surprised to see her. I thought I would just go home again, keep vigil another time, as I had the night before and the night before that. She was a small woman, wasn't she?" He looked somewhere past Lanie as if seeing her mother in some other dimension. His attention returned to her. "I waited until she was halfway across the street. It was just past dusk, not a soul around."

There was a buzzing around her head, a roaring in her ears.

"I stepped on the gas," he told her. "For a split second, we made eye-contact. She looked surprised. Confused, maybe. The impact made just the slightest sound. Only a gentle bump. He drew his coat more tightly about him. "We should leave now. It's getting chilly. Why are you looking at me like that, Jenny. I did it for you."

His eyes had changed and he was someone she didn't know. No longer the kind, warm Mr. Frawley, not Tim, as he'd asked her to call him, but something else. Something dark and dangerous. A wisp of cloud drifted past the sliver of moon, and a chill gripped her. She stood in shock, her heart a frantic weight in her chest, keenly aware that she was alone in a cemetery with a killer.

And then a voice spoke to her. Her mother's voice. *You're an actress, Jen. Act. Save yourself.* A warm, caring voice, as it had been before her father left. A voice not inside Jen's head, not in her imagination, but right here, just at her left shoulder.

Now breathe deeply. Smooth. Meet him where he is.

"I'm just so surprised, Tim. That you would avenge me like that. That you cared about me that much."

She saw him relax visibly, the smile tug at the corners of his mouth. "Of course I did. I told you."

"I think I've always loved you, Tim. I just didn't know it." An involuntary shiver went through her that had nothing to do with the chill air. "You're right, it is getting cold. Shall we go?"

She kept up a light chatter in the car, mostly about the play, until he drew up at the curb in front of the hotel. She knew she couldn't carry this through dinner with him. "Tim, I'm awfully tired. Would you be mind if we skipped dinner and instead you pick me up for breakfast in the morning?"

He leaned over and kissed her. "Of course not. You get a good night's sleep. I promise I won't rush you, Jenny. I know you need time to get used to the idea of a life with your old acting coach."

"Ever sensitive, Tim. Thank you." She got out of the car, a soft smile on her face, not rushing. No hurry.

Inside her room with the door locked, she sagged against it and waited for her heart to settle down, for her gag reflexes to calm. Then, her hand shaking, she phoned the desk.

"This is Lanie Nichols, room 707. Please connect to me the Port Ainsley police department."

Good Boy Brownlow!

Judy Upton

Brownlow stuck his head out of the passenger window, grinning away with tongue lolling as if retelling some private joke to himself. I however was feeling anything but amused. We'd lost sight of the van a junction back, as our clapped out Clio struggled to keep up with the flow even in the slow lane. In our job, a car capable of at least a medium-speed chase is a necessity. Unfortunately, we were stuck with a knackered old rust bucket I'd spotted in my street with a handwritten 'For Sale' sign propped up on the dash. You might say 'they saw you coming,' only if you did, I'd retort that for two hundred quid, you could also say I got exactly what I could afford. That's the main trouble with being a freelancer. The pay's lousy.

We'd spent the entire morning parked up in the aforementioned Clio, staking out a ritzy new café in downtown, Hove. I'd been alerted to the fact there'd been two dog thefts, a Springer and a Frenchie from outside this establishment in the last week. Brownlow and I were now lying in wait, hoping the perpetrator would return to the scene of the crimes.

For the first couple of hours no one tethered up a dog outside, so there was nothing to do but neck nasty homemade coffee from my thermos, whilst developing a serious espresso envy of those lucky souls who were inside, guzzling a far superior blend. Now I know you're probably thinking I could've used Brownlow as a decoy. I could've tied him up outside the coffee shop and returned to lying in wait. You are, I must point out at this point, only thinking this because you don't yet know much about Brownlow.

Firstly the majority of stolen dogs are pedigrees or designer breeds like Cavapoos or Sprockers, while Brownlow is simply a large mongrel. Secondly, Brownlow is a specially trained pet detection dog. He can track a lost cat, dog, rabbit or just about any other creature from the smallest whiff of their scent. Thirdly and most vitally, I love that shaggy, slobbery, breath-reeking mutt. Dog thieves are ruthless, dangerous people. They often dump dogs they can't sell on a roadside, sometimes even from a moving vehicle. Sometimes too, the dogs are pinched for breeding purposes, and then left to die when they become too old to produce lucrative litters of puppies. Some breeds of dog can sell for thousands or tens of thousands of pounds, so it's a profitable if cruel business.

I was stuck in a tiny car with a large flatulent dog and the cold dregs of my economy brand instant coffee, but stakeouts like this are a big part of the job. At lunchtime the café started to get busy. It was soon standing room only and the windows had steamed up. That's when a young woman arrived and tethered a gorgeous Pomeranian puppy outside. It was cute as a button and fluffy as a snowflake. Now the bait was in place, the trap was set and my fingers were crossed that something would happen.

My plan was to let the dognapper approach and discreetly take photos of him or her. I'd then get out of the car and shout to cause the thief to flee, and hopefully get a car number as the person drove off, empty-handed. In the event, it all happened far too fast for me to execute my plan. The guy swerved his white van to a stop right outside the café. He leapt out, grabbed the pup and was back in and speeding off before I could even get a useable photo. Of course we were straight in pursuit, but as I said, unfortunately we lost him on the London Road, just outside of town.

I'd like to report it was Brownlow who spotted the van again, but despite him being the one with his head out the window, it was me. There it was parked up in a lay-by just before the turn off towards Haywards Heath. I pulled straight in behind. It was the only place to stop, being as it was a dual carriageway. The driver would've seen me, and had no doubt already clocked me tailing him from Hove, but there wasn't much I could do about that. At least now I could jot down his number plate. That's if I had got the right van of course. One battered white Ford Transit does look very like another. That was a problem. I don't have a great relationship with the police. I always seem to wind them up the wrong way. There's one officer in particular I always get on the wrong side of. Either that or she's just someone with a very bad attitude. *Time waster.* Can you believe that's what she calls me? Time waster is *not* what the owners of twenty-seven cats, fourteen dogs, three rabbits and a Chinese Water Dragon call me, you can be sure. 'Heroine' and 'National Treasure' would come closer to the mark.

My issues with the cops meant I couldn't immediately ring them and say I'd located a van that looked a bit like one involved in a dognapping. They've a law called *wasting police time*, which they like to mention almost every time I call 101 about a stolen pet. I wouldn't dare dial 999. I'd probably be threatened with a life sentence.

I got out the car, leaving Brownlow safely locked in and warily approached the van on its passenger side. From what I'd glimpsed during the lightning fast canine heist, the perpetrator was working this job alone. As I reached the van's window, I was ready to give a cock-and-bull story about a malfunctioning sat nav and my needing directions to Horsham. There was however no one in the front of the van. Then I heard the whine of a scared puppy coming from the back. I'd found the little Pom!

I tried the passenger door of the van and wonder of wonders it was unlocked. The Pom was in a flimsy chicken-wire cage just behind the seats. After taking a quick look around, to ascertain the driver wasn't returning from the call of nature or whatever else he was doing, I scrambled in. Tugging open the lid of the cage, I grabbed the puppy. It wiggled and licked at my face as I clambered out backwards.

"Ms Gorrage!" hollered a familiar voice. My heart sank. It was rural crime officer, PC Gemma Carmichael, in other words my arch nemesis. "Breaking and entering a parked vehicle?"

"No, it was left unlocked. I was checking on the welfare of a Pom I believe to have been stolen from outside 'Coffee Actually' half an hour ago". Carmichael scowled her female-Judge-Dredd scowl, all sharp haircut and sharper cheekbones beneath her peaked cap. "This van flagged up as having stolen plates" she said, explaining the reason for her sudden materialisation. She wanted to speak to the driver.

"You and me both, pet."

"You – walk with me," growled Carmichael. I followed her as she purposefully strode across the lay-by, the wriggling Pom still in my arms. Suddenly she stopped. We both did. There was a man lying face down on the ground and there was a big red stain with a hole in it through the back of his baseball cap. In shock, I dropped the poor Pom in a puddle. Carmichael looked at me.

"This your work, Ms Gorrage?"

Some things do take a lot of explaining. It was so late by the time I'd temporarily finished helping the police with their enquiries, I was treated to the dawn chorus during what should've been on Brownlow's before bedtime walkies. I was still half-asleep over my morning yoghurt and choco-flakes when the Pom's owners called. Having also had a long conversation with the blatherers in blue, they'd been told about the pet detective's interference and found me via my socials. Despite the official purveyors of the law trying to paint me in a bad light, they were incredibly grateful to have Candice back and wanted to give me a generous reward. I said I'd accept my standard finder's fee, which I charge to anyone who has actually hired me, but not a penny more. That seemed only fair.

The police had said they would probably want to 'chat with' me again about the dead dognapper, which I hadn't been too happy to hear. At least as Carmichael had been attending officer at the incident, she hadn't been the one interviewing me. If she had, I'd probably still be twiddling my thumbs in the custody suite. Who but the police would call a cellblock a suite? Gemma Carmichael is a rural crime officer, but she's a PC, not a detective. The dead guy would be the responsibility of the Serious Crimes folk. But, in a way, as he'd been stealing an animal shortly before his demise, he was still part of my remit too. At least that's how I saw it. If I could find out who had killed him, it would mean the police would have someone to charge rather than half suspecting me, as I feared they currently did. They would, I reflected, be less likely to cause a miscarriage of justice where I was concerned, if they'd been helpfully spoon-fed all the facts.

My cases usually begin in one of two ways. Either a pet owner sees one of my advertisements – on socials, my website, or in the local vets' waiting rooms – and gets in touch. Or I trawl the Sussex lost animal websites and offer my services. Now though it was not a missing animal but a murderer I was trying to find. It would, I decided, be a good idea to first try to discover a little more about the victim. I had judged him a dognapper and in all likelihood he was, but there was also the remote possibility that he was in fact the original owner of the Pomeranian, stealing it back after he'd had it stolen from him. Brownlow and I had encountered one such case in the past. I didn't know the deceased's name and unlike the police I couldn't trace his licence plate. I do however spend more than a little time pursuing clues online, and that was the place to start.

If I presumed for a moment that the dead dognapper *was* stealing the animal to sell on, to either a private home or an unlicensed breeder, then there was a good chance he had recently offered other animals for sale. There are certain marketplace websites that sell puppies, though it's hard to tell the legitimate breeders advertising there from the crooks. If you know what you're doing however it isn't impossible. I tend to search on certain terms. One is 'last of the litter'. When you visit to see this pup, it's sitting there alone, the owner is apologetic but you can't see the mother as his or her partner is currently walking it, and the pup's father belongs to a friend.

The puppy is adorable and they've another person lined up to view straight after you. Before you know it, you've handed over a wad of cash and left with a stolen pooch and a handful of bogus paperwork. When I'd last looked, the Springer Spaniel and French Bulldog who'd previously been pinched from outside the Hove café were not being advertised. The search on 'Last of litter' brought up nothing but a similar one of the words, 'reluctant sale of much loved pet' did. The 'cherished' animal that was 'due to unforeseen circumstances' being offered to a good home was a Springer. I checked my records and someone using the same mobile number had 'reluctantly' sold another 'much loved pet' a month before.

I called the dog seller. She sounded friendly and plausible enough on the phone. She offered to bring the dog to me, but I said I'd been told I must see it in its own home. After initial hesitation, she agreed. I'd shut Brownlow out in my garden while making this call. I didn't want her to hear any doggy noises in the background while I was laying it on thick about how this would be my very first dog and that I was offering a 'forever home'. She told me how adorable the Springer was, telling me his name was Sam, and that she'd 'cried buckets' when she'd heard they had to move and could no longer keep him. It all sounded authentic, but she was certainly no actor. There was no emotion in her voice.

The woman with the Springer for sale lived in a village just outside Brighton, in a terrace with a garden. In her thirties, she wore a wedding ring, had expensively dyed blonde hair and wore a sweatshirt with a designer logo. She offered me a cup of tea and brought the dog in. I'd seen the photos of the missing canine and the markings looked identical. The dog was a little subdued for a Springer, and he appeared ill at ease. As a dog expert I could tell by his body language this wasn't his home. The woman's husband was away on business she said. This puzzled me. I'd assumed she'd have been told by now he was lying in the morgue. I started to think I'd got things a little wrong. This was not simply a couple trying to make a bit of illegal cash. This was actually a larger dognapping racket and this woman was just the gang's 'fence' selling on the animals, and with no personal relationship with the actual thief. Perhaps she'd not even been told of his demise.

After some chat and fussing over the dog, I finished my tea and she got around to mentioning money. I made an excuse to visit the loo and while up there opened the bathroom window. There were two recently erected sheds the garden. Odds on, they housed at least one or more stolen dogs.

I returned from the loo, phone in hand and a worried expression on my face. Posing as a concerned mother, I explained I'd just received a call from my daughter's school. She wasn't well, I said and I needed to collect her. Clearly I couldn't take the dog right away, but I'd be back and would collect the animal later that day. I would pay then.

Back home. I called the Springer's owner and let him know the situation. The man said he loved the dog and would pay anything to get it back. I advised he ring the seller, posing as a buyer and gazump me by offering well over the price I'd been offered. "Get the dog first, then contact the police." That was the safest way. He might lose the money, if the investigation went awry, but he'd have his companion back and that, to him, was priceless

On the online lost pets' pages there were a lot of posts from another man. This one had, had an Irish Setter taken from his garden. Again it was in Hove. Judging by his comments he was very angry indeed. The dog was he declared 'a valuable working animal'. 'Working' doesn't mean it stocked shelves in the Co-op, in case you're wondering. It means he took it shooting as a gun dog. A man had been found dead in a lay-by with a bullet hole in his head. This clearly merited further investigation.

I rang the Irish Setter's owner. He seemed wary when I told him I'm a pet detective, but eventually agreed to meet. I suggested the café the dogs had been stolen from. While the original thief couldn't turn up to the scene of the crime, if the thefts were down to a gang, there was the possibility one of his colleagues might arrive, either still on the rob, or trying to find out who had killed the Pom's kidnapper.

*****

Alex Goodman, the owner of the setter, was middle-aged and worked as a financial advisor, but liked to see himself as a 'country person'. I interpreted this as 'likes to shoot anything that moves'. He wore a tweed jacket and had fox-head cuff links. I imagined his green wellies and waxed jacket were in the Land Rover he'd arrived in. He drank Earl Grey and talked a lot of bluster and hot air. He kept saying he'd "like to get his hands on" whoever had taken "Old Rex", and became very red in the face as he did so. I understand dogs and cats, but I'm no human psychologist. Surely though if Mr Goodman had dispatched the dognapper, I reasoned, he wouldn't have still been so worked up about it. He agreed to hire me to find Rex, after a long haggle over my daily rate and finder's fee. It's always the well-off ones who don't want to pay up.

*****

I couldn't sleep that night, and it wasn't only due to Brownlow sleeping on my leg. That dog is such a fidget. I awoke choking with the smell of one of his sulphurous emissions. As I rolled over, to escape the pong, I heard a floorboard creak on the landing outside. I froze. Brownlow too tensed up and uttered a soft 'a-woof' under his breath. I crept out of bed, but as I did so the bedroom door opened. A figure stood in the doorway. Brownlow got up and jumped off the bed, half-wagging his tail, unsure whether a friend or foe was visiting us. Me, I was absolutely petrified. By the streetlight filtering through the curtains I could see a revolver pointed in my direction.

"I couldn't believe it when I saw you," a woman's voice said, speaking softly and calmly. The hairs on the back of my neck stood up. I recognised that voice. It was the woman who'd tried to sell me the stolen Springer. Surely the police couldn't have visited her already? They were usually so slow with these things. That's why I'd suggested the owner buy back his dog.

"How… how did you find me?" I stammered.

"While you were in the toilet, I looked in your handbag. Your diary has your address on the front page. So stupid." I cursed myself for this careless lapse. It seemed though that while she had found my address, she hadn't glimpsed my business cards, tucked away in one of the pockets. She wasn't here because I was a pet detective who was on to her. "I just couldn't believe it when you showed up," she continued. "I mean you're nothing special, are you? You're older than me and you dress like your granny" Normally, I wouldn't have stood for this kind of personal attack, on myself or my poor old nan, who was actually quite fashion forward. Having a gun pointing at my head though, kept me from telling her exactly what I thought of her own vulgar, over-flashy look. "I'd never have imagined he'd look twice at someone like you. I didn't even suspect there was another woman. Not for a long time.

But then I found the messages on his phone. And I wasn't having that. No way. Nobody cheats on me."

"So you shot him? Your husband?"

"Bullet through the head. And the next one's for you, you selfish slapper. Think I was daft did you? Did you really think I'd believe you were there to buy a dog? You were looking for him. Wondering why he hadn't turned up this time, at that nice little country hotel where you were getting so cosy." Hell certainly hath no fury, I thought to myself.

I started to explain I had no interest in this woman's dog-stealing husband, but she yelled at me to shut up, her voice high and dangerous.

"Brownlow," I said. He still stood grinning and wagging his tail, the soppy mutt.

"Brownlow – jump!" The woman screamed and tottered backwards, as Brownlow leapt on her, barking loudly right in her face. Serve her right for favouring heels over sensible brogues. Moving fast, while she was off balance, I knocked the gun from her hand and kicked it as far as I could across the room. At that moment PC Carmichael burst in, taser drawn. I hadn't even known a rural crime officer carried such a thing. What did she normally taser – sheep? If I had known she was licensed to zap, perhaps I wouldn't have given her so much backchat over the years of our fraught acquaintance.

PC Carmichael, as it turned out, had been tailing the dognapper's wife. From the attitude of her superiors when they showed up ten minutes later, this fighter of countryside crimes had been seriously exceeding her rural remit and treading on her superiors' toes by making her own investigations. It sounded like she was in for a dressing down at the very least.

The worst thing was, as the police left with their prisoner, I heard Carmichael justifying her actions by saying that she had "prevented a member of the public from being killed."

I wanted to say, *No, PC Carmichael, that was Brownlow.* But I didn't say anything. I didn't want to create even more bad blood between us. This city is barely big enough for me, her and her ego as it is.

Instead I said, "Good boy, Brownlow," when they'd all gone. "Good boy!"

The Usual Unusual Suspects

Eve Fisher has been fortunate to have had almost 30 stories published with *Alfred Hitchcock Mystery Magazine*, as well as additional publications in other mystery, science-fiction and fantasy magazines. Her short story – *Collateral Damage* – appeared in the Murderous Ink Press anthology series, CRIMEUCOPIA – *We're All Animals Under The Skin*

Alexander Frew comes from farming and mining stock in the county of Ayrshire, Scotland. He went to the same Academy as Sir Alexander Fleming, the man who discovered penicillin, but it is fair to say that on leaving at the age of fifteen he failed to make the same societal impact. He wrote poetry and short stories in the 80s, then joined Borderline Theatre in the 90s and had several plays performed in an old church in Ayr. He also started South West Writers, and had three books for children published at the turn of the century. This led exactly nowhere, and after a fallow period he started self-publishing and produced a series of poetry booklets, CD's and performances in conjunction with the group.

After having an adventure story accepted by Hale in 2012, Alex has published some twenty books in the Western genre. He has also had a science fiction book published this March *by Mocha Memoirs Press*. His first, and greatest love, is the short story and he is trying to get better because it is harder to write a short story than a short book.

Tom Johnstone is the author of the collection, *Last Stop*

Wellsbourne and two novellas, *The Monsters are Due in Madison Square Garden* and *Star Spangled Knuckle Duster*, all published by Omnium Gatherum Books. His stories have also appeared in such publications as *Black Static #68* (TTA Press), *Best Horror of the Year #8* (Night Shade Books), *Terror Tales of the Home Counties* (Telos Publishing), *Nightscript VI* (Chthonic Matter) and others. More information at tomjohnstone.wordpress.com

John M. Floyd's work has appeared in more than 300 different publications, including *Alfred Hitchcock's Mystery Magazine, Ellery Queen's Mystery Magazine, Strand Magazine, the Saturday Evening Post*, and three editions of *The Best American Mystery Stories*. A former Air Force captain and IBM systems engineer, John is also an Edgar Award finalist, a four-time Derringer Award winner, and the author of nine books.

Andrew Humphrey has been widely published in the Independent Press over the last twenty years or so, most notably in magazines such as *Crimewave, Black Static, The Third Alternative, Bare Bone* and *Midnight Street* – and Nick Royle's Nightjar Press in 2020.
In addition he has had a novel, *Alison*, published by TTA Press in 2008 and also two collections of short stories – *Open the Box* and *Other Voices* – courtesy of Elastic Press. *Other Voices* was one of the winners of the East Anglian Book Award in 2008.

Joan Leotta plays with words on page and stage. Her short stories have appeared in *Betty Fedora*, overmydeadbody.com, the *Lawyerist*, and in two recent Guppy anthologies. She is a

poet, short story writer, essayist, CNF writer and novelist. On stage she tells folk and personal tales of food, family, and strong women.
She thinks up her best plots for mysteries while walking the beach.

Gary Thomson resides in Ontario, Canada where in his rec moments he blows Beatles and blues on his Hohner harmonica. His short fiction has appeared in *Horla e-zine, Wellington Street Review, AgnesandTrue,* among others.

Eamonn Murphey has been a reviewer for sfcrowsnest for several years and has published more than forty short stories in small magazines. His latest book *Federation and Empire,* a future history short story collection, is out now from Nomadic Delirium Press.

Matias Travieso-Diaz Matias Travieso-Diaz is an engineer and attorney, born in Cuba and retired after half a century of professional practice in Washington, D.C. Following retirement, he has taken up creative writing and authored many short stories of various lengths and genres. His stories have appeared or are scheduled to appear in about forty short story anthologies, magazines, audio books and podcasts in the United States, the U.K., Canada, Australia and New Zealand. A collection of some of his stories has also been accepted for publication.
https://www.facebook.com/matias.traviesodiaz
https://twitter.com/mtravies
https://mtravies.wixsite.com/mysite
https://www.amazon.com/-/e/B08L8QMT27

Madeline McEwen is a blow-in to the Bay Area from the UK, bi-focaled and technically challenged, who has enjoyed publication in a variety of different outlets both online and in traditional print. Her fiction and non-fiction focuses primarily on disabilities [ableism] and humor.

She has numerous short stories and a few stand-alone novelettes. Her latest short story, *Stepping on Snakes*, appears in the *Me Too Anthology* edited by Elizabeth Zelvin published by Level Best Books, and *Benevolent Dictatorship* published in *Low Down Dirty Vote Volume II* edited by Mysti Berry.

She and her Significant Other manage their four offspring, one major and three minors, two autistic, two neurotypical, plus a time-share with Alzheimer's.

In her free time, she walks two dogs and chases two cats with her nose in a book and her fingers on the keyboard.

http://www.madelinemcewen.com
http://www.amazon.com/-/e/B00Q41VUFI
https://www.pinterest.com/macmaddy/pins/
https://twitter.com/MadMcEwen
http://www.facebook.com/madeline.mcewenasker

Lyn Fraser currently resides in the U.S. but has also lived in London and Brighton. At present she teaches a course in crime fiction for the adult education program at Colorado Mesa University and has served as a hospice and palliative care chaplain. Publications include short fiction in literary reviews, a mystery novel, and an academic textbook.

Ella Moon is actually three writers stacked on top of each other wearing a trenchcoat. Together, they have stories in publications including *72 Hours of Insanity: Writer's Games Vol. 7 & 9*, Red Penguin's *A Heart Full of Love*, and online at *Little Old Lady Comedy* and *Defenestration*. One or the other of them can usually be found ignoring the advice of the other two and buying more books and/or mugs and/or sweaters.

Gina L. Grandi is a professor in the theatre and dance department at Appalachian State University. In her former life, she was a public school teacher in San Francisco and a teaching artist and arts administrator in New York. She is currently the co-founder and artistic director of *The Bechdel Group*, a theatre company dedicated to fostering writers writing for women. Her writing has appeared in *Cicada, 100 Word Story*, *Apex Magazine*, and *Fine Linen*. Gina has a BA from Vassar College, a PhD from New York University, and an extensive finger puppet collection. She can be found on twitter at @yonderpaw, lurking about in a middle-aged way.

Louise Taylor has recently been published in the *Bodies in the Library* anthology (Flame Tree Publications) and *Pulp Modern*. She also has a story in the upcoming *WhoDunIt* anthology (Jersey Pines Ink).

Originally from the UK, Louise grew up in northern California and presently live in Paris, France, where she teach high school English. Follow her at: https://twitter.com/LouiseMTaylor2

Judy Penz Sheluk is a former journalist and magazine editor, and is the author of the bestselling *Glass Dolphin* and the *Marketville Mystery* series. Her short crime fiction appears in several collections, including *The Best Laid Plans, Heartbreaks*

& Half-truths and *Moonlight & Misadventure*, which she also edited.

Judy is a member of Sisters in Crime, International Thriller Writers, the Short Mystery Fiction Society, and Crime Writers of Canada, where she serves as Chair on the Board of Directors. Find her at www.judypenzsheluk.com.

Joan Hall Hovey is a Canadian author, living and writing in Saint John, New Brunswick. Her novels include *And Then He Was Gone, The Deepest Dark*, and *Night Corridor* among others. Available on Amazon and most online bookstores. Her short stories include *Dark Reunion* which appears in *Investigating Women*, published by Simon & Pierre, Canada.

Joan also has the short story, *Freeing Henry*, in CRIMEUCOPIA – The lady Thrillers.

To learn more about the author, check out her websites at http://amzn.to/M7mVAR and www.joanhallhovey.com

Judy Upton is an award-winning playwright with plays produced by the Royal Court, National Theatre, Hampstead Theatre, Birmingham Rep and BBC Radio 4 etc. *The Bulbul Was Singing* was a Radio 4 Drama of the Week (2019). She's had two feature films and a TV drama produced, plus a novella *Maisie And Mrs Webster* published by W&N in 2018. Her first full length novel will be published by Wrecking Ball Press in 2021. Further details can be found on Judy's website at www.judyupton.co.uk.

16 stories ranging from the 14th to the 21st Century, all from women authors whose forte is crime.

Featuring *Karen Skinner, Hilary Davidson, Pauline Gostling, Linda Kerr, Kate Miller, Tiffany Lindfield, Lena Ng, Ginny Swart, Sandrine Bergèss, Michelle Ann King, Amanda Steel, Kelly Lewis, Paulene Turner, Claire Leng, Madeleine McDonald and Joan Hall Hovey.*

Paperback Edition ISBN:
9781909498198
eBook Edition ISBN:
9781909498204

18 authors take time to look under the skin of the people who sometimes inhabit their heads, and put what they find down on paper.

Featuring John Gerard Fagan, Nick Boldock, Weldon Burge, Chris Phillips, Dan Meyers, Jeff Dosser, Eve Fisher, Emilian Wojnowski, Fabiyas M V, Lamont A. Turner, Edward Ahern, Robert Petyo, Al Hagan, Caroline Tuohey, Steve Carr, Bobby Mathews, Michael Bracken, and June Lorraine Roberts.

Paperback Edition ISBN:
9781909498235
eBook Edition ISBN:
9781909498228

9 781909 498242